The Witness

KW-015-497

MARY TANT'S WEBSITE

http://www.marytant.com

Lincolnshire
COUNTY COUNCIL

discover libraries

This book should be returned on or before the due date.

MDS

2014

31. 01. 16

MAY

0 8 APR 2020

023

To renew or order library books p
or visit https://lincoln:
You will require a Personal
Ask any member o

The above does not apply to Read

MARY TANT

The Witness

Threshold Press

First published 2014 by Threshold Press Ltd,
Norfolk House
75 Bartholomew Street,
Newbury Berks RG14 5DU
Phone 01635-230272 and fax 01635-44804
email: publish@threshold-press.co.uk
www.threshold-press.co.uk

British Library Cataloguing in Publication Data
A catalogue record for this book is available from the British
Library ISBN 978–1–903152–33–1

Designed by Jim Weaver Design

Printed in Great Britain by Berfort Information Press, Stevenage

FOR JENNY
WHO TURNS MY WORDS
SO BEAUTIFULLY
INTO PICTURES

Roscombe Village

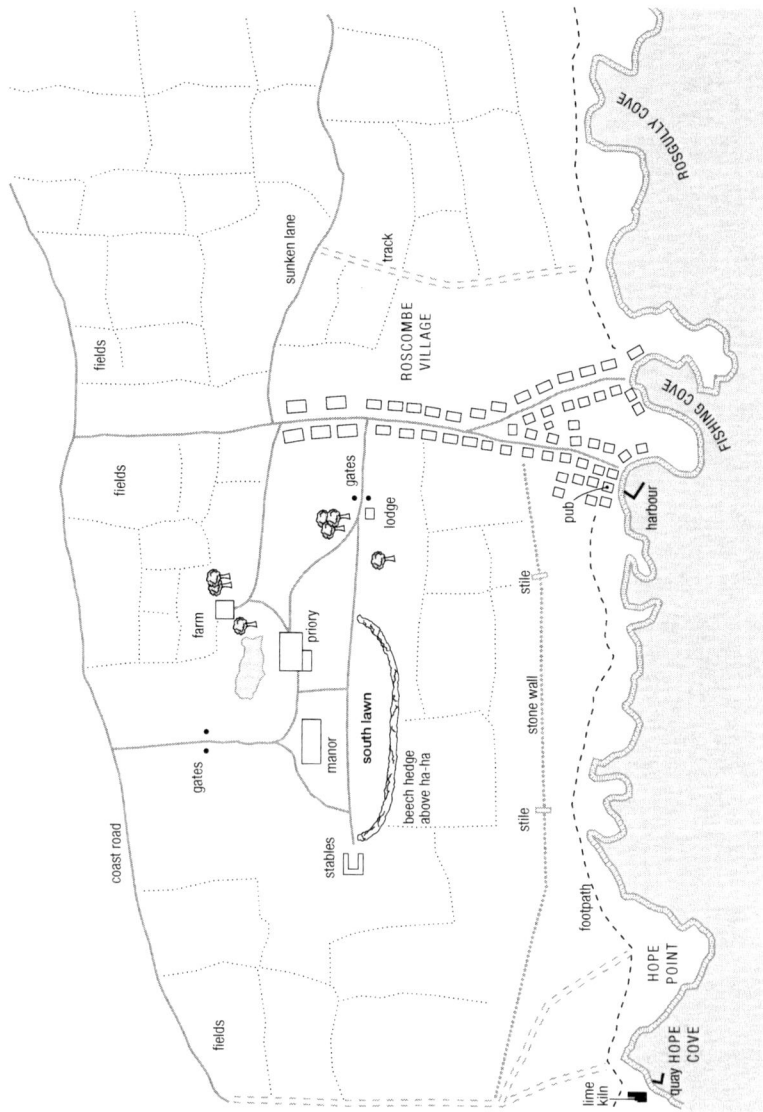

N

coast road

fields

fields

fields

gates

sunken lane

track

farm

priory

gates

lodge

ROSCOMBE
VILLAGE

stables

manor

south lawn

beech hedge
above ha-ha

stile

stile

stone wall

footpath

pub

harbour

FISHING COVE

ROSGULLY COVE

HOPE
POINT

HOPE
COVE

quay

lime
kiln

Rossington Manor and Priory

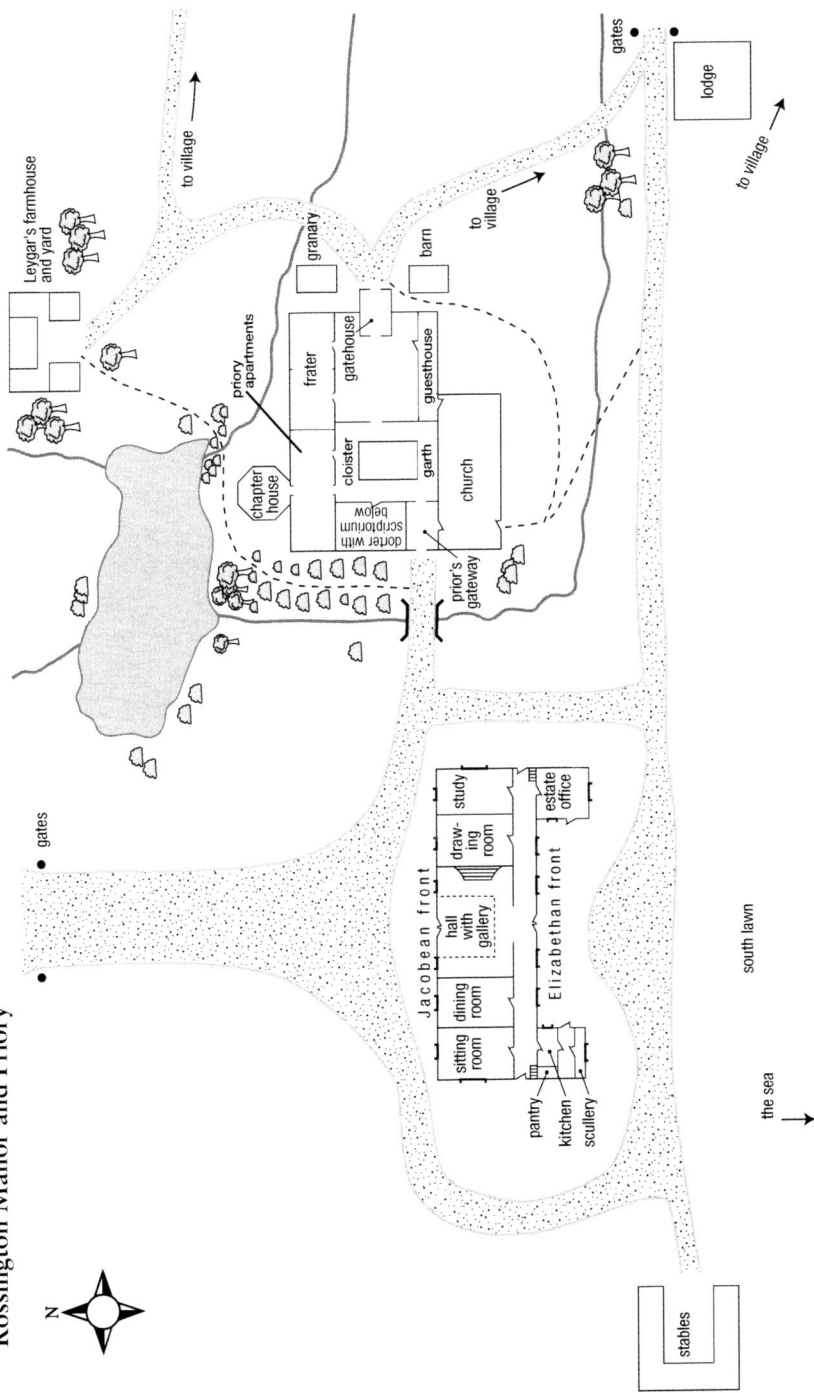

N

Leygar's farmhouse and yard

to village

to village

priory apartments

granary

gatehouse

frater

guesthouse

chapter house

cloister

garth

church

dorter with scriptorium below

prior's gateway

barn

to village

gates

lodge

to village

gates

Jacobean front

sitting room

dining room

hall with gallery

draw-ing room

study

Elizabethan front

pantry

kitchen

scullery

estate office

south lawn

the sea

stables

ONE

The bramble tendrils wrapped around her legs, hooking their barbs into her cut-off cotton trousers and tightening as she struggled to free herself, panting slightly. Sweat trickled down her flushed face, her long black curls were damp, clinging to her head and neck as she brushed them back with a shaking hand.

Heavy crashing in the thick undergrowth behind her made her turn quickly towards the man who was following her. He was breathing heavily as he lumbered towards her, glaring furiously as he waved the machete in his hand. 'What the hell do you think you're doing?' he demanded. 'Don't go wandering off the path like that. God know where you'll end up. This place is like a jungle.'

Anna Evesleigh's dark blue eyes sparkled with anger as she returned his glare. One hand waved wildly around the tangle of trees, bushes, climbers and long grass that surrounded them. 'What path, Mike? There isn't one. The route I chose through this jungle you've led us into was just as good as yours.'

Mike Shannon, increasingly distinguished as an archaeologist, was a frightening sight as he rested his hands on his hips. His shirt was torn, flaps of faded blue cotton hung limply across his chest and arms. His red hair, nearly always tousled, was at this moment in wild disarray, knotted with pieces of bark, twigs and leaves, and even a green beetle. His square freckled face was scarlet with exertion and his eyes blazed with fury. The light of anger faded as he considered the woman in front of him.

Anna was unusually dishevelled for a woman who had a natural elegance. Her white shirt was stained with green and brown, and clung to her shapely figure as she bent over, trying again to disentangle the brambles. 'I should have known this was a terrible idea as soon as you mentioned it,' she muttered.

Mike burst out laughing. 'I'm tempted to take a photo,' he said. 'The glamorous actress Anna Evesleigh in her spare time.' His expression darkened. 'Rather different to the one of you with Hugh in the paper this week.'

'For goodness' sake, Mike,' she said. 'Stop burbling and give me a hand, or I'll be trapped here forever.'

He dropped the machete and stepped forward, bending down beside her. His fingers, she noticed, were cut and bleeding even before he began to pull the brambles roughly off her trousers, cursing in an undertone as he wove each strand back into the bushes that nearly surrounded them. Ah well, she thought as snags appeared in the cotton, surrounded by a pattern of bloodstains, the trousers were ruined anyway. No point fussing now.

Anna began absentmindedly to pick the twigs out of his hair as she thought about their expedition. She really should have been more careful, she thought ruefully. Mike's ideas always led to trouble. She had, she realised, been thrown off her guard by his willingness to join her for lunch with Berhane, her old school friend. Mike had certainly met Berhane before. He had also recently provided Anna with some useful historical background for the community play that Berhane had commissioned Anna to write for the small moorland community where she lived. But Mike never normally volunteered to attend social events.

Yesterday, bumping into him unexpectedly in Coombhaven near her family home, Anna had casually mentioned that Berhane was staying with her and that they were going out to lunch before Berhane returned home today. It had surprised her immensely when Mike had demanded to come to lunch too, to make sure that his information was not distorted. A faint suspicion had flick-ered across Anna's thoughts; maybe Mike was once again falling in love.

And that, she realised, was why her mind was not alert enough when Mike had suggested that after lunch, when they had seen Berhane set off, they should look for this place on the way back. And, the thought crept insidiously forward, the idea of a hidden garden was so romantic she hadn't been able to resist agreeing to come with him. So here they were, she thought glumly as he stood up, rubbing his hands down his jeans and leaving smears of blood on them. It hadn't even been on the way back. They must have come at least ten miles off the direct route to her home. And the June sunshine was bakingly hot again this after-noon, creating a sauna-like atmosphere under the trees, searing her skin when she was out in the open.

'This is hopeless, Mike,' she said, stepping cautiously away from the bushes into the long grass that reached well above her knees, brushing irritably at the insects that buzzed in an eager cloud around her face. 'We've no idea where to go. I can't even see any sign of a garden, let alone a house. I only hope we can find our way back.' She glanced over her shoulder, relieved to see that the passage he had hacked out was very obvious, littered with trampled grass and chopped branches. A strong smell of crushed greenery drifted around them, not unpleasantly, she thought.

Mike had retrieved his machete and stood with it propped against one leg, looking around at the uncompromising screen of tangled growth, his sweaty brow furrowed in thought. 'Most of the garden is in the valley that leads to the sea,' he muttered, pulling a photocopied map out of his back pocket and opening it up to stare intently at the squiggle of lines. 'We've been going downhill for some distance. These West Country valleys aren't usually very long, so this must be the outlying woodland and the garden itself should be near. As long as we keep going down we can't go wrong.'

'Let's hope we don't fall in the sea,' Anna said crossly. 'That would just put the finishing touch to the day.'

He glowered at her. 'If you carry on like this I'll probably push you in when we get there. Go back to the car and wait if you can't stand the pace. Good God, woman, this is the opportunity of a lifetime and you stand around moaning about a bit of difficulty.'

She bit her lip to keep back a sharp retort. 'Mike darling,' she managed to say sweetly, 'I know anything you're involved in will be difficult. I certainly couldn't leave you to get into trouble. You know how easily you do.'

He was scowling now, remembering the times when they and their friends Lucy Rossington and Hugh Carey had fallen into unexpected and dangerous situations. And how often Anna's self-defence skills had come in useful. His lips twitched. 'Ah well,' he said, his expression lightening, 'the worst trouble always happens when we're all together.'

'Mmm,' Anna said, looking suddenly sad. 'But the way things are with Lucy and Hugh now I'm not sure how much that will happen again. Their relationship seems to have gone downhill since she was injured last year.'

He glanced intently at her and opened his mouth. He shut it again with a snap of his teeth. 'Let's concentrate on finding this damned garden, not stand around gossiping about other people's marital problems.'

'I'm not …' she began hotly, but he cut across her words.

'Stay behind me,' he instructed, picking up the machete.

'Mike,' she said in alarm. 'Do be careful. I'm sure you shouldn't have that thing.'

'I'm not planning to swing through the trees,' he said. 'How else would we get through?'

There was, Anna conceded as she quickly stepped further back, some truth in that. For the first time she wondered why Mike was so determined to find this garden. Gardens and even eighteenth century houses that stood in them were not at all in his line of work or one of his general interests.

'Mike,' she asked, 'why are you so keen to find this place?'

There was no reply, possibly because he had not heard the question above his grunts of effort as he swung the blade and the crashing of branches falling to the ground, followed by the crunching of his progress forward. A large buzzard flew heavily out of a tree just in front of him, making Mike swear audibly as he came to a startled stop for a moment.

Anna felt as though she had been trailing behind him for several hours when she looked down at her watch, blinking the sweat out of her eyes. Only three thirty, she saw in stunned surprise. They had left Mike's car in the cliff car park just after two thirty, and had surely been in this wilderness for several hours. She felt a sense of relief that they were doing this on a sunny summer's day, when it would be light until late unless the weather changed unexpectedly. However enervating the heat was, it was still better than struggling through here in dim light and the heavy rain that had fallen for days earlier in the month. She lifted the watch to her ear, trying to hear it ticking above the pounding of her heart, wondering if it had stopped. Giving up, she stepped forward and gasped in horror.

Mike lay sprawled on the ground in front of her, the machete lying under his body. She hurried forward as fast as she could, and almost fell herself when she tripped over something hard on the ground. Mike rolled swiftly aside as she stumbled towards him.

His eyes were wide with alarm as she landed beside him. 'For God's sake,' he growled, 'look where you're going.'

Too out of breath to retort, Anna could only turn her head and glare at him. As he got to his feet her eyes ran over his heaving chest, but she saw no sign of heavy bleeding. She glanced quickly at the machete and saw that it lay in front of a fallen log that must have protected Mike as he fell.

She felt his hands on her shoulders and said quickly, 'I'm alright. Just let me get up.' She pushed herself ungracefully up onto her hands and knees and stood up straight with an effort.

He was not looking at her, but standing, his arms hanging by his side, staring around. She looked too, aware of birds singing everywhere as she realised that they were actually in a clearing. The trees here were not the oaks that had grown so thickly on the upper slopes, towering out of the bushes and brambles, trailing great screens of ivy. She drew in her breath sharply as her eyes fell on the tree that grew tall in the centre of the glade, reaching well above the jumble of azaleas and rhododendrons that flowered in a profusion of pinks, highlighted here and there with a blaze of scarlet. A nuthatch, elegant in grey and pink, was working its way up through the branches of the central tree, which held up goblets of creamy yellow. A tulip tree, she knew, but it was huge and very old, far older than any other she had seen.

Mike grunted with satisfaction. He was not gazing at the beauty in front of them but had gone back to the edge of the woodland. Anna turned to stare in surprise at his bent back. He had pulled aside fallen branches and clods of earth, scattering them around him. He stood up, brushing his dirty hands together. 'Iron railings,' he announced. 'That's what we tripped over. Probably the fence that divided the garden from the woodland.' He came to stand beside Anna, who was looking again at the overgrown shrubbery in front of them.

'I had no idea that things would still be growing here,' she said quietly. 'Let alone anything like this.'

He glanced at her, surprised at her tone. His eyes followed her gaze, seeing for the first time not just the proof of the garden that he had been searching for, but the colours and shapes of the flowers that grew in such profusion around them.

Anna moved forward slowly, bending to sniff at the flowers and Mike became aware too of the heady scent that filled the glade. He waited with unusual patience, watching the dishevelled woman as she moved from bush to bush, but after a while his eyes lifted to scan the far side of the clearing. He pulled the map out again and stared at it, trying to get his bearings.

The crackle of paper attracted Anna's attention. She turned to look at him. 'Do you think it's all like this?' she asked, still in a hushed tone. 'A secret garden, with the trees and plants still flowering, although not a person comes to see them now.'

'I've no idea,' he said, but his voice was remarkably gentle, with no trace of his usual irritability or frequent hostility. 'I'm trying to work out where we are. Would you say,' he glanced at her enquiringly, 'that this was the shrubbery?'

'I don't know,' Anna said. 'I don't really know anything about gardens.' She looked about thoughtfully. 'I suppose it is, after all these are shrubs, aren't they?' She added hastily, seeing a hint of glower appearing on his face, 'Azaleas and rhododendrons. Not flowers in a border, I mean.'

The glower vanished as he nodded his head. 'That's what I thought,' he agreed. 'The map's no use now, it doesn't show the layout of the garden, so we can only go by guesswork. As far as I know, this place was first planted in the late eighteenth century, when the house was built, and revamped seventy or so years later. It wasn't a great estate, its landscape manipulated by Brown or Repton. It was the home of a family who sponsored plant-hunting expeditions for at least a couple of generations. So I reckon lawns surrounded the house and led to paths down to the shrubbery and on to the arboretum that filled the valley.'

'Wow,' Anna commented. 'I'm impressed, Mike. I don't even know who Brown and Repton were, but I'm sure you're right.'

He glanced at her suspiciously, but saw no trace of irony on her flushed face. He nodded a trifle self-consciously. 'They were garden designers, I suppose they'd be media celebrities today.' He peered at the map again. 'So we must be about halfway from the house. And I want to be a bit further up. Really, we've judged it very well.'

Anna frowned. 'Why?' she demanded. 'Is there something here you're particularly looking for?'

He ignored her, skirting the clearing and staring into the bushes that grew around it. Faintly flushed white roses threaded through them, making an impenetrable but lovely thicket. At last Mike paused, using the machete to prise chunks of soil and grass from the ground.

Anna waited at a safe distance, well away from the clods that flew up all around him. When he stopped, dropping the blade and bending to scrape with his hands at the ground, she went to join him. 'What is it?' she asked.

'A path, I think,' he said. 'A level surface anyway.'

He straightened up as she looked down, unable to see anything except disturbed earth. 'This way.' He pushed through the bushes, not using the machete now, letting it hang from one hand.

As Anna followed, her scepticism faded. Although branches scratched her arms and face, and roots and leaf litter booby-trapped her feet the route did seem easier. She rounded a large bush, honeysuckle tendrils teasing her hair, and almost bumped into Mike. He put out an arm to catch her and for an instant held her still against him as they stared ahead.

A fox prowled across the wide tussocky field that stretched in front of them, with small trees dotted haphazardly here and there. The animal stopped to stare back at them, before continuing its leisurely way across what had once, Anna realised with a shock, been a lawn. The mounds beyond it, thickly covered with purple flowering wisteria and scarlet roses, were the remains of the house. The plants were also creeping high up the tall ivy-clad columns that must be chimneys.

Without waiting for Mike she moved through the long grass, almost in a dream, taking no notice of the green woodpecker that flew up in front of her, yaffling in alarm. Mike, that most unromantic of men, that most prosaic of archaeologists, smelt the scent of warm sweet grass rise up and mingle with the headiness of honeysuckle, and for an instant the unkempt woman and the scene of dereliction before him shifted. It was another woman who walked there, her long skirts swishing over the neatly mown stripes of the lawn, her lace-trimmed parasol screening the dark hair piled beautifully above her head. Beyond her, sunlight glittered off the windows in the grey stone house, tables stood on the wide terrace. A dainty Italian greyhound pranced out from the shelter of her skirts to skip up the steps, towards the shadowy figure who emerged from the open French windows.

Anna had reached the front of the ruined building and the imaginary scene vanished from Mike's mind. He shouted at her in alarm. 'Anna, stop there!' He stalked after her, grabbing her arm and roughly pulling her back.

'Mike, let go,' she protested. 'You're hurting me.'

He released her at once and glowered. 'Don't be so stupid,' he said angrily. 'There'll be all sorts of hazards here. Holes for you to fall into, broken stones to trip you, loose bits of masonry just waiting to fall on you. That's why I didn't want to come down the old drive. It's best to avoid the house and buildings.'

She frowned. 'So what did you come for?' she asked. 'I don't believe you wanted to find the garden. It must,' she guessed, 'be something archaeological.'

Again he ignored her, turning to stride through the grass to the eastern edge of the lawn. Here he walked along the bushes that fringed it, turning aside suddenly to push his way through them.

Anna followed reluctantly, stopping once to look back at the house before she plunged into the bushes behind Mike, suddenly anxious not to lose him and be left here alone. The undergrowth was thinner than she had expected, and she could see that the trees growing in it were unusual. Their shapes were unfamiliar, the leaves and barks unrecognisable, although Anna acknowledged to herself that she was far from an expert. Perhaps this was the arboretum Mike had mentioned, although it was obviously not where he was expecting it. He had, she realised suddenly, clearly done some research on the house and garden.

A sudden shout alarmed her, mingled as it was with the sound of a heavy fall and the rattling of stones and rocks. Mike, one moment only a short distance ahead of her, had vanished and a jagged hole had opened up in the ground.

Anna hurried forward, almost swept off her feet when a branch swiped across her head. Blinking tears of pain away, conscious of a trickle of blood running down her face, she cautiously approached the edge of the hole, warned by the gleam of steel that the machete lay half hidden in the long grass.

Mike was sprawled unmoving at the foot of a slope of rubble, almost obscured by a cloud of dust that rose to settle over Anna's sweaty face and damp hair. Stones and pebbles still rolled downwards, and little rivulets of earth trickled towards the bottom of the hole.

Anna stood frozen, wondering frantically what to do. If she tried to get down to Mike, she was afraid there would be another fall of earth, and then they might both be trapped down there. It would be best, she thought, to go for help. But could she find her way out of the garden? Perhaps she should skirt the house and find the drive he had mentioned. Surely that would be easier than retracing her steps, even if she could.

She hesitated. She could not leave him like this. Suppose… Her thoughts broke off. Pulling herself together she called his name urgently. 'Mike! Mike! Can you hear me?' She bit her lip until she tasted blood, then caught her breath.

The figure below her stirred, struggling feebly. Then with an abrupt movement Mike rolled over, shuddering off a layer of soil and stones, spitting earth out of his mouth. He said gruffly, 'Of course I can hear you. I'm not deaf. It's better not to move until this kind of fall's over.' His hands went up to rub his eyes.

'Don't, Mike,' Anna shouted. 'You've got all sorts of muck in them. Don't rub it in.'

He lowered his hands, blinking hard. 'Alright, Florence Nightingale. Any other useful advice?' he demanded belligerently.

'Check your ribs and your legs before you move,' she instructed. 'And your head.'

Mike ignored her, getting abruptly to his feet. He swayed, putting one hand to the side of the hole to support himself.

'Mike,' Anna said, looking for a way that she could safely take down to him, 'don't move, you fool.'

He rested his head against the rough earth, only looking up

when he heard her treading cautiously around the rim of the hole. 'Stay away,' he shouted.

'I'm just seeing if I can find a broken branch or something,' she said, 'to help you up.'

'Don't bother.' He was scanning the slope. 'I can manage.'

She hurried back to see him edging up the side of the slope, his back to the more solid wall of the hole. At least, she hoped it was solid.

The first few steps went well, then the earth beneath his feet shifted, sliding him back a short distance. Anna held her breath fearfully, but Mike kept his balance and tried again, stepping delicately upwards once more. He lowered his full weight carefully, his hands spread against the earthen wall. The slope under his feet quivered but did not move. He stepped again and again until his shoulders were just below Anna's grasp.

She had lain down flat on the ground above, her arms reaching down towards him, her eyes fixed on the slope that he was navigating. As he stepped up again the soil heaved and slid and she knew he would fall.

He flung his arms upwards and she grabbed them, holding him with all her strength for a fraction of a second. With a tremendous heave against the wall, he catapulted himself out, landing heavily half across her body.

Anna looked anxiously at Mike as he drove his battered red Passat estate along the narrow lane. His shoulders were hunched, his hands clutched the steering wheel as he carefully negotiated the route between the high banks. He knew and so did she that the thick greenery screening the banks concealed unforgiving granite boulders. Not, she thought, that a few more scratches and dents would be noticeable on his car.

She had cleaned them both up as well as she could with tissues and the small amount of water Mike had in a bottle in the car, but he still looked as though he had been in a fight. Blood oozed sluggishly from a cut on the side of his head, matting his red hair into a flat patch above one ear. His face and hands were scraped and bruised, as were the portions of his sunburnt chest and arms that gaped through the rents in his shirt.

'Are you sure you're alright, Mike?' she asked again as he slowed the car, groaning, as they approached a side turning.

'Of course I am,' he growled. 'I've had worse accidents than that. But I don't know where the hell we are.' He peered at the wooden fingerpost signing a place called Genarran. 'Well, I've never heard of Genarran,' he said, turning the car into the side lane, which seemed even narrower than the first one to Anna. 'But let's hope they've got a decent pub. Or any pub at all,' he added morosely. 'I'm really not fussy as long as I can get a pint of beer.'

'Mike,' Anna said quickly, 'you really shouldn't drink alcohol after a knock on the head.'

'I didn't knock my head, I cut it on a rock as I fell,' he argued. 'A quick beer will help to anaesthetise the pain. And,' he went on, casting a swift glance at her, 'I want to find out more about that garden. They're bound to have stories about it locally.'

'But surely that's all they'll be,' Anna said. 'Stories, not facts.'

'True.' Mike began to nod, and stopped as a stab of pain shot up his neck. 'But stories often grow up around one or two basic facts in places like this. And it's those facts that could be useful.'

Anna had seen him wince, and knew perfectly well why. She knew perfectly well too that if she persisted in arguing about it he would just insist on doing what he had said he would. She bit her lip, looking out of the side window as she tried to think of a way of diverting him. She flipped her long curls over her shoulder, feeling the grit in her hair as she touched it. With a sigh she reached for her bag and pulled out a brush. Lowering the sunshield and sliding open its mirror she lifted the brush and then gasped in horror as she saw her reflection.

'I still look dreadful,' she exclaimed, leaning forward to peer at her face. The hectic flush had disappeared, but scratches ran across her skin, while the rose and cream complexion was marred by smears of mud and green slime that looked like bizarre war paint. Her hair was as matted as Mike's and hung like tattered banners on either side of her face.

'You didn't clean up too well,' Mike commented, not looking at her as he brought the car out onto a wider village street.

'Neither did you,' she snapped, trying in vain to tug the brush through her hair. She gave up, shoving the brush into her bag, closing the mirror and pushing the sunshield back, before turning towards him.

He was pulling the car to a halt outside a grey stone cottage in the centre of a short row of other grey cottages. This one was slightly larger than its neighbours, and a faded signboard swung heavily from a post in front of it, announcing it to be The Lanyon Arms.

'Mike,' she said urgently, 'we can't possibly go in there looking like this.'

He turned to stare at her in surprise. 'What does it matter?' he demanded. His eyes ran over her, and his mouth twitched. 'Nobody here's going to know you don't normally look like this.'

Anna glared at him, unable for once to find words to express what she wanted to say. Before she could, he said abruptly, 'Stay here if you want to. I'm going to get a drink.' He turned away and opened the driver's door, levering himself out with a muffled curse.

She only hesitated in her seat for a moment, long enough to realise that she was not only thirsty but very hungry too. Moving cautiously, aware of all the bumps and knocks that she had taken that afternoon, she swung her door open and got out of the car.

It was not a particularly attractive street, she thought, looking swiftly around. It ran past the pub, with cottages of different shapes and sizes lining it, all fronting directly onto the street. They were generally in their bare granite state, which even in bright sunlight had a faintly gloomy effect. Yet the walls were bright with rambling roses and honeysuckles, while pots full of scarlet geraniums stood on steps. The green branches of trees formed a backdrop behind the houses on both sides, and as she looked over the small fields that lay to the south she was sure that she saw a distant glimpse of the sea through a screen of leaves.

Anna looked round and saw that Mike was already at the pub door, almost obscured by the profusion of flowers, yellows, creams, blues, growing in the flanking tiers of tubs and cascading down from the hanging baskets. She called him quickly, unwilling to enter the place on her own. As he glanced back impatiently, a bubble of laughter rose in her chest as she realised that only with Mike would she dream of going anywhere in so dreadful a state.

He held the door for her, but she urged him through it, more than happy for him to be the first to go into the small lobby and enter the wide bar room beyond. And the reaction he got more than justified her forethought.

First one head turned, then another and another, drinks held still in hands, mouths frozen open in mid sentence. It took less than a minute until all the people in the room, mainly men, were staring at them in varying degrees of shock and disbelief.

Anna the actress, used to performing in front of hundreds of people, took the attention in her stride, restraining herself with difficulty from playing the role of injured heroine to the full. Mike, used to academic audiences, was quite oblivious to this fascinated one, his mind focused intently on the beer on offer at the bar counter.

The landlord leaned forward over it, a cloth in one hand, a glass in the other, his sombre dark face wrinkled in concern. 'Has there been an accident?' he asked.

'No, no.' Mike waved the question away. Seeing the landlord's expression change, losing its air of concern and beginning to look cautious, Mike added quickly 'We just got a bit lost when we were out walking and ended up struggling through what felt like a jungle.'

'Lost,' an elderly man standing in front of the counter ejaculated, watching Anna sink onto a bench by the open window. 'You both look as though you've fallen down a cliff.'

'And scrambled back up again,' his companion added gruffly.

'Where were you then?' he asked curiously as Mike shouldered past them to order a large glass of red wine and a pint of Bolster's Blood Porter.

'We went down from the cliff path into a valley and came across what must have been a garden,' Mike said as the landlord passed the full wine glass over to him. He heard a hissing intake of breath as he watched a pump handle being lowered and the stream of beer pouring into a tankard, and was aware that both the men by his side were staring at him.

Watching the scene from her seat, Anna noticed how different the men appeared at first glance. The thick walls and open windows made the bar a naturally cool room, but the crowd of drinkers and the lingering heat of the summer day still raised the temperature enough to make Anna feel quite warm. Yet the older man wore a light jacket over his open-necked shirt and trousers with a neat line in them. He was probably around eighty, his grey hair still thick and tidily brushed, his pale eyes bright with interest in a tanned and lined face. He seemed sprightly enough in spite of the walking stick propped against the bar counter beside him.

His companion was younger, Anna judged, his black hair only lightly streaked with grey, his face less aged, but more sober, lacking the laughter lines that graced his companion's. He was much more casually dressed, in jeans and a green t-shirt, but he was of a similar stocky build to the older man. Perhaps he was the older man's son, or a relation of some sort; there was a certain likeness in their movements and expressions too, Anna noticed as she studied them. They looked like prosperous local farmers.

Before she could speculate further the landlord put Mike's beer down on the counter and said to the older man, 'Sounds like Elowen, doesn't it, Aaron?'

Aaron nodded slowly, his eyes on the glass he held in his hand. 'You must have been in the old Lanyon family garden,' he said, looking up at Mike. 'I didn't know the footpath there had been reopened. Had you heard, Cal?'

The other man shook his head. 'It's been closed off for years,

Aaron, completely overgrown, I know for a fact.' He eyed Mike. 'You must have had a real struggle to get through that lot. There can't have been a human foot stepped in that place for decades.'

Mike carried the drinks over to Anna, who leaned forward to take hers. She was interested now, and said lightly, 'How mysterious it sounds. Is it haunted?' Before she could remind him, Mike had gone to fetch menus.

The two men were leaning back against the counter, nursing what Anna guessed to be glasses of amber whisky. They were talking to her now, ignoring Mike as he returned to the table, planting a menu firmly in front of her and settling down on a stool with his own copy. He took a deep gulp of beer, feeling enormous satisfaction as it trickled down his dry throat.

Cal said, 'I wouldn't be surprised if it were haunted, the deaths there've been.'

Anna's eyes sparkled. 'Who died there?'

'Not there,' Aaron said quickly, 'but it hasn't been a lucky place. So many of those associated with it died or had bad luck.'

'Do tell us,' Anna said. 'I feel we've earned the story.' She held out her scratched hands, with the palely painted nails chipped and broken.

Tut-tutting, Aaron took a sip of whisky as Mike shifted his stool to look at him. 'It was a beautiful place once, long ago, when the house was first built and the gardens made. The Lanyons owned Elowen estate then, and it was a younger son who made it what it was when it came to him after his brother died. The brother was a soldier, died in the war with America long ago. The Lanyon men weren't lucky as soldiers.'

'The younger one did okay though,' Cal said. 'He married an heiress, a merchant's daughter, and used all her wealth on the place. That's right, isn't it, Aaron?' He glanced at Anna, lowering his voice slightly. 'I've never had much time for all that history stuff, but it's a shame to see good land going to waste.'

'Yes, it's good land right enough,' Aaron agreed. 'History's got a place, though, boy, it's part of what we are. And we're part of that place.' He sipped his whisky before continuing more strongly, 'The Tregonans, my father's family, farmed there for centuries, holding their land from the Lanyons. My father bought it after the war, the Second World War, when the old lady was selling off the estate. I remember it as if it was yesterday. Dad was the only local bidder, the others,' his fingers whitened around the glass, 'were outsiders, men who'd done well out of the war. Dad got it too, and I think the old lady was glad. Though,' he added reflectively, 'she can't have got as much as she'd hoped for. Twenty thousand pounds for the whole lot, four hundred acres it was, with the farmhouse and buildings too, although they were barely habitable for animals, let alone us. He put us on iron rations for all his life to pay for it, but it was a bargain. And for all that, he did better than the old lady, holed up until she died in a couple of rooms with the family house falling down around her and the wilderness creeping closer and closer.'

'Who was she?' Anna asked eagerly. 'The old lady.'

'Mariot Lanyon, she married her cousin Grenville Lanyon, and was prouder than he was of Elowen and the family. She was distraught when the place was requisitioned during the war for the Americans. She tried everything she knew to keep them out, and insisted on living in the head gardener's cottage when she didn't succeed. When she did at last get it back she was desperate to keep the place going for her son Denzil. He was a marine, and did some brave things. You wouldn't believe the stories that were told about him when I was a lad. His mother was that proud of him, and he was the last of the Lanyons.'

'No, he wasn't,' Cal interrupted unexpectedly, 'there was the girl.'

Aaron nodded. 'Denzil's wife, but she wasn't a Lanyon. And she went away years ago with the boy. Off to Canada, to a place he inherited there.' He glanced at Anna. 'I did hear he died there, so you see there's nothing mysterious about the house, and no hauntings. For all there were a lot of deaths, they didn't happen at Elowen.'

'What about Denzil?' she asked. 'Did he come back?'

Aaron shook his head. 'No. He'd been listed missing in 1944, after the D-Day landings, and he didn't come home again, although his mother never gave up hope that he would. Piece by piece she sold off the land, room by room she retreated in the house, and the garden …' He shrugged. 'She'd given up on the garden even before the war. They couldn't keep it going after the previous one, the First World War. All the gardeners then signed up with Grenville Lanyon, Denzil's father. They were all in the mounted cavalry, taking the farm horses along with them, poor creatures. And they were all killed, every man of them, on the Somme, along with Sir Grenville. He was twenty-six, and never saw his own child. Denzil was born after news came of his death.'

He glanced at Cal. 'You'll not remember, with your lack of interest in history, but when you were a youngster I took you to the garden, to see the memorial Lady Lanyon raised to her husband and the gardeners who didn't come back.'

Cal winked at Anna. 'Down by the lake in the valley. I'll never forget being stung by nettles and scratched by gunnera. And I nearly fell in the water, it was so overgrown I couldn't see it.'

'You never could look where you were going,' Aaron said mildly.

'What's it like?' Mike asked. The men glanced at him in surprise, and he said, 'The memorial.'

'Not what you'd think,' Cal said. 'It wasn't a cross or a slab, but a figure of a man carved in granite, a young man in working clothes, waistcoat hanging over his shirt, sleeves rolled up, cap on his head, leaning on a spade and looking down over the valley where they had all worked. He had a dog pressed against his side, a lurcher it was.'

'Sir Grenville loved that garden, and the dog loved him. They said it pined away and died after his death, and Mariot Lanyon chose to remember his faithfulness when the memorial was designed,' Aaron said quietly.

Anna felt tears filling her eyes and blinked hard. Mike glanced quickly at her and away again. 'What happened to the house?' he asked.

Aaron shrugged. 'Denzil's widow left with her son, went to Canada with him as I said. She never liked it here, Amethyst,' Aaron snapped his fingers triumphantly, 'that was her name. It's many years since it's been spoken here. By rights she was Lady Lanyon too, but nobody ever called her that. She was a lovely little thing too, a singer in London entertaining the troops like Vera Lynn when Denzil met her.' His eyes misted. 'Her voice was the most beautiful thing I'd ever heard, she used to sing and play the piano sometimes when she first came. I heard her once when my dad took me up to the house with him when he had to see the old lady.' His expression was sad.

'It must have been grim for her here,' he said quietly. 'No friends, none of the life she'd left, and the old lady couldn't stand her, she wasn't good enough for her son, you see. But Lady Lanyon tried to keep her here because of the boy, the Lanyon heir. And it was the old lady that had the money. It was only after the boy came into this Canadian place, Toronto, I think it was, a property of some kind, that Amethyst had chance to leave. And she took it so fast that we didn't even know she and the boy had gone until old Lady Lanyon told the vicar.' Aaron shook his head disbelievingly. 'That must have been in the early 1960s. It must have been grim for the old lady, but she lived on alone in the house after her maid died until she died herself, sometime in the 1980s I reckon. Cal and my girl Bryony were well grown up then, and thought nothing to it, the death of one old lady. But then nobody had seen much of her for years, some people thought she was already dead. I've no idea where she got her food from in those last years, she never came to the village shop.' He turned, putting down his empty glass.

'Here, let me get you another,' Mike offered. 'You're telling Anna such a good story that it's keeping her mind off her bruises.'

'Thank you.' Aaron accepted the offer simply.

Cal shook his head when Mike looked enquiringly at him.

'Thanks, but no, I'm on call later.'

Anna held out her empty wine glass and Mike reached across for it. 'Are you a doctor?' she asked.

Cal grinned. 'Nope. I'm part of the lifeboat crew. If there's a call tonight, or any night this week, I need to be fit to go out.'

'The story doesn't get told much now,' Aaron said, ignoring Cal's comment. 'They're all forgotten, I suppose, the Lanyons, and their house and garden. The garden was used for a bit by the locals after old Lady Lanyon died, and before that too, I reckon. The house was broken into a couple of years after her death, young people I guess, looking for a bit of excitement. I expect that was how the fire started.'

'What fire?' Mike demanded, looking round sharply from the bar counter.

'Kids mucking about, I reckon,' Aaron said, looking surprised at Mike's vehemence. 'It was a right job for the fire engine to get down there, the drive being so overgrown by then. The fire had taken such a hold when they did reach the house, that there wasn't much they could do. It was a sorry end to the place. I don't reckon anyone goes there at all, not even down the drive now.' He glanced wickedly at Cal. 'His lot used the drive as a Lovers' Lane when they were young,' he commented. 'Not the sort of place I'd have wanted to take my girls to.'

'Catch any of them taking the risk,' Cal said jokingly. 'It was the creepiness that added to the fun when we went.'

'Who owns the place now?' Mike asked, trying to sound idly curious as he passed a glass of whisky to Aaron. 'Denzil's widow if she's still alive, I suppose.'

Anna glanced quickly at Mike as he put her wine down on the table. He met her look with a warning frown.

'Not her, no,' Aaron said. 'The place was entailed, so I think it must have gone to some cousin or other. He's never been down here though, just left the place to disappear off the face of the earth. I don't even know his name or where he lives.'

'You'd have thought he'd want to sell it,' Anna said, her eyes on Mike as he returned to the counter for his own drink. 'Maybe somebody could restore it.'

Aaron laughed. 'Who on earth would want to spend money on a place like that these days? There's little of the house left, and the garden's a jungle. No,' he took a sip of the amber liquid in his glass, 'it's already had its time, soon it'll just be nothing more than a local legend.'

The pub door banged open and a tall slender woman entered the bar room. 'Dad, I'm sorry I'm late,' she said in a toneless voice.

Anna blinked. The woman had a long face, made even longer by the thick straight black hair that hung down to her waist on either side of it. A striking white blaze ran through the hair above her forehead. Artificial, Anna thought at once, even though the woman must be in her late fifties and probably greying naturally, but it's very effective. She certainly was not at all like her father.

The woman ignored Cal as she stopped in front of Aaron. Her curiously blank eyes stared expressionlessly at the glass in his hand. 'You'll have to leave it,' she said. 'I've got to get on.'

'My daughter, Bryony,' Aaron said. 'She's come over from Coombhaven with my weekly shopping. She's got a place of her own there, the Witches' Shop.' He snorted with laughter. 'Did you ever hear of such rubbish? Still, there's people pay good money for what she sells. And she never did take to farming, our Bryony, she must be a changeling. But no sense in wasting fine whisky, girl.' He lifted the glass to his lips and drained it. 'Especially when it's my fee for a good story.'

Bryony did not respond or question this, just stood waiting, her eyes on Aaron. A man came to stand behind her, one hand on her shoulder as he stared round the group of people in front of her. Cal was leaning against the counter, gazing into his own glass, but the newcomer's eyes passed over him and Mike to fix appreciatively on Anna.

'Aren't you going to introduce us to your friends, Dad?' he asked jovially.

Aaron looked at him, chill disapproval very obvious on his

face. 'This is Bruce Riley,' he said shortly to Anna and Mike, 'no son of mine. Just Bryony's partner. At the moment.' The last words were said softly, but still Anna caught them.

She looked with more interest at Bruce. The fair skin was reddened over his cheeks, weathered from sun and wind, his light hair was carefully brushed forward in an attempt to hide its receding line. His patterned shirt screamed of South Sea Islands, with life-sized parrots prancing through garish vegetation, exposing skinny sunburnt forearms. He showed no awareness of Aaron's patent dislike, as he winked at Anna.

'I've been telling this couple about Elowen,' Aaron was saying, picking up his walking stick. 'Only right since they stumbled across the garden.'

There was a flicker then on Bryony's face as she looked out of the corner of her eyes at the man next to her. Bruce had stiffened, his smile becoming fixed.

They don't want to hear about it again, Anna guessed. I suppose they've got bored with family stories that have been endlessly repeated. Aloud, she said, 'Thank you very much, Mr Tregonan. It was cheap at the price. Wasn't it, Mike?'

'What?' Mike started. 'Oh yes. A good story.'

Cal was watching the elderly man leave with his daughter and her partner. Not a word was said in farewell to him, not a word was said between the departing trio as they went out of the room.

'They're not much alike, are they?' Anna said lightly to Cal. 'Father and daughter, I mean.'

'No.' Aware that he must have sounded curt, Cal smiled tightly, turning to face her. 'No, they're not, never were. Neither are Bryony or I, for that matter, for all we're cousins and grew up together. But if you're interested in that garden it's her bloke you should talk to,' he added. 'Bruce. Works in Tourist Information in Coombhaven. Knows everything about everywhere. Or thinks he does. He's never mentioned Elowen yet, that I know of, so I guess he didn't know about it before today. But he'll be pumping Aaron now, and by tomorrow he'll be talking about the place as if he was born there. To hear him you'd think he'd lived in this area all his life, not just a couple of months. He and his cousin moved down here, wanting a better life, so Bruce says. They're pretty matey, the two of them, not like Bryony and me. But it's Bruce that does the talking, the other bloke never gets a chance. So,' Cal warned, half joking, 'only get him started if you've got the odd morning to spare. Anyone wandering into his office must have a hard job getting out again, the way he goes on. And like as not he'll have put them right off wherever they'd wanted to go, and given them a full schedule of places they'll never see, nor want to. Ah well,' he put his glass down on the counter, 'I must get off too. Take my advice, listen to the stories about it but don't go near Elowen again. That place was never any good.' Raising a hand in farewell he left, the bar room door banging behind him.

Anna looked at Mike as he came at last to join her at the table. 'Well,' she said, 'did you get what you wanted?'

'Possibly,' he replied, running his eyes down the menu. 'I could see you were. I suppose Elowen's history will appear in one of your plays.'

'Do you know, Mike,' she said in surprise, 'I hadn't really thought of it. I'm just fascinated by the place.'

'Hmmmph,' he mumbled. 'Well,' he added more strongly, 'if we're going to eat, let's get on with it.'

'This menu's not at all bad,' Anna commented. 'I'll have the poached salmon. It's just right for this weather.'

'One thing about you, Anna,' Mike said, getting to his feet again, 'you never fuss about getting fat, you're always able to eat.'

'One *good* thing, Mike?' she asked with mock astonishment as he reached the counter.

He ignored her, even when he returned to the table and sat down heavily on the stool opposite her bench.

Anna eyed him curiously, respecting his thoughtful silence for a while, watching him as he scanned the old framed photographs on the wall. As far as she could see they showed village scenes and people, there was nothing that looked like Elowen house or garden.

'Come on, Mike, you know I won't tell anybody,' she said at last in a quiet voice. 'Why are you so interested in the garden?'

'I'm not,' he said crossly. Making an effort, he spoke in a subdued growl, 'I suppose you'll just nag on until you get an answer. Well, marked on the map there's an underground chamber, a fogou. I just wanted to see what's there, what it looks like now. I didn't,' he grinned suddenly, 'really plan to make my obeisance flat on my face in front of it.'

'Was that what you fell into?' she demanded.

'Ssssh,' he hissed, glancing over his shoulder. 'Just the entrance, not the chamber.'

'Mike,' Anna pointed out patiently, 'just choose your words carefully and speak normally. If you behave like a pantomime villain you'll attract everybody's attention at once.'

He scowled at her. 'I don't want to talk about it here. Anyway,' he went on abruptly, 'what were you doing with Hugh in London? You seemed to be having a good time when that newspaper photo was taken.'

She stared at him in surprise, moving her glass out of the way as a woman arrived with the meals. 'Thank you,' she said, as her salmon was put in front of her. When she and Mike were alone again she said, 'You know that Hugh's publishing company is doing well. In fact,' she added thoughtfully, 'I sometimes think that's part of the problem with Lucy. She had to give up her career to help her brother keep the family home, and now Will is off in India doing interesting things. Then Lucy married Hugh and they did up Withern. Hugh's doing what he wants to with his publishing and doing it brilliantly. But Lucy's got time now to feel stranded, realising that her botanical work down here is small beer compared to what she could be doing. And at university she was expected to do great things.'

Anna caught Mike's sardonic eye and went on quickly, 'Anyway, I went to an award ceremony at the weekend for one of the books Hugh published earlier this year. That's when the photo was taken. And,' she added evenly, 'I was having a good time. I like parties and Hugh's always great company.'

'He's Lucy's husband,' Mike pointed out as a large steak was put down on the table before him.

'He was my friend too, long before he met Lucy,' she snapped, her eyes flashing, as she cut into her fillet, 'and he needs support right now, although I suppose you haven't noticed that.'

'Don't be stupid, Anna,' Mike said. 'Hugh and I go back years as well. But I can't see how swanning around with him is going to help him and Lucy get back together.'

'I thought he might like a chance to talk about it,' Anna said. 'I'm sure he misses Lucy, now that she's doing this seed bank job in Hampshire. She's only gone for three days each week, as she can work at home for the rest of the time, but Hugh always seems to be away when she's back. I just hoped I could point out that isn't a great idea if he wants things to get better between them.'

'And did he want a cosy heart-to-heart?' Mike asked shortly.

'No, he didn't. He spent most of the evening chatting to some bloke he used to work with, a barrister, I think.'

'Did he show signs of wanting to talk to you?' Mike persisted

'No. Oh, alright, so he won't, he's a bloke. Has he talked to you?'

Mike stared at her, as he put a large piece of meat into his mouth. 'Of course he hasn't. Hugh's not going to discuss his marriage problems with me. But,' he said thickly, pointing his fork emphatically towards her, 'don't get between them, friend or not. They've got to sort it out themselves.'

'Well, I know that,' she said crossly, stabbing at the green beans that edged her fish. 'But I want to help. And anyway Lucy asked me to go with Hugh to the ceremony. She found at the last minute that she couldn't make it and didn't want to leave him in the lurch.'

Mike's eyes widened in disbelief. 'For God's sake, Anna. Don't be so ready to fill the gap then. Maybe she would have made a bigger effort to go if she couldn't rely on you to cover for her.'

'Maybe,' Anna said thoughtfully. 'But maybe it would just have forced more choices on them too quickly.' She lapsed into silence, concentrating on her meal.

Mike watched the thoughts and emotions chasing each other across her face as he swallowed the last mouthful of steak. 'Well?' he demanded after a couple of minutes.

'You could be right,' she admitted reluctantly. 'But how can I refuse when Lucy asks me to help?'

He laughed. 'Anna, you've always got something on. Just make sure you're busy. Surely you've got plenty of blokes on tap. *Inspector Elliot* is bound to be available if you call.'

'Rob's pretty busy at the moment, and anyway,' she hesitated, 'somehow things haven't been the same since that business in the spring, when he left us all in danger.'

Mike was silent, knowing that Anna would never be convinced that Rob Elliot had only been doing what he had to. 'Well,' he said, 'there must be plenty of others who'll come running.'

'It's kind of you to think so, Mike,' she said lightly, laying her knife and fork down, 'but it's not quite like that. And I don't want to lie if I'm free and I wouldn't want to encourage some bloke just to make use of him, so I'm stuck.'

Mike opened his mouth, caught her eye, and decided against the derisive comment she knew he was about to make. 'I suppose,' he said slowly, grudgingly, 'we're friends of a sort. I'll be around if you need an excuse. Purely,' he added hastily, 'to make sure you can avoid leaping to Hugh's side to fill in for Lucy.'

Her eyes were alight with laughter as she picked up her glass. 'Alright, Mike. It's a noble offer. Of course, everyone will think we're a couple, but if you can stand it, I won't worry.'

His face darkened. 'I suppose you're right,' he said irritably, snatching at the menu. 'Well, I've never worried about what people think, and I'm not going to start now. Just as long as you don't get the wrong idea.'

'I won't, Mike, don't worry about that. You're definitely not my type.' She added quickly as his eyes narrowed, 'But we'll have to be convincing for Lucy and Hugh. They're bound to suspect a rat otherwise.'

'Hmmm.' Mike tugged at his knotted hair. 'Well, look, Hugh's coming to lunch at my place tomorrow, you'd better come too. I'm working at home,' he explained, catching her look of surprise. 'I've got a damned excavation report to finish by next week, and I'll never get it done otherwise. And I've got to write up some of the finds we're making at Ravenstow Abbey. Their sponsors want some idea of what they're getting for their money.' He lifted his tankard and drank heavily.

'Yes, alright,' Anna said quickly, aware that he would sink into a litany of despair over his paperwork if she let him carry on. 'That's really convenient as I'm seeing Philly Leygar at the manor in the morning.'

Mike looked puzzled for a moment, then his expression lightened. 'Of course, she's working on this year's Rossington Play, isn't she? I suppose you're getting on with that.'

Anna nodded. 'Yes, it's all written up. Philly helped with the research this year, so I want to run the plot past her before we start auditions next week. She's busy with the admin of the manor's holiday apartments right now, so it's easier for me to go to her. And I want to go over the lie of the land around the South Lawn again, working out entrances and exits.'

Mike grunted. 'The play's about the mule chest in the manor, isn't it?'

Anna looked taken aback. 'Yes, that's right. Fancy you remembering,' she marvelled.

'Don't push it,' Mike advised, 'if you want us to exude an atmosphere of sweetness and light for Lucy and Hugh.'

A gurgle of laughter broke from Anna. 'I'll try not to. You don't rise to the bait as well as you used to, so it's not as much fun anyway.' She leaned forward, her blue eyes suddenly intent. 'I know, Mike, I'll come a bit early tomorrow, and Hugh can find you listening to the plot of the play. That'll really surprise him, and,' she went on quickly, 'I'd really appreciate any comments from you. Useful comments, that is.' She gave him a minatory glare.

He looked amused. 'I'm amazed that you think I could make any,' he commented.

'Well, you've been helpful over the play for Berhane,' Anna admitted. 'I do like to get the historical facts right.'

Mike snorted with laughter. 'I never thought I'd hear you say that.'

'Stop it, Mike,' she ordered, 'and concentrate on our private plot. I know,' she said, suddenly excited, 'it's Midsummer's Eve tomorrow, let's go somewhere for a meal, and casually invite Hugh to come too when we see him at lunchtime. It's Friday, so Lucy will be home too. She's normally back by Thursday evenings, but I know she's got to work at the seed bank until late tonight. Still, she'll be home by midday tomorrow, so I'll see if she can come too and then we can make it a foursome. And,' she leaned forward, her blue eyes sparkling, her creamy complexion flushed, 'let's make it an adventure.'

Mike was watching her, enjoying her plotting, noticing that the scratches and bruises on her face were barely visible in her happiness, that her tangled black curls still fell attractively around her cheeks. He was so intent that he almost did not hear what she was saying. 'What?' he demanded abruptly, jerking his head up. 'What did you say?'

'Mike, you must concentrate,' Anna chided. 'We can take a picnic to Elowen, and find a nice spot to sit.'

'Sometimes, Anna, I know you need your head tested,' Mike said. 'Where the hell will we find a nice spot there? On the broken stones of the terrace, waiting for a bit of the house to squash us? In the long grass, bitten by insects, and an adder or two, if we're really lucky? Or perhaps we could go wandering down the valley and see if we can find the lake to fall into.'

'Don't be so gloomy,' Anna said buoyantly. 'There's bound to be somewhere, an old wall or something safe enough to suit you.

But just think, Mike. Hugh will be fascinated by the house, and Lucy won't be able to resist searching for wild flowers. They simply won't have chance to be awkward with each other.'

'Hmmm,' he mumbled reluctantly, 'maybe.'

'And you'll have chance to explore your old fog thing a bit more,' she suggested, with the wiles of Eve.

'Fogou,' he snapped. 'Or to you, an underground Iron Age chamber.' He relaxed unexpectedly into a reluctant smile. 'I know that's a bribe,' he said, 'but alright. Though I can't see what you'll get out of it.'

She shrugged elegantly. 'I love the feel of the place,' she said lightly. 'So romantic, Mike. Lucy and Hugh will see why we want to go there together, maybe it'll trigger off the right mood for them too.'

Mike stared at her, memories of the afternoon's exploration running through his mind. He began to roar with laughter, almost falling off his stool.

TWO

Anna looked out of the window of the old porter's lodging in Rossington Priory's gatehouse to the courtyard below, the late morning sunshine warm on her face, the scent of jasmine all around her from the tiny white flowers starring the stone wall. White also splashed the scarlet dress she wore, that fitted her shapely figure nicely, flaring out just above her knees, creating a patch of colour against the grey wall and the greenery that screened part of it. Not a sound was to be heard except the bees that hummed close to her ears. Nothing moved below except the butterflies that flitted over the flowers.

It never failed to surprise her how well the old priory buildings had been converted into holiday apartments, and she looked out with satisfaction over the ones she could see. Here in this entrance courtyard, and in the cloister garth beyond the wall, the only real signs of change showed in the curtains at the narrow windows of the old buildings, and the tubs and pots of plants that demarcated the outdoor space for each apartment.

Out of sight lay the garth, which she had just been exploring. It had been turned into a tranquil garden, studded with the stumps of the pillars that marked the paved pathway around its perimeter. The carrels where the monks had worked on the illuminated manuscripts that once made the priory famous had been left open, with basket chairs and tables for those who wanted to enjoy the tranquillity of the place.

Beyond them lay what Anna had grown up knowing as the scriptorium, although Mike had once taken the time to debunk this idea, declaring that it would really have been a library. But still, Anna thought happily, the old name has stuck to it. It was now an apartment sleeping four, like the dorter above it, which would once have housed several monks. Current holidaymakers accessed it via the restored staircase that the monks would have used to reach the church for the night services. It pleased Anna to think of that, and her thoughts wandered on along these lines to the octagonal chapter house at the northern end of the garth. Did it see more chatter when the monks used it for their meetings than it did now as the sitting room of an apartment that encompassed the old infirmary and warming room?

She calculated for a moment, four people in each apartment, which made twelve people around the whole garth. Her brows knitted as she leaned out of the window, breathing in the jasmine scent and doing more sums. Here below the gatehouse there were two apartments in the priory's entrance courtyard. The smaller Frater to her right incorporated the old dining room into the kitchen, and had retained the pulpit from which a monk read to his brethren as they ate in silence. In their childhood Anna had much enjoyed reading to Lucy and her brother Will when she had constructed a game around life in the priory. Although, she acknowledged to herself, almost laughing out loud, her reading material was far different, certainly more amusing, than the biblical works the monks had listened to.

Anna brought her mind back to the present and the figures she was working out. Frater slept two people, but the two-storey Guesthouse apartment across the courtyard on her left incorporated the old sacristy and slept eight, so that made ten people altogether here, plus the garth's twelve. Twenty-two in total. She wondered how many of them would come to the annual summer play she devised, based on local historical events and staged on the South Lawn of the neighbouring manor, Lucy Rossington's family home.

As she leaned against the windowsill, the jasmine tendrils tangling with her long black curls, Anna's quick imagination peopled the scene below with the monks who had once lived and worked here. Heat and steam poured from the kitchen as the brothers filed silently into the frater for their meal, pausing outside to wash their hands in the lavatorium set into the outer wall, planted now with tumbling crimson geraniums. She saw the priory's final sacristan poring over their last treasure, wondering where to hide away from the king's men the precious chalice that would be found centuries later by Lucy's brother Will. Nearby, in an earlier century a lady swept hastily into the guesthouse, the gold of her girdle clasp flashing, as her sweating horse was led away by a groom.

It came as a shock to Anna to actually hear present day voices in the courtyard below. Recognising one of them, she leaned further out of the open window, planning to call to Hugh Carey, Lucy's husband. His figure, clad in chinos and a white shirt, was unremarkable, being of medium height and medium build, but Anna looked down on his head with affection, noticing that his thick brown hair was unusually dishevelled. She guessed that he must have been walking on the cliffs; in spite of the general June heat there was normally a breeze of some sort blowing there.

For a moment Anna was puzzled, knowing that Hugh rarely took time off from his publishing business. He had worked hard to get the business going when he had first started it a few years ago, having given up a potentially golden career as a barrister. Now that it was taking off he was working even harder, it seemed to Anna.

Her puzzlement increased. Why, after all, was Hugh here anyway? If he wasn't working in his office in the barns of the old farmhouse at Withern that he and Lucy had restored, it seemed odd to find him here at the priory when Lucy was away. As Anna considered this Hugh moved and she saw the camera dangling at his side. That was it, she thought, strangely relieved. He had always been keen on photography, like everything else he undertook he was very skilled at it and was especially keen on wildlife shots. No doubt there was some bird around that he was trying to take a picture of. Her eyes narrowed slightly. But still, how did he have time? She was convinced that part of the problem between him and Lucy was down to his endless working.

Anna had just opened her mouth to call to Hugh when she saw that he was looking over his shoulder, waiting for somebody to follow him through from the cloister garth. She moved back into the room without speaking, her eyes narrowed as she saw the woman who appeared behind Hugh's shoulders. Small, with short light brown hair, she conveyed an aura of self-possession that caught Anna's attention. The woman moved in a pantherish style, with long almost loping strides, and her camisole top revealed tanned muscular arms and a generous bosom. Her legs, emerging from very short shorts, were well shaped and very brown.

Anna frowned, watching the woman laugh up at Hugh as he made a comment, gesturing at the lavatorium set into the wall of the frater. She could not catch their words, but it certainly sounded as though they knew each other well. Anna's frown deepened. She had not seen Hugh look so relaxed and happy for a long time.

Leaning against the window frame she caught Hugh's next sentence, as he stopped by the door that led into Frater. 'Let's get out the map and I'll show you where I mean. It's just the right place.'

Anna did not hear the woman's reply, but she did see Hugh's face. Intent and interested, very interested. She felt a jolt of shock as she heard Hugh say, 'We'll go first thing tomorrow.'

Lucy was returning today, Anna thought crossly. What was Hugh thinking about? They were never going to improve things between them if Hugh went gallivanting off with another woman on one of Lucy's few days at home. It was bad enough that he often seemed to have work trips that clashed with her homeworking, but this would be a really deliberate avoidance of his wife.

Hugh opened the apartment door and went in as Anna watched in surprise. The woman followed, closing the door firmly behind her.

As Anna stood staring out of the window another woman spoke in the room behind, making Anna start violently. 'Sorry,' Philly apologised as Anna swung quickly round, 'I didn't mean to startle you.'

Anna stared at her as if she had not seen the young woman before. Philly's short dark curls made a halo about a face which glowed with health, but the eyes that were a lighter blue than Anna's were beginning to look uneasy.

'Are you alright, Anna?' she asked anxiously. 'You look as though you've just seen a ghost.'

Anna achieved a light laugh. 'This would be the right place, wouldn't it?' Until she spoke she had managed to put out of her mind the traumatic events she had been through here a couple of years ago. Now the memories flooded back, almost submerging the room as it was now. With an effort she concentrated on what she could see.

It was only a small room, this place that once the monastic porter had occupied. Two neat desks sat at right angles at the far end of the room, almost filling it. Philly's was loaded with papers in neat piles around the laptop in the centre of it. The other one was Will's, unoccupied now that he was in India, so Anna had appropriated it and covered the surface with her notes and a manuscript stack.

Nearby, just behind the window, three small armchairs fitted tightly around a low coffee table, on which stood a glass jug filled with sweet peas. As she picked out each item in the room Anna's eyes focused on the flowers and she became aware of the brightness in this room, which had once been so ominously dark.

She shook her head, smiling at Philly, as she moved forward to smell the flowers. 'I was miles away, you know what I'm like, off dreaming about the past. Did you bring these from home? They smell heavenly.'

'Yes, Mum always grows them. Let's have another coffee, and sit down at the table,' Philly said, filling the kettle at the sink behind a screen in the nearby corner. 'I'll just close down this booking list. I was working on it when somebody arrived.' She crossed to her desk as she spoke and jabbed at the keyboard of her laptop.

Coming back across the room, depositing the laptop on the coffee table, Philly disappeared behind the screen again just as the kettle began to boil. 'I'm sorry to disappear as soon as you arrived, but we've just had an unexpected booking, a man who picked up our details in Coombhaven and called by to see if there was a vacancy. I was discussing his requirements with Mum. I expect you know,' her voice sounded faintly enquiring, 'that she's doing the housekeeping for the priory apartments. And I didn't expect the new leaflets to be delivered today, so that held me up when I saw them downstairs. I just took a few minutes to sort through them and put them out. Did you meet Clive when he dropped them off? If he's coming over from Coombhaven he brings things we want here on his way to the farm, he's good like that.'

'Clive?' Anna queried. 'I didn't see anybody. But I wandered around the priory for a few minutes. I expect he came then. Who is he?'

'The plumber,' Philly explained, peering round the screen. 'If he knew you were here he wouldn't want to disturb you. He's quite shy, really. You probably don't know him, he's lodging in the village with Tilly Barlow. I reckon,' she sounded amused, 'that Tilly's got her eye on him. She's always coming up here to meet him, bringing him lunch, taking him to see the sea. He's doing some work for Mum and Dad at Home Farm, and I know he was going to Coombhaven today to get some new pipes.' She went on, seeing that Anna looked puzzled, 'Mum's going to do bed and breakfast with three of the rooms, otherwise they just stand empty most of the time. Clive's putting small ensuite bathrooms in each room.'

'Why does he bring the leaflets then? Is he promoting his work too?'

'Oh no, his cousin or something works at the Tourist Information Office in Coombhaven, and I asked if they could let me have a few to fill some gaps. Sometimes he comes over with things himself and goes down to the pub with Clive. But I guess he's busy now the tourist season is picking up, so he must have handed them to Clive to bring out. Clive's quiet, but a nice chap. He's a newcomer, but I think he wants to live around here permanently. Dad reckons he's doing a good job, so he ought to find plenty of work.'

'Are the leaflets for the apartments then?' Anna asked, trying to keep her mind on what Philly was saying, as she collected her papers from Will's desk.

'No, they're just stock things for the information room downstairs. It's surprising how popular that's been with visitors. I have to keep replacing leaflets, as well as adding new ones when they're sent in.'

Anna realised what Philly had said earlier. 'You've an unexpected guest then? Did you say it was a man?'

Philly came back round the screen holding a tray with a cafetière and two mugs, bringing the aroma of ground coffee with her, as well as a biscuit tin. 'Yes, that's right. He's taken Dorter in the cloister garth. I haven't found out yet how he heard of us, but it's quite a relief to have another booking. We've had a spate of last minute cancellations recently, and I was getting to be afraid all the apartments would be standing empty. I've spoken to Lucy and she's coming over later to discuss it, but things are improving a bit now.'

'I saw a woman just now, going into Frater,' Anna said casually, as she put her papers down on the table and pulled out one of the armchairs. 'Is she new too?' she asked, sitting down gracefully and stretching out her legs to admire her scarlet pumps.

Philly plonked the tray down. 'Yes, she's another unexpected one. At least,' she amended as she sat down opposite Anna, 'she didn't book ahead. Hugh made the booking for her, I think she's an old friend of his.'

'Oh?' Anna infused as much curiosity into the word as she could.

'You take yours black, don't you?' Philly asked, pouring out the coffee. 'I didn't put any milk in one of the mugs.'

'That's perfect,' Anna said, and waited with bated breath. As Philly opened the laptop she was forced to say, 'I saw Hugh too, just now. I didn't realise he came here much from Withern these days.'

'He doesn't normally, but he's been backwards and forwards since he brought Celia down from London at the beginning of the week,' Philly commented, her fingers flying over the laptop keys. 'And I've mentioned the booking problems to him too. I don't really think he'll deal with them though, so I expect Lucy will when she's here.'

'I'm sure she will,' Anna said. She tried again. 'This Celia, she looked interesting. Do you know anything about her?'

'Not really,' Philly said. 'She put down artist as her occupation on the booking form, but she didn't say what kind. I assumed she did something for books as that's what Hugh's business is about.'

'Oh yes,' Anna said, her spirits lightening, 'you're probably right.'

Philly looked up suddenly, with a flash of white teeth as she grinned. 'Stop it, Anna, you've got enough characters in this year's play without working on another one. That's what you're doing, isn't it?'

'I'm always doing it,' Anna agreed. 'Still, you're right, we should concentrate on discussing this year's play. I think we've covered everything pretty well already though, unless you've got any more questions. All we need to do otherwise is fix the schedule for auditions and rehearsals.'

'There are just a few points I want to check,' Philly said, scrolling down her screen.

Anna bent forward, her attention now almost fully focused on the work they were doing. Part of her consciousness listened for the sound of Frater's door opening, but still she almost started when she heard a loud rapping. Looking up, she saw that Philly had noticed it too.

'It sounds as though Celia's got a caller,' Philly commented. 'I wonder if she's in.'

'I'll have a quick look and see if she answers,' Anna said quickly. Ignoring Philly's surprised expression, Anna got swiftly to her feet and crossed to the window. She drew in her breath in surprise when she saw who stood at the apartment door. There was no mistaking the plump woman dressed in a long bright blue skirt, hanging so unevenly that it drooped on the ground at her heels. Dangling loosely from her shoulders was a heavily embroidered white top that glittered with metallic thread, and made her resemble, as usual, an exotic bird with a crown of wispy curls fading now from blonde to grey. What on earth, Anna thought, was Tilly Barlow doing here?

The door opened and Hugh appeared, apparently unfazed by the presumably unexpected visitor. Anna heard the sound of voices, the lazy drawl that Hugh adopted when he was annoyed, the light breathless tones of Tilly's, a distinct Welsh lilt that must be Celia's, but she could not distinguish the words. Tilly handed over a box and the conversation ended. As the door began to close Tilly's high titter rose to the window of the porter's lodging where Anna stood. She saw Tilly step back and stare for a moment at the apartment before turning away, almost tripping over her skirt hem.

A flicker of movement under the archway that led to the cloister garth caught Anna's attention. She looked towards it, but could only see a dark shadow just beyond in the garth, where somebody stood quite still. Whether they were male or female, old or young, it was not possible to distinguish. Nor could she tell whether they were watching Tilly or facing the other way and enjoying the view across the garth to the little church at its southern end.

It must be the new arrival, Anna thought without much interest, enjoying the ambience. What a good job they didn't bump into Tilly, that would have marred the start of their holiday.

She returned to the table. 'Tilly Barlow,' she said in response to Philly's enquiring glance. 'I was surprised to see her here.'

Philly looked at her watch. 'I think she only works mornings in the Art Shop, so she's probably finished for the day. It is nearly lunch time. And if Celia's an artist, Tilly may have brought her some paints and stuff.'

Anna was astonished. 'The time's flown by,' she said, beginning to gather her papers together. 'I'm due at Mike's for lunch. I know,' she said with an impish grin as she saw Philly's surprise, 'but he's being very useful over this community play I'm working on for Berhane, and he's even given me a few tips for this year's Rossington one. Somehow he doesn't seem as irritating as he used to.' She looked across the table at Philly. 'We have finished anyway, haven't we? If there's something else you want to go over I could call in this afternoon. I'll be at the manor anyway, I just want to run over the lie of the South Lawn again, but I'd better not do it now. I don't expect Mike's noticed the time, but if for once he has his temper won't improve if I'm too late.'

'I'm fine with it,' Philly said. 'It all seems pretty straightforward.'

'Then I'll see you next week for the auditions.' Anna closed the lid of her laptop. As it clicked she heard Frater's door opening, and was dismayed to hear two voices, Hugh's and this woman, Celia's, coming nearer as they crossed the courtyard together and then fading as they passed under the window and went out through the gatehouse.

She glanced at Philly, who had not seemed to notice. 'I'll be off then,' she said lightly. 'Thanks for the coffee, Philly. Have a good weekend.'

'You too,' Philly replied, taking her own things back to her desk. 'See you next week.'

Anna went carefully down the narrow worn treads of the stairs, thinking how lucky it was that she had left her car outside Mike's cottage and walked up. If she moved quickly now she might catch up with Hugh and meet this Celia, she thought as she hurried across the small room below that had once been where the priory's porter sat watching arrivals and departures. She heard soft footsteps passing the open door and looked up sharply to see a man moving past the tiny window. It was too gloomy under the arch of the gatehouse to distinguish much except the dark glasses and straw hat that he wore, but she guessed he was the new visitor, moving on to tour outside the priory buildings.

In her hurry Anna did not spare a glance for the leaflets and brochures piled neatly on the tables in the porter's room, quite forgetting she wanted to check through the garden and history ones to see if she could find any mention of Elowen or the Lanyons who had lived there. The ancient studded wooden door stood ajar, as it always did when Philly was working upstairs.

Anna slipped through it into the wide shaded passageway under the gatehouse. Both the gates were open, the main carriage one that she used now, and the narrower pedestrian one that flanked it. Once outside the old priory buildings the sunlight dazzled her eyes for a moment. She stood blinking on the track outside as a horrible thought struck her. Surely Hugh wasn't bringing this Celia to lunch with Mike too?

Her vision cleared, and she looked to her right, expecting at least to see Hugh sauntering ahead of her down towards the manor's back drive with its lodge and the gates out into the village. This section of track, heavily rutted for most of the years that Anna had used it, was now freshly tarmacked, and she remembered that Lucy had explained the priory guests were encouraged to use this entrance, to avoid clogging up the higher track that led to the Home Farm where Philly Leygar lived with her parents.

Anna's view was obstructed by the large barn to the south, a massive stone building two storeys high, whose roof slates were thickly lichened in yellow and bronze. She stepped further out onto the track, where the thick shrubbery that edged the grass verge had been thinned and cut back. There was now a clear view further down the track, but nobody was in sight. Puzzled, she looked around.

A few quick steps took her across the track to peer through the laurels that screened the car park. Hugh's silver Audi was there, so he had not driven away. There was only one other car, a plain black Golf. Strange, Anna thought, two separate guests should surely have two separate cars. Oh no. She closed her eyes briefly. Hugh had brought Celia down in his own car, so the woman wouldn't have one of her own here. Anna's mind whirled. Maybe Celia'd gone walking again with Hugh. Or perhaps she might have gone off on her own and Hugh was racing down to Mike's. That must be it.

Reassured, Anna stepped back onto the track and glanced beyond the huge granary that stood on the north side of the priory gatehouse, facing the barn. It was still raised high above the ground, even though the soil levels had gradually risen around the stone toadstools that supported it, but from where she stood Anna had glimpses of the lake that was generally hidden by thick banks of rhododendrons.

Sunlight glinted suddenly off the dark glasses worn by the man moving across one of the gaps in the bushes. So the visitor was going round the priory, Anna thought. It was lucky, she thought with a flash of humour, that he was doing it now. The path through the bushes could be very muddy in bad weather.

From the corner of her eye Anna saw a flash of colour on the far edge of the track, just opposite the rhododendrons. Looking quickly round she saw Tilly emerging from behind a wide oak trunk to stand under the tree's branches. She's been watching Hugh, Anna guessed at once, so he must have disappeared into the shrubbery too. She always has been a nosy woman, but she won't be able to crash through that without being heard.

But what on earth was Hugh doing, Anna wondered crossly. It was unlikely he'd have business at the Leygar's farm further down the track and Philly would surely have mentioned it if he had. Anyway he wouldn't be going there by the lake path, it was a very long way round.

The rhododendrons were still spotted here and there with late blooming flowers of red, purple and white, but were hardly worth showing off to a visitor if Hugh still had Celia with him. The lake is quite pretty, Anna thought fleetingly, now the water-lilies are out. And it was the old priory stews. That's it, she decided, Hugh's giving Celia a guided tour of the priory. Well, Mr X would probably join in when he caught up with them.

Anna glanced at her watch. Ten past one. If he's noticed the time Mike's going to be furious that neither Hugh nor I have turned up. But, she guessed hopefully, he won't have done if he's working. I don't expect he's even got lunch ready yet. Just as well I dropped off some food this morning. Still, I'd better get a move on. And, she thought grimly, if Mike was worried about me going out with Hugh, wait until he hears about this Celia.

Just as she turned to walk off Tilly came out from under the tree and saw her. There was no way Anna could move away without offending her. She gritted her teeth as Tilly waved gaily and called out.

'Hello, Tilly,' Anna said as the bright figure pattered up to her. 'I'm afraid I can't stop, I'm meeting Mike for lunch.' Reluctant as Anna was to give Tilly food for gossip, she knew Tilly would not risk bumping into Mike, whose brusque manner disconcerted her.

'Oh, that's alright,' Tilly said breathlessly. 'I'll walk down part of the way with you. I'm just waiting for my friend. He's up at the Leygars, but he'll soon catch me up.' She emphasised the pronoun, glancing at Anna from the corner of her eye. 'You are a dark horse,' she added playfully.

'What?' Anna glanced at her, and quickened her step. 'Oh Mike, you mean.' She shook her head. 'Hard luck, Tilly, nothing's going on there, we're just working together on a job and we're both so busy it's easier to do it over lunch.'

'Oh yes, of course,' Tilly said hastily, panting a little as she hurried to keep up with Anna. 'And I'd never gossip, you know, such an awful thing to do. I expect,' she went on, a waspish note in her voice, 'Hugh's working with that woman at the priory too.

They must be very busy, he didn't sound at all pleased when that man caught up with them just now.'

'Celia, you mean?' Anna sounded surprised. 'I should think Hugh's just giving her the priory tour. She's staying in one of the apartments.'

'Oh, do you know her too?' Tilly said, disappointed. 'Of course, I expect you would, living in London as well.'

'Mmm,' Anna said noncommittally, wondering what Tilly was talking about.

'I'd love to have seen her latest exhibition,' Tilly went on, 'but it's so difficult to get to London when you live such a long way off. The trains are so expensive now, and of course it would be such a long day. Anyway,' she hurried on, rather pleased to have Anna's full attention as they reached the back drive to the manor and turned down it towards the village, 'I was telling her she should have one here in the West Country, I'm sure plenty of people would like to go to it. Anyone interested in art would know Celia Vaughan. Of course, she's quite well known for her photographs as well, but it's the paintings I think are best. If you and Hugh tell her how popular an exhibition here would be, I'm sure she'd listen to you.'

'How did you meet her?' Anna asked curiously, ignoring the emphasis on Tilly's last word, as they passed the lodge.

'Oh, she came into the shop yesterday, and I knew her at once, I've seen her picture in magazines,' Tilly said, without drawing breath. 'She has her own paints, of course, but she needed a particular brush and wanted to stock up on some colours. She said she'd come away in a hurry, and had left a few things behind. I think she was surprised at how good our range is, she even ordered a few canvases too, so I dropped them off on my way home just now. And,' Tilly tittered, twisting one of her wispy curls around a finger, 'I may just have been playing Cupid too. Somebody else came into the shop looking for her. Although,' Tilly sounded disappointed, 'I wouldn't have thought he was her type.'

Anna ignored this too, biting her lip to stop herself from

asking any of the questions that were jostling around in her mind. Anything would be grist to Tilly's rumour mill. As they passed through the gates that opened onto the village street, Anna said lightly, 'I didn't know you were working in a shop.'

Tilly said, distracted at once, 'Not just any shop, of course, but the Art Shop in Coombhaven. It's got a very good reputation, and Lily, the owner you know, relies on me a lot. I get my own things there too, and of course it's nice to have a bit of discount. Things are so expensive now, and my pictures aren't selling as well as they used to, there just don't seem to be so many tourists about, and they're more careful about spending than they used to be.' She drew a breath, the colour in her red-veined cheeks deepening.

Anna took her opportunity, glancing at her watch and saying quickly, 'I'd better run, Tilly. If I don't turn up soon Mike will be coming to look for me.' With a wave of her hand she set off at a brisk pace, leaving Tilly, her mouth half-ajar, her eyes staring.

Anna was conscious of Tilly's avid gaze following her down the narrow pavement. She was glad when she had gone far enough down the sloping village street to feel free from that unsettling observation.

Slowing her pace, Anna became aware of the gentle burbling of the brook that ran in a broad channel between the narrow pavement and the street, with here and there a flat paving slab covering it to let people cross. Low granite cottages lining both sides of the street were nearly all painted in white, but occasionally a splash of yellow or pink broke out. Their frontages were bright with geraniums in pots on the steps and in troughs below the small windows. Here and there in narrow strips of front garden hollyhock spires surged upwards with tiers of coloured flowers, while feathery tamarisk billowed in fleeting glimpses of back gardens. These cottages had once chiefly been homes to fishermen, when Roscombe had its own small fishing fleet based in the cove next to the harbour at the foot of the street. There were still a couple of working fishermen living here, a few more retired ones who still came out to survey the weather every morning, and descendants of others too, although most of these now worked in nearby Coombhaven or Corrington.

Mike, Anna thought, as she approached his cottage near the harbour, was one of only a few newcomers. And as yet, as far as she knew, the village had escaped the curse of second homes.

She was fairly sure that Mike would not have gone in for prettifying his cottage, so she felt a start of surprise as she stopped by his gate, wide open as she knew it would be. Roses flowered in profusion, red, white, pink, cream, mingling with golden honey-suckle, all rambling in a tangled mass over the whitewashed cottage walls and stretching up to the roof. The scent almost overwhelmed her as she knocked on the front door.

When there was no reply she sighed and turned the door handle. As she had guessed the door was not locked, so she pushed it open and went down the shallow step into the sitting room. She had known this place well at one time and saw immediately that the lime-washed walls and ceiling were just the same, and that the pale wooden beams had not been altered. A slight frown drew her eyebrows together. Even the plain oak coffee table and brightly patterned throws draping the armchairs seemed to be the same. A suspicion crossed her mind that Mike had bought the contents too.

Anna called his name, surprised that he had not heard her come in. A grunt caught her ears. He was obviously in his dining room, the long room set back a little from the street that had originally been the wheelwright's shop, and had given its name to the cottage.

She crossed the sitting room, surprised at its neatness and cleanliness. She would never have guessed that Mike would live in such tidiness. Even the hearth of the open fire was decoratively occupied with a large basket of patterned pottery pieces. As she reached the door to the right of it that led into the dining room she suddenly wondered if there was a woman in Mike's life that she had not heard about.

The room beyond was completely different, and exactly what

Anna had been expecting. There was a long central table, a dining table, Anna presumed with a spurt of laughter. It was covered with papers and books, spread out with no hint of order. The dining chairs were pushed back higgledy-piggledy, each piled high with more stacks of papers and books. Even the floor was covered with similar heaps, with pathways between them. The two side tables were different though, they held an odd assortment of bowls, jars and glassware, all, she guessed from a quick look, very ancient. They were the only things in the room that did not seem to be covered with a film of dust.

What really caught her attention was the new spiral staircase that rose up from the far end of the room to a mezzanine floor that stretched across the room like a balcony. Mike was working just below it, at the far end of the dining table, his head bent over his laptop, which was so overwhelmed by the sea of papers that Anna was surprised he could use the keyboard.

She began to work her way towards him, treading carefully through the heaps of papers. As she approached he raised one hand irritably, swatting her away. Resignedly she moved past him beyond the staircase to a pair of French windows that stood open onto the back garden. As she looked out she felt a start of surprise again at the care that had clearly been taken with it.

Sunlight streamed down over the neatly mown lawn, the flowerbeds that had once been a tangle of overgrown shrubs had been cut back. Only the gnarled apple tree was familiar, although the canopy of leaves hid the clusters of mistletoe that she knew grew there. A small brick outbuilding was barely visible at the bottom of the garden behind the purple-flowered arcs of a buddleia, bursting upwards like an exploding firework. Anna was just wondering why Mike did not use the outbuilding as an office when she heard him push back his chair. Turning, she saw him stretching his arms above his head, flexing his neck up and down.

'That's it,' he declared with satisfaction. 'Another report bites the dust. I may,' he added, 'catch up on myself one day.' He seemed to realise who he was speaking to, and a frown gathered on his face. 'Is it lunchtime already?' he demanded. Without waiting for an answer he stood up, arching his back. 'Where's Hugh?'

'That,' Anna said emphatically, 'is quite a story.'

He stared at her, uncomprehendingly. 'Don't play games,' he snapped. His stomach rumbled loudly. 'Let's eat and you can tell me all about it. Hugh can join in when he gets here.'

'Mike,' Anna said, struck by a sudden thought, 'Hugh hasn't rung you, has he?'

The archaeologist looked at her in surprise as he joined her by the French windows. 'Why should he? He knows where I live.'

'I thought he might want to bring somebody else,' Anna remarked. 'Just see if he's called, will you?'

Muttering irritably he strode across the garden towards the back door and pushed it open. Anna followed him into the kitchen as he seized the phone receiver, pressing the buttons, and watched him he listened. 'Eight messages,' he grumbled, scowling at her as he stamped up and down the room.

'Well,' she demanded impatiently, 'is one of them from Hugh?'

He waved a hand furiously, pressing the receiver close to his ear and stabbing repeatedly at one of the buttons. The gesturing ceased abruptly, and he held up his hand, his expression suddenly alert as he listened.

Anna watched expectantly as Mike dropped the receiver onto the kitchen table and glared at her. 'I'm sure you already know what he's got to say. He can't make lunch. Something's cropped up.'

'I didn't know, but I was afraid it might be that. And it's someone that's cropped up, not something,' Anna corrected. 'A woman called Celia Vaughan, staying at one of the priory apartments. I saw Hugh with her this morning when I had my meeting with Philly.'

'Well, Hugh could have brought her too,' Mike said crossly. 'All this effort and planning, and he doesn't even turn up.'

'He seemed,' Anna said carefully, 'rather keen on keeping her to himself.'

Mike groaned and ran his hands through his hair. 'God, and I was worried about you. Don't tell me we've got to fend off another woman. No,' he held up a hand again, stopping her from speaking, 'let's eat this food and maybe I can bear to hear about it then.'

'Alright,' Anna said, looking round the kitchen, again taken aback at how neat everything was. 'Where did you put the things I brought?'

'In the fridge.' Mike had already opened its door and was pulling out packages. 'Here's your stuff. I got beef and ham from the shop this morning, and some bread and cheese. There's raspberries and cream from the farm shop as well.'

'I didn't know you could get so much locally,' Anna said in surprise as he sliced open the meat packages and slid the contents into a jumbled heap on a plate. With an effort she refrained from tidying it or commenting, and carefully did not add that she was surprised too that Mike had bothered to get it. 'I wouldn't have brought this if I'd known, but at least I haven't got duplicate things. There's just salmon and salads, with a vanilla cheesecake.'

'All this effort and Hugh doesn't turn up,' Mike said morosely, dropping the loaf onto a breadboard. 'Still,' he added, 'with your appetite not much will go to waste.'

Anna smiled brilliantly as she put out the food she had brought. 'Of course not,' she replied, refusing to let him needle her. 'Are we sitting outside, or will it be too hot for you?'

He snorted with laughter as he carried plates to the back door. 'For God's sake, Anna, I'm outside in all weathers on an excavation.'

She had found a tray and stacked it with more food, plates and glasses, taking out of the fridge the bottle of wine she had also brought that morning. Following Mike out of the kitchen she crossed the garden to the large metal table near the apple tree.

He glanced at the wine. 'Do you really want to open that?' he demanded. 'I've got beer in the kitchen.'

Anna hesitated. 'Yes,' she said finally, 'I do fancy a glass of wine. But you have beer. I can always leave the bottle for another time. I wouldn't mind some water too, in this heat.'

He looked startled but loped off to the kitchen, returning with a glass of water and a bottle of beer by the time she had laid everything out on the table and propped the tray on a spare chair. She sank down into another chair, surprised to find a comfortable cushion shielding her from the metal seat. She seemed, she thought wryly, to be in a permanent state of surprise. Maybe she hadn't known Mike as well as she thought after all.

'Really, Mike,' she said, leaning over to help herself to some of everything, 'I had no idea you lived in such comfort. Is there a woman on the scene that I haven't heard about?'

He stared at her, chewing the mouthful of beef he had just taken. Swallowing hard, he picked up his beer bottle and looked at her over its top, his eyes narrowed. 'Where have you been, Anna? René's been around for a long time.'

Anna did not have time to analyse the pang that struck her so unexpectedly. 'Oh?' she said, achieving an idle curiosity that she was proud of. 'Now Lucy's away so much I never seem to hear what's going on locally. What's René like?'

'Well, she's a force to be reckoned with,' Mike commented. 'A human dynamo. Little and full of energy.' He burst out laughing. 'About sixty, red hennaed hair, with what sounds like thirty grandchildren, but I don't really listen when she's rambling on about them. Amazing,' he commented wryly, 'how well she can clean when she talks all the time. I usually make sure I'm not here when she comes in.'

'Mike,' Anna exclaimed, her eyes sparkling with laughter, although she tried to sound reproachful. 'How could I know you'd have a cleaning lady? It's perhaps the most surprising thing I've ever heard. But,' she glanced around the garden, 'surely she doesn't do this too.'

'Of course not,' he said thickly through a mouthful of bread. 'Sends her old man. And one of the grandchildren cleans the car.

I'm surprised, with your eagle eye, that you haven't noticed that it's always spotless these days.'

'Umm,' Anna murmured, sipping her wine. She had not noticed yesterday. That was definitely a hit for Mike. 'How did you find this paragon?'

'I didn't,' he said. 'Will's housekeeper did, you know, whatshername up at the manor who runs the afternoon teas now. She came down soon after I bought this place and said René would be coming in to help, and the others just drifted in as part of René's train.' He grinned. 'I didn't really have much choice. You know what Gina,' he snapped his fingers triumphantly at remembering the name, 'you know what she's like. Bossy.'

He reached across, spearing some more ham onto his own plate. 'Anyway,' he said, 'stop going off on a tangent. Who's this woman of Hugh's you're fussing about?'

'You're a fine one to talk,' she said. 'You thought I'd be getting off with Hugh just because I went to a couple of shows and this ceremony with him.' She shook her head to stop him from answering. 'No, really, Mike, I am worried about this Celia. I've never heard of her. Have you? After all, you've known him longer than I have.'

Mike shrugged. 'No,' he admitted reluctantly. 'I've never heard of the woman. But then,' his expression brightened, 'I've got an appalling memory for names.'

'Little and nondescript to look at,' Anna said ruthlessly. 'Welsh from her accent. But she's got a presence, a self-confidence that gives her a distinctive air. She wouldn't stand out in a crowd for her looks, but you wouldn't miss her.'

Mike looked startled. 'No, I don't think I've seen her then,' he said. 'But what makes you think she's a problem?'

Anna leaned forward, one hand fiddling with the stem of her glass. 'Mike, at the beginning of the week he brought her down from London to stay without any warning at all, booking her into one of the self-catering apartments at the priory. Frater, too, one of the best ones. Philly says he's been there every day since.' Anna frowned. 'So why,' she asked, almost to herself, 'would he only be taking her round the priory today? He's had plenty of time for the tour before now.'

'What,' Mike demanded, 'are you talking about?'

'Well,' Anna said slowly, 'they were in her apartment for a bit, then they went off together out into the grounds. Through the rhododendrons, so I thought Hugh must be showing her around. But he's had loads of time to do it already, and it's one of his favourite things to do with visitors, so I can't believe he hasn't already done it. So what were they doing?'

'Not what your prurient mind is thinking,' Mike said. He added bluntly, 'He's got lots of more comfortable places to take her.'

Anna blushed. She cursed herself as she felt the hot colour rising in her cheeks under Mike's amused eyes. 'Alright, what were they doing then?' she demanded.

'A simple walk,' he suggested. 'It's busy on the cliffs at this time of year, so they probably went through the parkland.'

'And he's got time for that,' Anna pointed out furiously, 'when he can't find time to go walking with Lucy, because he's too busy. Actually,' she remembered suddenly, 'he had his camera with him, and Tilly Barlow says this woman's an artist and photographer, so maybe that's what they were doing, photographing one of Hugh's precious birds.' Mike looked incredulous, but Anna went on just as angrily, 'What's happened to all his precious work if he can spend the week over here?'

She saw Mike looked flummoxed, and pressed on, 'You didn't see them, Mike. Hugh was really interested in her. And,' she finished triumphantly, 'she's why he couldn't come to lunch today. Why didn't he just say so, if it isn't an issue? And I heard him arranging to meet her tomorrow. What's Lucy going to think of that?'

'Well, it's not our business, is it?' Mike said feebly. 'They'll have to sort it out themselves.'

'You can leave it like that if you want,' Anna said forcefully.

'But they're both my friends and I'm going to help them.'

'Whether they like it or not,' Mike muttered. 'Oh alright,' he said ungraciously, 'what do you want to do?'

'I'm going back to the manor this afternoon. I've got to check a few things on the South Lawn for the play. You know, entrances, exits, positions, just the final details really before rehearsals start. If Hugh's still around I'll find him, and make sure he comes to our picnic at Elowen this evening. He hasn't replied to my text. Lucy has, though, and she's keen to come. You could bring her as she says she's staying at the manor over the weekend to sort out a few problems with the bookings. And I want to make sure Hugh doesn't bring this woman.'

'I'll come up with you,' Mike offered. 'I'd like to see her too.' He caught Anna's eye and said hurriedly, 'It's always best to know the foe.'

'Okay, but don't say anything to Hugh about it. And don't blether on about the state of Elowen's garden. We don't want to put him off.'

'As if it would,' Mike said blandly. 'I'll stick to the building, that'll get him. I just won't say that it's nearly all ruins.'

Anna laughed suddenly. 'Mike, you could make a good conspirator after all.'

The sound of an angry voice startled Anna and Mike as they approached the priory gatehouse. They glanced at each other, knowing that it was Hugh they could hear.

'Come on,' Mike said, lengthening his stride. 'I don't often hear Hugh lose his temper. Let's see what's going on.'

Anna was beside him as they passed through the open gates. From the shade under the gatehouse arch they could see into the courtyard, where three people stood, brightly lit by the sun's glare.

Hugh stood in front of the woman Anna knew to be Celia Vaughan. His posture was belligerent, Anna recognised with a shock, and his attitude was aggressive. 'She's here for some peace and quiet, not to be bothered by other residents. So try your luck somewhere else,' he was saying.

The man who stood before him was unknown to Anna, although she recognised him as the man she had seen passing the porter's lodge earlier. His eyes were still screened by dark glasses, his face shaded by a wide straw hat, his clothes similar to Hugh's own except for the colour, chinos in dark blue, a pale blue shirt, although they looked newer.

'Okay, cool it, mate,' he said roughly. 'I was only passing the time of day, trying to be friendly like. Sorry I bothered.' He turned on his heel and stalked back into the cloister garth.

Hugh turned, putting a hand on Celia's bare arm. As he did so he saw Anna and Mike standing under the arch of the gatehouse. The anger flared on his face again for a moment, quickly masked as he regained his self-control.

'Trouble with the tourists?' Mike demanded, walking forward.

Anna followed him, feeling an unexpected relief that he was dealing with the situation. For one of the few times in her life she had not known how to react. She glanced up at the office in the gatehouse. Philly was just visible at the window, no doubt seeing whether she should come down. Anna wondered suddenly if Hugh was aware of how loud he had been.

Hugh shrugged, looking at Mike as the archaeologist stopped in front of him. 'Not really. Some of them have different ideas of how to spend their time, that's all.'

'Who is he? Is he staying here?' Anna asked as she reached the little group.

'Unfortunately,' Hugh said shortly. 'A late booking in Dorter. I thought the whole place was empty for the week, but Philly seems to have had a spate of last-minute bookings.' He sounded exasperated.

'Really, Hugh, it's nothing to worry about, he was just trying it on,' Celia broke in, her tone decisive. 'He wouldn't have persisted. Not,' she added, 'that I'm not grateful that you got rid of him. But he's the kind who'd always have to try.'

Anna looked at her enquiringly, achieving a friendly smile she was proud of. 'Are you staying here too?' she enquired mendaciously.

'Yes,' Celia said, gesturing behind her, 'thanks to Hugh, who found me such a neat little bolt-hole.'

'In hiding, are you?' Mike demanded genially.

'Just getting away from life for a bit,' she replied. 'Look, Hugh, I won't keep you from your friends.'

Hugh's glance at Anna and Mike was unusually cool. 'I'm sure they're here about their own business.'

Anna raised an eyebrow haughtily. 'Of course. We won't intrude on you.' She turned away, but was brought up short as Mike caught her arm.

'What?' she asked.

'Have you asked Hugh about the picnic?' he said, pulling a wild face at her, his shoulder turned away from Hugh and Celia, screening his expression.

'I expect Lucy's been in touch with you about it,' she said, looking stiffly at Hugh.

'No,' he said shortly.

'Well, Anna's set on celebrating Midsummer's Eve tonight,' Mike said blithely, 'with a picnic at a mystery location we've stumbled across. No need to bring anything, the village shop does a picnic hamper so we'll get enough for four. Lucy's coming, she'll love the garden, and we've got an old house, Georgian I reckon, for you.'

'It sounds tempting, Mike,' Hugh said, with a tight smile, 'but not tonight, I'm afraid.'

'For heaven's sake, Hugh,' Celia said encouragingly, 'you can't miss an opportunity like this. A magical mystery tour.' Her eyes were mocking. 'Perhaps one of you will end up turned into an ass.' Her gaze lingered momentarily on Anna's flushed face.

'Well, why don't you come too?' Hugh asked. 'Who knows, there may be nightingales to give it a real midsummer touch.'

Mike still had his hand on Anna's arm. Feeling it stiffen, he slipped his own arm around her shoulders, pulling her against his side.

She was so taken aback that the words trembling on her tongue were not uttered. Even in her own surprise, she was aware of the startled look on Hugh's face.

'Just the place, I'd say,' Mike said. 'I think that's what we heard last time we were there, wasn't it, Anna?'

'Mmmm,' she managed, trying not to laugh as she saw Hugh's amazement deepen.

'Tempting though it sounds,' Celia said, her dark eyes resting on Anna and Mike, 'what I really fancy is a night in, washing my hair. You can tell me all about it afterwards, Hugh. Maybe you can show it to me another time.'

'Well, let us know, Hugh,' Mike said abruptly. 'We'd better get on. Anna's got to sort out some details for the next play, so we can't hang around.'

'Alright, then,' Hugh said, not really disguising his relief that they were leaving. 'What time is this picnic?' he asked unenthusiastically.

'Well, I'm not sure,' Mike admitted without concern, 'but as Lucy will be at the manor and Anna's staying with me I can take them both when we're ready. You can come with us if you're still here.'

Anna's start of surprise was stifled at birth, and not for the first time she was grateful for her theatrical training. She smiled at Mike. 'That's a good idea.'

Hugh was obviously disconcerted. 'I didn't know Lucy was planning to stay here,' he said, struggling to hide his shock at Mike's comment.

'Maybe you haven't been looking at your messages,' Anna said lightly. 'She texted me about it this morning.'

'Why is she staying here?' Hugh sounded suddenly suspicious.

Anna looked steadily at him. 'You'd better ask her,' she replied evenly, and was pleased to see a flicker of anxiety in his eyes.

'I've got to get back home to Withern and spend some time in the office. I could go from there but it sounds as though it'll be easier for me to join you here later on and follow you,' Hugh said. 'What time are you thinking of going?' he asked again.

Mike glanced enquiringly at Anna. 'Sixish?'

'Yes, that'll give us plenty of time. Wear your oldest clothes, Hugh,' she advised, subduing an unworthy inclination to let him tear his chinos and light linen shirt to shreds. After all, she didn't want to give him an excuse to back out.

He nodded, and turned away to where Celia waited. Although she had not moved from the spot she had withdrawn from the exchange, flicking through a leaflet she held in her hands.

Mike drew Anna away through the arch that led into the cloister garth. The lawn here had been divided by narrow paths into four small squares, each with its own wooden bench. Lavender edged the paths, filling the air with its scent, while the bees working over its flowers made a gentle background humming in the enclosed space.

The flags of the cloister walk had been carefully replaced, the illuminators' carrels open to the light and air as before, although the monks' stools had been replaced by basket chairs. Anna glanced around to see whether the man whom Hugh had confronted was visible, but saw no sign of him. The only people around were an older couple, who were sitting quietly in two of the chairs, a pile of Philly's leaflets on the table between them. The man leaned forward to pick up another one and looked over to Anna, suddenly aware of her presence.

'Good afternoon,' he said politely, a friendly smile on his round face. 'Lovely place, isn't it? The Tourist Office was a bit cagey about it for some reason, but my Karen fell in love with the pictures. We're in the old Guesthouse. It's a bit big really, but Karen likes the thought of staying where people did in the old days. A bit different to living where the monks did. I wouldn't be quite so sure about that.'

Karen had glanced up while he spoke, her eyes running indifferently over Anna and Mike before she returned to the leaflets she was examining. She couldn't have been more nondescript if she'd tried, Anna thought, with her faded hair and bleached skin, beige trousers and top.

'Are you staying here too?' the man enquired. He dropped his leaflet and stood up to retrieve it. On his feet he was seen to be a short man, sturdily built, his face reddened from stooping when he spoke again. 'I'm Eddie Armitage, and this is my wife Karen.'

'Hello,' Anna said in a friendly fashion, rather taken with this enthusiastic visitor, and considerably amused by the pencil-thin moustache that ran above his full lips. 'No, we're not staying here, just passing through to the manor. But I'm sure you'll enjoy your visit, it's a lovely place. I've known it for years.'

'You're just the person I want then,' he said, pleased. 'I don't suppose,' he hesitated, then hurried on, 'do you know anything about the birds round here?' He patted a pair of binoculars, shiny and immaculate, that stood on the table near him. 'I'm just starting out. Bird-watching, you know. But,' he confessed, a shadow passing over his face, 'I don't know much about it, although I've got a good book. I wondered where it was best to look for something exciting.' He gazed at her hopefully, his eyes wide.

Anna felt Mike shifting impatiently beside her, and said quickly, 'I'm afraid neither of us knows much about birds.' A sudden thought struck her. 'But,' she said blithely, 'you're in luck. Hugh Carey's an expert and he's in and out of the place quite a lot at the moment. If you catch sight of him he's the man to ask.'

Mike grunted. She wasn't sure if it was amusement or horrified disbelief. But before he could say anything, Karen Armitage looked up at them. She held out the leaflet she was clutching. 'This pub down on the quay,' she asked earnestly, 'is it any good for food?'

'The Lobster Pot?' Anna queried.

Karen glanced at the leaflet and nodded emphatically. 'Yes, that's right.'

'It's very good,' Anna said encouragingly. 'They make their own meals and Bryon is a great cook. He's the owner's son.'

'Oh,' Karen's face fell. 'A young man then. I expect he'll be doing fancy stuff.'

'Some of it is, I suppose,' Anna said. 'But he does good plain meals too, fish of course, and beef from a local farm. We go there a lot.'

'Yes, well,' Karen sounded dubious.

Before she could ask more, Mike intervened, 'You should try it out for yourselves.' He took firm hold of Anna's arm. 'Sorry to leave you, but we're getting short of time. I'm sure we'll see you again.'

He tugged Anna forward and she moved with him, casting a brilliant smile over her shoulder at the couple. Eddie returned it gratefully, one hand caressing his binoculars. Karen ignored it, her attention on another leaflet she had spread out on the table.

A movement above caught Anna's eye and she looked quickly upwards to the windows of Dorter. But nothing moved behind the tiny panes of glass, nothing showed whether anybody stood there watching them.

THREE

Lucy Rossington paused, panting slightly, in the shadow of one of the trees that lined the overgrown avenue leading through Elowen's parkland. There was a strong scent of lime from the tiny flowers that dangled among the leaves over her head and a faint buzzing from the bees that were still working there in the early evening. She looked ahead to here Mike was vigorously treading down grass and nettles. He had almost reached the ivy-clad walls of the ruined house, and showed no sign of slackening his efforts, in spite of the heavy rucksack on his back.

'He is useful to have around, isn't he?' Anna said lightly as she joined Lucy. 'All that energy. It comes in handy if it's directed in the right way.'

'Is that what you're doing?' Lucy asked curiously, glancing at her friend.

Anna had taken a more leisurely approach than Lucy and was only slightly pink in the face. Her black curls sprang with vibrant life around her face, which was only slightly marred by the scratches she had acquired the previous day. She was dressed in thick denim jeans, with a heavy cotton jacket over a long sleeved t-shirt in her favourite scarlet. Her brilliant smile flashed out as she answered. 'Of course. I certainly wouldn't want to fight my own way into the garden.'

'It's hardly my idea of a romantic evening,' Lucy commented

dryly.

A gurgle of laughter escaped Anna, and her eyes sparkled. 'It's hardly that,' she said.

'But you and Mike have got,' Lucy paused delicately, remembering tempestuous confrontations between Anna and Mike in recent years, 'umm, friendly all of a sudden, haven't you?'

'I suppose so,' Anna said lightly. 'He isn't quite so difficult when you learn the knack of managing him. And he can be very useful.' She gestured gracefully along the wide swathe Mike had made down the avenue.

Lucy pushed damp strands of chestnut hair out of her eyes and leaned back against the trunk of the tree. Her figure was boyishly slender in thick jeans and a shirt, her shoulders draped with an old green jumper.

Anna glanced at her, still taken aback at the change in Lucy's hairstyle. The long smooth bob had gone, the hair was cropped short with a long fringe left over the hazel eyes. The new cut suited Lucy's small pointed face, lightly browned by the sun. Those hazel eyes had been watching Mike's progress, and now swung round to meet Anna's stare.

'I can't quite get used to it,' Anna admitted. 'Your hair. But it really suits you.'

Lucy's lips made a small dismissive moue. 'It's practical. I'm so busy I just don't have time for longer hair.'

'What does Hugh think about it?' Anna asked.

'He didn't say,' Lucy said indifferently. 'I'm not even sure he noticed, he was in such a rush.'

'What for? What was so important that he couldn't come with us?' Anna demanded. 'I'm not sure he'll find his own way here later on. I don't think I'd have been able to follow Mike's directions.'

'There was some problem at the priory,' Lucy said. 'Philly's been in touch with me about various issues, and I need to talk to her about them. Late cancellations, that sort of thing. But this is some new difficulty, I think, with one of the holidaymakers.' She looked faintly surprised. 'I didn't know Hugh was involved with the apartments, and he didn't stay long enough for me to ask him about it. But,' a slight frown touched her face, 'he's always so absorbed in his publishing business that I can't see how he's finding the time.'

Anna's heart sank. Before she could respond an angry shout startled them, and a lithe form ran towards them down the avenue.

Ben, Lucy's tricolour collie, came to an abrupt halt in front of her. His long pink tongue hung out of his mouth, which gaped open in a panting smile. His golden eyes sparkled.

'All these scents and sounds, and here you are hanging around,' Anna commented. 'It's easy enough to read Ben's mind.'

Another shout rang out.

Lucy's gamine smile lit her face. 'You don't have to read Mike's though,' she said. 'You only have to listen to him.'

Anna made an expressive gesture with her hands, raising her own voice to call back. Years of theatre training gave it a penetration and volume that carried just as well as Mike's shouting, and he fell silent.

'Come on,' Lucy said, pushing herself away from the tree. 'We don't want to put him in a bad mood when he's doing all the hard work.'

'And he's got the food,' Anna said as they set off, picking their way along Mike's trail. 'And the wine.'

She waved her hand at her own rucksack, and the one on Lucy's back. 'I've only got the tablecloth and cushions, and you've got the crockery and cutlery. We won't survive on those.'

'I hadn't expected this picnic to be so grand,' Lucy said, skirting a clump of nettles, glad of the walking boots Anna had advised her to wear.

'It's a special place,' Anna said. 'I wanted the evening to be special too.' She thought crossly of Hugh, who was again spoiling the plans she and Mike had made. Oh well, she dismissed her annoyance, I'm still glad we've come. She watched Ben's plumed tail, tipped with white, floating like an ostrich feather through the grass, luring them on in his wake. Well, there's one of us who's completely happy with the expedition, she realised.

Lucy stopped so suddenly that Anna nearly bumped into her. 'Look,' she said, 'a hummingbird hawk-moth. There on the red valerian in front of the house.'

Anna let her eyes follow Lucy's pointing finger. Hovering over the plants in a blur of wings was what looked like a small humming bird, dipping its beak into the flowers.

As Lucy moved on Anna's gaze lifted to the walls of the house in front of her. They stood higher here than at the back, in places up to where the roof had once been, but there was no trace of the stone they were built of, smothered as they were with greenery. But on this side of the house the wisteria was producing huge racemes of pink flowers. The climber's long branches fought for space with a vast rambling rose, its wide blooms a rich cream tinged with a deeper shade of pink. The ivy that crept through both of them clung more tightly to the house's structure, but was only visible in patches at the lower levels.

Anna drew in a deep breath, assailed by the sweet scents released by the warmth of the midsummer heat. A bellow startled her, and she looked round guiltily, fearing that Mike had come to collect her. But he had gone out of sight round the end of the house, and Lucy had gone with him. It was Ben the collie who came gambolling up, keen to fetch her to the others.

She bent to stroke his head and he turned immediately, willing her to follow him. It was with reluctance that she left the front of the house to stand sightless and alone, but still, she thought whimsically, with its soul.

The track around the eastern side of the house was clear enough. Mike had found remnants of a paved path that led to the back lawn to emerge from the shadow of the house under the low gnarled branches of an ancient fig tree.

As Anna passed Ben, who had paused under the tree to sniff an interesting smell, she saw Mike and Lucy standing on what she guessed had once been a terrace. Here and there the top of an ornamental urn or vase protruded above the grass that grew thickly over the old stones. Lucy was examining a plant that wound its tiny leaves decoratively around what looked like the base of a ruined pillar. She did not seem to be listening to Mike, who was staring up at the house, saying, '... difficult to know without some research. Of course ...'

Anna tuned him out too, staring around the wilderness in front of her. She could see the spot where she and Mike had come in yesterday on the far side of the hayfield that once had been a lawn, and the route they had ploughed through it to struggle out after Mike's fall. Her nose wrinkled as she thought how little she wanted to battle around or through all that scratchy grass again.

'Well, let's get going,' Mike said gruffly, making her start. He was standing beside her, his square face scarlet with effort, his red hair tousled and untidy. He was looking beyond her, along the eastern edge of the lawn, where scraggly holm oaks topped a series of Cornish hedges, the stones of their double walls lichened with silver circles, almost like prehistoric runes. The hedges seemed to be screening tiny disused fields, and Mike's gaze ran over them without interest, and moved on beyond the lawn to the shrubbery that hid the fogou.

'Oh no,' Anna said emphatically as Ben brushed past her in search of his mistress. 'This is not an archaeological expedition, Mike. Look,' she took his arm, turning him towards her, 'here beside the fig. There's some kind of stone bench curving around against the hedge bank. We can use that.'

'If it's safe,' he grunted. 'Hmm.' He moved towards the bank, his rucksack catching in the branches of the tree as he passed under it. Muttering, he retreated, shrugging the rucksack off his back and letting it fall carelessly to the ground.

'Mike, do be careful,' Anna said. 'Don't break the bottles.'

He was not listening, standing at the far edge of the bench and scraping away at the wall of the Cornish hedge with the blade of the penknife he had pulled from his pocket.

Anna raised her eyebrows, looking at Lucy with resigned amusement. 'I suppose we'll never stop him.'

'Let's get things unpacked,' Lucy said prosaically. 'That bench is a good size, and it looks safe enough to me.' She let her own rucksack slide off onto it with a sigh of relief. 'That was heavier than I expected.'

Anna dropped hers onto the ground and began to unzip it. 'You should have left Hugh's share for him to carry,' she said, pulling out a brightly patterned tablecloth 'or let me take some of it too.'

'There wasn't much point in relying on Hugh,' Lucy said, watching the collie sniff at each of the rucksacks in turn. 'He probably won't turn up at all.'

Anna glanced at her in concern, but before she could speak, Lucy went on, 'Let's put the cloth across the centre of the bench, then we can sit on either side where it curves round.'

Anna placed the cloth neatly down and Lucy began to put out the plates, as Ben lifted his head momentarily to watch them.

'I thought so,' Mike said triumphantly, stepping back from the hedge and stumbling, almost falling, over his rucksack as Ben shot hastily away from it. 'It's a proper bank further along, but here behind the bench, under the moss there's a mortared stonewall. Some kind of outbuilding, I expect.' He turned, about to walk along the bank. 'There must be a way in somewhere.'

'No, Mike,' Anna said forcefully, grabbing his arm again. 'Let's get settled and eat. We can explore later.'

He hesitated, then caught her eye, remembering why they had come. 'Oh alright,' he said reluctantly, adding with forced jocularity. 'Let's get it all set up for Hugh's arrival. Then,' he grinned malevolently, 'we can let him carry all the debris back and do the washing up. Latecomer's penalty.'

Anna released her grip and he bent over his rucksack. 'Let's see what you've got for us, Anna.' He glanced at Lucy. 'The village shop's picnic hamper wasn't enough, so she added to it. I shouldn't have told her about the farm shop, I probably won't find anything decent left there for the next few days.'

His eyes fell on the blue and white tin plates, and plastic wine glasses that Lucy was laying out. 'I hope you remembered the candles, Anna,' he added with false earnestness.

'Of course, although they're only nightlights,' she said, refusing to rise to the bait. 'You can light them later on when it's darker, but do get out the food now, Mike. There's beer in there too, for you. I didn't think you'd want wine.'

He grinned again, with genuine amusement this time. 'Okay, darling.'

Lucy darted a quick surprised look at him, but he had bent again over the rucksack, elbowing Ben aside to pull out boxes and foil-wrapped packets.

'Here you are,' he said cheerfully, handing them over to Anna. 'Let's see what we've got to eat.'

She began to prise off lids, revealing a pile of gleaming brown sausages, stacks of little quiches, a heap of pink prawns, a thick round of local brie, and releasing a strong scent of mint from a mound of tabbouleh. 'There are French sticks in the foil, they'll be a bit battered, but that won't hurt,' she said. 'Can you unwrap them, Mike, then open the wine, and there's a big box of salad still to come.'

He obeyed without a word, and she smiled at Lucy. 'Why don't you dot the nightlights around? It might be worth lighting the citronella ones now, in case of midges, but I thought they'd all be pretty later on.'

'It's pretty now,' Lucy said, one hand resting on the head of the dog who had come to stand beside her. Mike snorted in disbelief, and she amended her comment. 'Well, it's a stunning place, like something time has forgotten. And the flowers are lovely. It's a shame nobody ever comes to see them.'

'Well, maybe the wild animals enjoy them,' Anna said lightly. 'There are beaten tracks all over the lawn, so there must be plenty of foxes and badgers and deer that make their way through the long grass and call this place home.'

'They're probably more comfortable here than we're going to be,' Mike said prosaically as he struggled with the cork of a wine bottle. 'For God's sake, Anna, invest in a decent corkscrew, can't you?'

'It's yours, Mike,' she said. 'I borrowed it when I was packing the picnic. I'll get you another one, if you like.'

The cork slid out and he lifted the bottle, pouring wine into three of the glasses.

Anna frowned. 'Hugh's not here yet,' she pointed out.

'I fancy a glass myself tonight. It must be the romantic atmosphere,' Mike said meaningfully, passing one glass to her and one to Lucy. He took up his own and sat down heavily at one end of the bench.

As Anna came to join him he looked taken aback, getting quickly to his feet. 'Look, you hold this,' he said, passing his glass to Anna. 'I'll pull up a lump of wood from over there,' he gestured vaguely along the bank, 'and sit in the middle here. We don't want to leave Lucy isolated over there on her own.'

He strode off, oblivious to Anna's furious glare. How like Mike, she thought, to underline Hugh's absence.

'How like Mike,' Lucy said, sitting down on the other side of the repast, with Ben settling at her feet, 'to want better access to the food. At least,' she looked past Anna, 'it's distracting him from exploring the place just yet. How on earth did you come across it?'

'It was one of Mike's little surprises,' Anna replied, watching Mike tug a large round stump towards them. 'A gentle afternoon's stroll that turned into a hack through a tangle of undergrowth.' She regarded her closely trimmed, unvarnished nails ruefully as she spoke, and then looked up to the back of the house, hidden under the purple wisteria and scarlet roses. 'With this at the end of it.'

Mike planted the stump in front of the bench, between the two women, and sat down heavily. 'Are we going to eat?' he demanded.

'Let's wait a bit,' Anna said. 'We want to leave something for Hugh.' She looked towards the house again and suddenly she shivered.

'Are you cold?' Lucy asked with concern.

'No.' Anna rubbed her arms. 'Silly of me,' she said apologetically. 'I just keep getting the feeling we're being watched.'

'Well,' Mike said cheerfully, 'we can tell ghost stories if you like.'

Anna stared at him. 'Ghosts,' she repeated. 'I hadn't thought of that. I wonder,' she gazed at the house with more interest, 'if there are any?'

'Nonsense,' Mike said forcefully. 'The only things watching you are the foxes and deer that would normally be here without people around.'

'Yes, I should think so,' Lucy agreed. 'This place is virtually undisturbed by the outside world.'

'I know,' Anna agreed, but a small shiver ran again up her spine. In the distance a nightingale began to sing, its notes throbbing through the air.

Anna paused in her stroll alongside the hedge bank that screened the small square overgrown enclosures beyond the garden. Behind her, Lucy sat at the bench under the fig tree, gazing thoughtfully across the old lawn. Ben lay at her feet, but he was watching Anna's progress, torn between accompanying her and keeping his mistress company.

Anna looked away, intrigued by what she had found. There, half hidden by brambles and thick grass, just under the branches of an overhanging holm oak that had rooted in the bank, was a gateway leading into one of the enclosures. If there had once been a gate, it had long gone. All that remained was a tantalising view into another thicket of scrubby bushes, interlaced with honeysuckle and clematis. Blue periwinkle flowers starred the grass, and birds flitted through the branches with a fluttering of wings. A tantalising scent reached her nostrils, familiar but unidentifiable.

She was tempted, strongly tempted, to just look inside, intrigued to see whatever it was that lay out of sight.

Then she glanced surreptitiously at her watch. Eight thirty. She sighed and bit her lip in frustration, glancing back at the bench. There was no sign of Hugh, and she really did not think now that he would be coming. Oh well, she thought, Lucy and I want to eat. I'm surprised Mike was satisfied with just a few sausages before he wandered off. And now of course he's disappeared. All that casual 'I'll just have a stroll until Hugh comes'. Now I wonder, she touched a pensive finger to her painted lips, where in this huge hidden garden I'm going to find him. She smiled to herself. At least with Mike there was never much doubt where he'd be, with an archaeological site on offer.

She glanced back again at the bench under the fig, where Lucy leaned back, her legs stretched out in front of her, Ben now resting his head on her ankles. Her fingers were toying with the stem of her wine glass, her eyes still settled idly on the overgrown lawn in front of the house. She seems quite happy where she is, Anna decided. I'll leave her in peace. After all, she had a long drive back here from Hampshire this morning. And, she thought optimistically, with the nightlights lit, that's a really romantic spot for Hugh to find her, if he does bother to turn up.

Anna reluctantly moved on alongside the bank, following the route Mike had taken more than ten minutes ago. Without hesitation she walked on into the overgrown bushes that grew thickly beyond the lawn, following the faint track that she knew led to the fogou. At least she hadn't heard any sounds of disaster, she reflected. And if he'd tried to go down into the fogou she was sure there'd be another landslip.

A deer barked in alarm in the distant thicket to her right, and a blackbird flew off, shrieking his staccato alarm call. Anna paused, surprised. Surely she wasn't close enough to startle them. Her nicely pencilled eyebrows drew a shade closer. I hope, she thought, Mike hasn't gone wandering off over there.

Anna called his name, and was startled to hear him reply from her left, quite close to her. She pushed past a flowering oleander and there was the fogou in front of her. But Mike was nowhere to be seen.

She stepped closer to the edge with some care, and peered down the slope at the entrance to the underground chamber. Mike's tumble down it yesterday seemed to have altered the unstable balance of the stones and soil that must have been used long ago to partially fill in this sloping approach. The rubble against its entrance had shifted, now piled higher on one side than the other, exposing a narrow gap in the wooden planks that had closed off the chamber, a gap that was large enough for a slender person to pass through.

Her heart skipped a beat. Surely Mike wouldn't have been stupid enough to go in, not on his own. No, she realised quickly, he had called her from the open. So where on earth was he?

She looked round, scanning the thicket behind her, and her eye was caught by a movement of branches. 'Mike,' she called again, stepping forward and parting the shrubbery to peer through, 'do come back. We might as well ...'

Her voice broke off in an abrupt cry of surprise and fright as a heavy figure hurtled towards her, pushing violently past her. She staggered back, and felt the earth disappear from beneath her uncertain feet. Desperately she tried to throw herself forward, but she only succeeded in landing painfully face down on the slope of moving stones and earth that slid her inexorably towards the underground chamber.

More stones and soil fell lightly, then harder and harder on her unprotected head and body. Suddenly she was hit again, but this time she knew that it was a person, Mike, landing beside and partly on top of her, swearing furiously as he half scooped, half dragged her down the shaking slope.

Shoving hard, he forced her through the narrow gap into the chamber, and released her, letting her fall heavily to the earthen floor. Grunts, gasps of pain, and he followed her with a tearing of his shirt and jeans as he wriggled through the too small gap. He leaned back, blood streaming from cuts on his face, arms, chest and legs. Beyond him there was a faint gleam of light showing through the dust cloud created by the falling earth. The gleam grew dimmer, the rattle of stones and soil more muffled, until at last they were entombed in darkness and silence.

It was Ben who alerted Lucy. She had been gazing at the lawn, struggling at first to keep at bay her growing irritation at Hugh's tardiness. Gradually her eyes drifted across the scene in front of her, until she was wondering about the wild flowers that might be growing there and in the tangled mass of the garden that lay around it.

When the collie leaped to his feet, his ears pricked and alert, he startled Lucy. She sat up straighter, looking to see what he had noticed. It must be Anna and Mike returning, she thought, relaxing. Then the rumble of falling earth and rocks reached her, that terrible sound that was so horribly familiar, bringing back memories from the previous year that she preferred to forget. She froze for a few seconds, unable to shake them off.

Ben sprang forward, forcing her back to the present. This was now, not then when she had been falling with the thud and thump of soil and stones on her body. The past faded completely as she ran after the dog, following the route that first Mike, then Anna had taken.

Just as she reached the overgrown tangle of shrubbery beyond the lawn she saw Ben stop, his hackles raised. She got to his side and could hear the crashing of a heavy body in the bushes, blundering towards them. Her hand went out to Ben's collar just as the figure burst out in front of them.

Not a deer as she had feared, but a person dressed in black, a fleece hood pulled over their head. She caught a glimpse of distorted features and bulging eyes and then the figure lumbered towards her.

Ben's lips rolled back, exposing a gleaming set of white teeth, and a ferocious snarl filled the air, startling Lucy, and sending the person flinching away and around Lucy's far side. The collie struggled to free himself, desperate to follow as the person ran away towards the house.

Lucy's fingers had tightened unconsciously on the dog's collar, but now she had to make a considerable effort to hold him back. 'No, Ben,' she said sharply, aware of the fright sounding in her voice, knowing it would not reassure the dog. She took a deep breath and said the command again, more calmly and forcefully.

Ben's tugging slowed and stopped, but his hackles were still up and his body stiff. 'It's alright,' Lucy said gently, 'alright, Ben, you've seen him off.' She glanced anxiously through the trees, where a film of dust seemed to be settling over the bushes. 'We've got to go this way. We've got to find Anna and Mike.'

She pulled gently, urging him onto the track through the bushes, reasonably sure that this was where Anna at least had gone into the shrubbery. Sure too, beyond doubt, that this was where the man had come out. Her heart was pounding as she wondered what it was that he was running from. What it was that he had done. Even in her anxiety and fear her thoughts hesitated. He. She was saying he, but had it been a man?

She had no time to think any more about it as she rounded an oleander, for Ben had been tugging her ahead and now he stopped suddenly, so that she almost fell over him. In front of them azaleas dropped scarlet petals like tears over the large rectangle of newly turned earth in front of her. There was a shallow dip in it, where the soil and earth had sunk as far as it could go before it settled further. Lucy's heart that had been beating so hard seemed to stop, skipping a beat. The rectangle looked horribly like a large newly dug grave.

She sucked air into her dry throat and tried to call Anna's name. Only a croak came out. She tried again. This time it was a scream, Anna's name again and again. Lucy leaned precariously forward, trying to see through the cloud of dust that hung in the air, then spinning round to stare desperately into the bushes that grew so thickly all around. She called Mike's name. But there was still no answer. Nobody called back.

It was Ben's whining that stopped the hysteria she could feel rising inside her. With an effort she relaxed, looking down to reassure the dog, who had slipped out from under her hand when she began calling. But he was not looking at her. He was sniffing cautiously along the edge of the filled-in pit. He whined again and then began to bark. Short sharp barks.

Lucy moved quickly to his side. So that was it. This really was a grave, and Anna and Mike were down there. How on earth could they have survived such a fall of earth?

Her mind was crystal clear now, and one of Anna's comments came back to her, about why she and Mike had first come to Elowen. Mike had been looking for an underground chamber, a fogou, and had found it by virtually falling into it.

A chamber. Lucy's thoughts fastened onto that. If they were in there they could still be alive. She ran her eyes quickly over the ground. She knew at once that she could not deal with that amount of earth. She would have to get help. And that meant finding somewhere that had mobile reception. Or perhaps flagging down a car if she got as far as the lane.

She called Ben and turned to run back the way they had come. The collie came bounding towards her. Before he reached her she heard an ominous sound. An unpleasantly familiar crashing noise in the undergrowth. And it was getting closer. Somebody was coming towards her, coming quickly, not worried about conceal-ment.

Lucy looked round frantically. There was nowhere to run to, and nowhere to hide without making a lot of noise herself. Her lips tightened. And there was no time. Not if she was to get help for Anna and Mike.

She bent down and picked up a stout stick that lay in a heap of fallen branches. Grasping Ben's collar, she moved quietly to one side of the track that led to the clearing and waited, determined now to deal with the person who was coming. But Ben wriggled free of her grip, and in spite of her emphatic command he darted away towards the lawn.

Hugh Carey was not in a good humour as he picked his way along the track that his wife and friends had made down the overgrown avenue through the parkland. He had left his silver Audi behind Mike's Passat at the side of the still splendid entrance gate, but it had taken him longer than he had expected to find the place. Mike's directions had been cursory, and Anna had not done much to amplify them.

Anna was, Hugh knew, not pleased with him. This evening, for some reason he had not yet fathomed, had a special meaning for her. His black mood lifted slightly as he reached the front of the house, where the late evening sun lit the frontage as if spotlights had been turned on it. Elowen, that was it. He remembered now that he had meant to look it up, find out more about it.

His lips twisted in an ironic smile. It would have been wasted effort anyway. Mike would surely know all about it. Hugh's smile relaxed into genuine amusement. No doubt Lucy and Anna did too by now.

He looked curiously at the green-clad walls in front of him, trying to pick out any architectural features. But a quick survey convinced him that there was no chance of that at all. The greenery that covered the house hid any clues. And the flowers that made it beautiful, even in its ruined state, would have delighted the Romantic garden designers.

Romantic. A sudden thought struck him, startled him in fact. Surely Anna and Mike weren't going to make any kind of announcement tonight. They had seemed unusually close earlier that day, he remembered with a shock.

Hugh glanced at his watch, stunned to realise it was nearly nine o'clock. He had not meant to leave the priory so late, but Celia … His thoughts broke off as he moved on rapidly.

He skirted the house, identifying the path that Mike had found, and stopped abruptly in front of the overgrown lawn that spread out in front of him. To his west the sun was sinking in a sky streaked with gold and pink, turning the line of trees on the horizon into darkening silhouettes.

The glimmering flicker of tiny flames caught his eye and he turned to the left, seeing the dim corner under the fig tree lit by the nightlights, looking like a small cave with an inviting meal spread out on the coloured cloth that covered the stone bench. He noticed with a pang of guilt that they had not started eating without him. He had expected only the crumbs of the feast to be left.

He frowned. But where were they? Surely Anna and Lucy hadn't allowed Mike to inveigle them into exploring the grounds.

There was a heavy crashing in the bushes at the far end of the lawn, beyond the line of the Cornish bank that edged the eastern side of the lawn. Hugh moved out, standing on a hummock for a better view, and to be better seen if his wife or friends were looking that way.

At first Hugh thought the crashing was heading towards him, then he realised it was fading away, going in the other direction, westwards. A deer perhaps. He was about to call out when he heard a woman screaming in the shrubbery. Lucy. It was Lucy screaming.

Hugh began to run, too fast at first, stumbling over hazards in the grass and slowing his pace fractionally until he found the track the others had followed. Still the screaming rang out. Then it stopped and Ben began to bark. Short sharp barks.

A hard moving body hit Hugh in the legs and he staggered. By the time he realised what had happened, Ben was running around him, trying to hurry him on, virtually nipping at his heels.

Hugh pushed his way through the overgrown shrubs, even more concerned now, knowing that Ben would not normally have left Lucy. His chinos tore on brambles, he tripped painfully over a rope of honeysuckle that booby-trapped the track, sweat trickled down his neck attracting midges that bit viciously at his skin. He was panting as he rounded a flowering oleander, ducking as he felt the wind whistle around his ear from a stout stick aimed at his head. He spun round, struggling to keep his balance, his fists raised, in time to see the stick dropping from Lucy's hand.

She seemed a fragile figure, poised for a second against the pink blossoms on the oleander. Her face was milky white, her hazel eyes huge. And for the first time, oddly, he noticed her short hair.

They met involuntarily, each leaping forward at the same moment. His arms went out to hug her, relief surging through him that she was safe. But she held him off, her hands clutched hard on his arms, shaking him, words pouring out of her.

'They're under that. Anna and Mike. They're down there, they're under that. I'm sure they are.'

Hugh did not understand at first. Not until he turned to see the large rectangular pit almost filled to the brim with fresh soil. He moved, gripping her hands now, pulling her against him. 'What happened? Slowly, Lucy.'

Lucy struggled to regain her composure. She gulped hard, glad to feel Ben pressing against her legs. His warmth was reassuring. 'We were waiting for you, and Mike went off to look for this chamber. When Anna and I decided it was time to eat, she went to find him. Then I heard a crashing, and a man came bursting out of here, and there was dust and stones falling, and Ben was whining around the pit. I don't know what that man did, but I'm sure they're down there, Hugh. I called and called, and nobody answered. They can't be anywhere else.'

His arm was tight around her shoulders, and she was glad of that too. All their differences were forgotten, and once again all she knew was that he was Hugh, the man she loved, and that their friends once again needed help.

'If they're under that,' he said thickly, 'they don't stand a chance.'

'It's a tomb, Hugh.' In her anxiety to tell him, she turned and looked at him, realising at once that she had said the wrong thing.

'No, no, not that. It's not a tomb,' she picked her words more carefully, 'this is the entrance to an ancient chamber, a fogou. Mike told Anna, and she told me. If they're in that then surely they've got a chance.'

His eyes ran over the pit, then beyond it to what could be a slight curved mound where brambles and silver birch saplings grew thickly around a few larger trees. 'Yes,' he said, 'a chance, but ...' He stopped himself abruptly, biting back the words. 'Right, let's get to the cars. Mike will have a shovel in his boot, I've never known him not to have equipment in his car for a dig. God knows I never thought to be grateful for that. And you must get mobile reception or stop a car, then wait for the emergency services.'

He turned, pulling at her arm, and the three of them began to run as fast as they could. Out of the shrubbery, along the lawn, past the bench with its deserted picnic under the fig tree, round the corner of the house.

Hugh ran on in front, leaving Lucy to come as fast as she could. She ran quickly too, one hand clenched over her mobile, glancing at it repeatedly to see if that blessed symbol should appear, granting her enough reception to ring for help. Ben loped at her side, knowing this was no game, glad that there was action now.

Behind them, the dust had settled in the small clearing and the freshly filled pit lay still and silent. A blackbird alighted on the topmost tip of a nearby oak, and his clear notes rang out. Further away, down in the hidden valley a solitary tawny owl called, just once, almost experimentally. And deep in the shrubbery the sweetness of the nightingale's voice filled the encroaching night.

Anna lay sprawled on the earthen floor in the darkness, too stunned to move or think. Gradually she became aware of the coldness of the ground through her clothes, the gritty dust on her mouth and lips, the throbbing aches all over her body which would become bruises when they had chance to develop. Or worse. Cautiously she moved her arms and legs, relieved to find they worked. Still cautiously she pushed herself stiffly up onto her hands and knees.

Her mind was working again too. She must be inside the fogou. With Mike. Surely he had got into it too, just before the falling stones and soil had blocked the gap that he had pushed her through. She cocked her head, straining to hear in the silence. There it was, the sound she had hoped to hear. Another person breathing.

The spurt of gladness and relief was quickly capped. There was something wrong about that breathing. It was deep, laboured. And why wasn't he talking, swearing? He'd had enough to say when he was shoving her down here, protecting her from the deadly hail that was falling on her.

'Mike,' she called softly. Then she called again, louder, more insistently. Only the heavy breathing was to be heard when she fell silent.

Anna began slowly to stand, wincing with pain, her hands raised slightly above her head. She had no idea what size or shape a fogou was, and whether there would be enough room for her to stand upright. With a quickly suppressed shudder she remembered with sudden clarity a prehistoric tomb she had once visited in Wiltshire, dug into the ground and capped with stone. It had seemed horribly like this place.

It was with considerable relief that she finally stood up straight. Her raised hands just brushed the roof above and it seemed to be solid earth, ridged with tree roots. It showed no sign of movement, not even a trickle of soil fell when she touched it carefully with her fingers.

Now her hands went out in front of her as she inched her way forward, closer and closer to the sound of breathing. Her toes stubbed Mike's feet before her hands reached an earthen wall. Crouching quickly, Anna felt up his legs, over his body, realising he was slumped against the wall, half covered with a layer of soil and rubble. As she crawled alongside him to check his head she felt her sleeve catch roughly against wood. It must be the entrance, which had once been sealed off with planks. Mike had got through the gap in them just in time and then he must have collapsed, with earth falling through the gap on top of him until the entrance was blocked.

Anna frowned as her fingers skimmed lightly across his face, feeling the stubble on his chin sharp against her skin. He had not broken any limbs at least, so what was wrong? She drew in a sharp breath as she felt the warm blood that lay in a sticky trail down one side of his face. Her probing fingers found the source, a jagged wound on his forehead, just at the hairline.

She bit her lip hard as she felt under his jaw for a pulse. There it was, thank God, beating strongly. Surely that was good. Although she would at that moment have given a great deal to have him awake and aware too, cursing no doubt, but company, living company. He was still company, she assured herself quickly as she scooped soil off him with her cupped hands. She wasn't on her own. She didn't, she thought with another shudder, think she could have borne that. To be buried alive alone.

Stop it, she admonished herself, sitting back and digging her nails into the palms of her hands. Mike probably saved my life by getting me down here. Now I need to return the favour, so that he has chance to revel in being a hero. A smile trembled on her lips, although tears welled in her eyes, as she remembered how many times he had arrived too late, or been superfluous, at the scene of any action.

Right, she thought, blinking the tears away, I'm a heroine in a play. Not terrified Anna Evesleigh trapped here, but Anna Evesleigh playing a part. I've got to search for a way out of here. Who knows, there may be some hole or gap we can get through before the rescue party comes. And Lucy will be getting help, so there will be a rescue party. It was with a huge surge of relief that Anna remembered Lucy.

Then the blackness of spirit threatened to return. What about the person who had burst out of the bushes? What if Lucy had met him?

Lucy has Ben, Anna reassured herself. Ben won't let anyone hurt her. Now come on, Anna Evesleigh, renowned actress, get on with playing the brave heroine.

She left Mike's side with reluctance, loath to leave the only other living creature in this underground chamber, but standing up cautiously and stepping over him. She began to run her hands over the wall of hard compacted earth, up and down and across, careful to miss no part of it. There was nothing, not even a rabbit hole, and Anna lost track of time as she moved slowly along the boundary of the chamber. From time to time her feet crunched on small objects. At first she had investigated them eagerly, hopefully, although she didn't know what use they might be, but always she found them to be the dried little bones of rodents or rabbits who had died here.

She had no sense of the fogou's size either, and was unable to tell whether the wall ran in a straight or curved line, so when she stumbled over an obstacle she was sure at first that she had gone full circle and got back to Mike. Then cold as she was she felt herself turn even colder. It wasn't Mike. There was no feel of living solidity to the body she had found. Not a body, she reassured herself hastily, just an object. Mike said a fogou wasn't a tomb.

Most underground chambers hold bodies though, muttered that insidious little voice in her head that she was trying to ignore.

Alright, Anna said it out loud, the words almost deafening her in the enclosed space. Alright. If it's a body it's been dead for a very long time. It's not going to hurt me now. And an ancient body may have been buried with something useful, an axe, a sword, something that I can dig with.

She crouched down abruptly, her hands going to the shape in front of her. She ran her fingers over it lightly, their tips now unusually sensitised. Yes, it was the shape of a person. So yes, again she said it out loud, it's a body. But she was faintly puzzled as she felt more carefully along the bones of a leg. Surely the body wouldn't have been put in such a heap, it would have been laid out?

She nearly fainted when she touched a hand. A wizened dead hand, whose leathery skin still clung to the brittle fingers. Sudden realisation hit her, sending her backing away in horror. She had been feeling over clothes, modern clothes, or the remains of them, with buttons and zips. This wasn't an ancient burial. Somebody else had been left down here to die. That was why the bones were in such a heap. Whoever it was had been trying to get out, just as she was now.

How she got back to Mike she never knew. She was crouched by his side, his head resting on her shoulder, his hand in hers, when she next became aware of anything. Strange, it was almost as if she had been to sleep. In fact, she still felt very sleepy. And it seemed very hot down here now, when before she had been so cold.

I'll just have a quick nap, Anna thought drowsily, then I expect Lucy will be here with the cavalry.

FOUR

Lucy stood in the shelter of a large oak, one hand on Ben's collar, glad of the thick jumper she had brought with her and the jacket she had retrieved from Mike's car. It was well past eleven, and the summer night had turned extremely cold. Stars were out in the luminously dark midsummer sky. In the distance a single nightingale sang, the clear beautiful notes ringing around her ears. The air in the garden clearing was sweetly scented with jasmine and roses and honeysuckle, heady after the warmth of the evening.

It should have been just what she knew Anna had wanted, an evening of romance. Every element was there to make it that, even Mike had seemed to be playing his part properly. But the memory of that carefully planned picnic seemed like another lifetime now. Anna's careful choice of food, the sheltered corner on the bench under the fig tree, the flickering nightlights, they must all still be there waiting under the stars near the ruined house.

Yet Lucy felt as though she had fallen into a nightmare and was looking out on a war-torn landscape, where once there had been loveliness. The oleanders that had colonised the area around the fogou had been hastily pulled up and lay in scattered heaps among the trees. Scarlet and pink petals lay everywhere, but their beauty failed to hide the destruction around them. Brambles and bushes had been torn up as well, to provide access for the huge arc lights that now turned the clearing into a halogen-bright resemblance of day, and left the surrounding trees in a heavy blackness.

But Lucy's eyes did not rest on the spoiled loveliness around her. They were fixed on the pit in front of the fogou. The rescuers had been trying for some time to sink a ventilation pipe down to and through the planks that separated the underground chamber from the pile of earth and rubble. She saw the man supervising the job stand back and the other men working on it straighten, rubbing their hands down their trousers. They did not seem disappointed, so she hoped their efforts had been successful.

Before she could call Hugh to ask, there was a disturbance beyond the cluster of people standing near her under the trees, out of the way of the rescuers. The older man she had heard called Aaron came past, holding one end of a thick plank. The other end was held by a younger man, one who was surely related to Aaron as there was a strong physical similarity between the two. More pairs of men and women came through the trees, their faces starkly white in the artificial lighting, to lay similar planks in a heap close to the pit.

'Here's where we start,' Aaron said in his slow deep voice with the soft local accent. 'This end, away from the entrance. Then if that rubble shifts it should fall this way. But take it slowly, boys, we don't want to let any more earth collapse into the space we're making.'

The sirens of police cars and ambulances had brought out the villagers in force some time ago. They had come in dribs and drabs, knowing by local osmosis that there was trouble and what was needed. They came with blankets, spades, ropes, buckets, ready to be of use. After the early arrivals came the others, women mainly, with flasks of coffee and tea, bottles of water, tins of cakes and biscuits, even hastily cut sandwiches.

Lucy had been holding a chunky piece of French loaf for some time, unaware that she had been clutching it until it had grown limp, the sliced chicken inside it dangling over its edges. Ben had been eyeing it for a while, but now he stirred, turning his head away.

'Best eat that, my lover,' a voice said in her ear. 'You'll need to keep yourself going.'

Lucy started and turned. It was Aaron who stood beside her, his strong old fingers clasped around a mug of soup.

'Did they get the pipe down alright?' she asked.

He nodded. 'Aye, they know what they're doing, they've had enough experience with mine shafts and caves and the like. Now it's just a matter of time, taking it slowly and carefully, and we'll have your friends out. Though,' he shook his head disbelievingly, 'what they were doing down there beggars belief. It was only yesterday we were talking about it. I never thought they'd come back. 'Tis dangerous here, this old place hasn't been safe for years.'

'I don't think they meant …' Lucy began. Before she could finish Hugh was beside her, a warning hand on her arm, stretching the other hand down to greet the collie, who was patently relieved to see him, a known face among all these people.

'It's thanks to you, Mr Tregonan,' he said warmly, 'that we've got on so quickly. If you hadn't known this place so well we'd have wasted time seeing if we could get into the fogou another way, and then fetching planks from a distance.'

Aaron swallowed a great gulp of soup that was so hot the steam seemed to escape in little swirls from the corners of his mouth. 'The planks were easy. The old estate sawmill was just stopped in its work one day. Money ran out, I suppose. Anyhow, the old lady who lived at Elowen then, Mariot Lanyon she was, she upped and told the men to stop. They left it just as it was, work in progress and all.' He sighed. 'A lot of the stuff was pinched later on, of course, but not all of it. Lady Lanyon still put the fear of God into most people, and they wouldn't risk meeting her out here, old as she was by then.' He sighed, looking round appraisingly. 'I knew this place as a boy, before the old lady let it go to rack and ruin. When I last saw it, more than forty years ago it'd be, the roof of the fogou was several feet thick, with saplings growing over the top.' He waved a hand towards the trees growing beyond the pit. 'That's them now, thicker than my body, each of them. Take them down, and like as not the roof will fall in too.'

He saw Lucy's expression. 'But don't you worry, my lover. That isn't going to happen. Slow and easy, and we'll get in through the front, the way the old ones did when they built it. Young Cal there, he knows what he's doing. Part of the lifeboat crew, he is, my brother's son. He'll not lose his head. Still,' he drained his mug, 'I'd best get back and give them a hand with the digging. 'Twill get done faster if we all take a spell.'

Hugh lingered for a moment. 'Are you alright, Lucy?' he asked with concern.

She nodded. Her face was drawn tight to its bones, her lips pressed so closely together it looked as though they would never part again. With an obvious effort she opened them. 'Yes, I'm okay. You go on.' Her eyes passed to the activity behind him. Two lines of people had formed up, in one direction already passing buckets of raised rubble away from the pit out of sight to be emptied, in the other lightly swinging the buckets back to be refilled. 'I'll help over there. Ben won't be in the way if he stays beside me.'

Hugh turned to see what she meant. He nodded. 'Fine. I'll go and take my turn at the digging.'

Lucy watched him go, noticing suddenly the scratches on his hands, and his torn and dusty clothes. She glanced down at herself as she broke the French bread into pieces, feeding them one by one to the dog. She was in just as bad a state as Hugh was, and she knew why, it was the result of that frantic terrified run through Elowen's overgrown garden and parkland. She did not want to think about it, any of it. She stepped forward and the line of bucket emptiers parted to absorb her.

The handles of the buckets that passed through her hands blurred. She could not then or later say how many she had moved, with Ben lying close against her feet, keeping his head down, his golden eyes clouded with the anxiety he felt all around him. When the latest bucket was taken from her hand by somebody behind her and an arm pulled her away from the line she stood in, Lucy was dazed, not sure what was happening. Nobody in the lines reacted, they were all concentrating on the buckets, moving them as quickly as possible away and back to the pit.

Lucy looked up without any surprise into the grey eyes of Inspector Rob Elliot, a leading member of the regional crime unit. She accepted his presence unquestioningly, but realised dimly how concerned he must be. After all, he and Anna were good friends, in fact Lucy had once thought they were more than that. Rob's eyes were normally cool and reserved, but were now dark with concern as he stared down at her, his face drawn with worry. Ben got up without his usual exuberance and pressed quietly against Rob's legs.

'Lucy, tell me quickly what happened, then I'll go and give the diggers a hand. Strictly I'm on a new case over your way, but I heard about this and came at once.' He was stripping off his coat and putting it round her shoulders as he spoke.

'I mustn't stop,' she said urgently. 'There's so much rubble to move.'

'Tom's taken your place,' he said, gesturing towards the square figure of his detective sergeant, whose presence seemed to have energised the line of bucket handlers. 'But I need to know what's happened.'

'Anna and Mike are down there, in the underground chamber. I think they are. They aren't anywhere else.' Lucy brushed her hand wearily over her forehead. 'They went off, Anna was looking for Mike, then there was a man, and a cloud of dust over the pit. Aaron, he's local,' she gestured vaguely at the diggers, 'says the pit was only ever partially filled in after the entrance was barred, but he thinks the walls of the slope were maybe unstable after all the rain we've had recently, and that's why they've fallen in now.'

'The man.' Elliot fastened on the point. 'What was he doing?'

'I don't know.' Lucy frowned. 'Running away from here. If Ben hadn't been with me I think he'd have attacked me.'

'Would you recognise him again?'

Lucy shook her head. 'No. He was in dark clothes, with a hood over his head. And his face was covered by it. He was either furiously angry, or mad, or very afraid. I couldn't really see him properly, I suppose. He seemed very tall, but I'm not sure that he actually was. And really I'm not even sure it was a man.' She gripped his arm. 'Look, Rob, I've got to get back. I can't stand here talking.'

He put his own hand over hers. 'I know. But have something to eat and drink, otherwise you'll be of no use.' He looked around and saw a couple of women nearby, handing out hot chocolate from a large flask and passing round a box of cake. He waved an imperative hand, attracting their attention, and called, 'Can you bring something over here.'

He ignored Lucy's protests, and said firmly, pulling off the jacket of his beautifully tailored grey suit, 'You're not to come back until you've eaten a whole piece of cake and drunk a mug of chocolate. We can't,' he said firmly as he saw the mutinous expression on her face, 'waste time dealing with fainting women who should know better.'

Mutiny was replaced with shock as she stared after him as he draped his jacket over an oak branch and strode towards the diggers. Automatically she accepted the piece of fruitcake pressed into one hand and clasped the other hand around the beaker that was held out to her.

'He's right, my lover,' the older of the two women said reassuringly. 'You get that into you. Bryony makes a mean fruitcake. Mean's the word too, she never gives me the recipe no matter how often I ask.'

The light comment attracted Lucy's attention. She began to nibble at the cake, swallowing it without much interest, dropping a few crumbs for the attentive collie. She glanced over at the lines of people strung out from the fogou. Those with their backs to her were merely assorted black shapes, tall, medium, short, slender, rounded, bulky. Although many of them had shed their coats and jumpers, it was still difficult to see whether they were men or women. They were just people who, in a time of need, had fallen into place to help, swinging loaded buckets from hand to hand out of sight into the trees, keeping a constant movement going while there was still earth to move out of the pit. Opposite them the light shone on the faces of another line, but it was such a strange light that it distorted the colour and features it illuminated, and for an instant Lucy was reminded of a mediaeval painting of hell that she had once seen.

She tore her thoughts away from that mental image, turning back to the women who had stayed beside her. To her surprise she found that she had eaten the cake and drunk the hot chocolate.

'It was good, wasn't it?' the woman remarked, noticing her empty hands. 'Here, Bryony, give her another piece. Good job you were up to your Dad's with it. But you'll have to be baking him another, Aaron couldn't be going without a slice of cake to his tea.'

Bryony silently held out the box, where only a couple of pieces of cake remained. She said nothing, and kept her eyes down on the box that she was clutching. Ben glanced at her, black nostrils whiffling, then he looked away, totally indifferent to her presence.

Lucy was abstracted by the woman's silence. It was heavy, hinting at things waiting to be said. She looked over at Bryony, who was considerably taller than Lucy. Her thinness was obvious even under the strange scarlet cloak she wore, whose colour was dulled but still remarkable in the artificial duskiness under the trees. Her face was shadowed by the wide hood that she had over her head, partly concealing the colour of her long straight hair, all but the white streak that crowned her high forehead.

Seeing Lucy's attention the older woman, anxious to keep Lucy occupied, said brightly, 'Bryony's not one for talking. Perhaps it's just as well, we don't want her hexing us.'

Lucy turned startled eyes on the older woman, who smiled broadly, pleased at the result of her effort. 'Bryony's our witch, you know. Not really, of course,' she added hastily, catching sight of the local vicar passing through the group nearby. 'Although I'm not sure she didn't believe she was when she was a child. But she makes a nice living out of her witch shop in Coombhaven. And she always dresses the part.' She finished with a note of indulgence in her voice.

Bryony glanced at Lucy and away again, and Lucy was taken aback at the blankness of her eyes. They weren't looking at her now, though, but beyond to the lines of people that formed a human avenue up to the pit. A man was walking heavily over towards the women under the trees, his steps uncertain, his eyes momentarily confused by the change of light under the branches.

'Here, Cal, take something to eat,' the older woman said loudly, reaching out to grasp his arm and pull him closer. There's still some cake, and I'll fetch another flask. There's a couple more over in my basket.'

She had gone as she spoke, pushing Cal towards Bryony. Bryony's still figure seemed to have stiffened, her eyes were full on the man's face, but she said nothing as he looked back at her. She pushed the box at him, releasing her own grip as he took it.

Lucy was puzzled, aware of a strange atmosphere between them, but she had no inclination to dwell on it. 'How is it going?' she demanded eagerly.

Cal glanced at her as he swallowed a mouthful of cake. 'Not at all badly,' he said. 'We've shifted a lot of the rubble, and are putting in planks to hold back the rest where we can. And there've been no more falls from the sides. We can't be doing with that.' He nodded to Bryony, pushing the empty box back at her. As he turned towards the pit again he glanced aside at Lucy. 'Your friends, aren't they? Don't you worry. We'll have them out of there pretty soon.'

Lucy returned to the line with Ben, taking the place of an elderly man who was beginning to flag after nearly an hour's labour, and standing next to Sergeant Tom Peters' reassuring bulk. He was familiar from many incidents the four of them, she and Anna, Hugh and Mike, had been involved in. He was of middle height and middle girth, making him rather square in appearance, and in the strange lighting the high colour of his face was not noticeable. Lucy was fond of him, and could think of few people she would rather have beside her now. His blunt fingers touched hers briefly on the handle of the bucket she swung towards him, and she found the contact comforting.

She had no idea how much later it was when a triumphant shout brought all movement to an end, and Ben sat up sharply, his soft ears pricked and alert. The full bucket moving down the line towards Lucy was halted in mid swing, hanging heavily from somebody's hand before it was lowered to the ground. There was a slight movement forward, gaining in momentum as people realised what the shout meant.

Then Cal was there, his arms stretched out, forcing the rush to stop before it had properly started. 'No,' he shouted urgently. 'Stay back. Too much movement or weight over here and there could be another fall. We've reached the entrance. They'll be out shortly and then it'll be over. But stay back now.' He glanced over his shoulder, obviously anxious to return to the action.

Tom Peters moved, one hand briefly resting on Lucy's shoulder as he passed her, walking to the front of the lines. 'Detective Sergeant Peters,' he said to Cal, flashing his warrant card. 'You get back. I'll make sure we all stay here.'

His sturdy figure was firmly planted on the edge of the bright lighting that haloed the cluster of people who had drawn together at the fogou end of the pit. It was strangely similar in shape to many of the people around, but then he, like them, came from the old local farming stock. Peering past him Lucy saw that the pit was more than half empty, a firm bulwark of planks retaining the rest of the rubble as it had slid away from the entrance to the chamber. And there, glimpsed through the two men working in front of it, was the old wall of wood, which must have closed off the chamber for decades.

Lucy realised with a shock of surprise that Hugh was one of the men down there carefully prising the wood apart, enlarging a narrow gap. And it was Hugh who slipped cautiously through the gap as soon as it was wide enough to let him pass.

He emerged from the fogou almost immediately, one arm raised. Lucy felt herself sag with relief, the hand resting on the collie's soft head relaxed and the dog turned swiftly to lick it.

A ragged cheer rose from the watchers, swiftly stilled as the waiting paramedics moved forward, inching their way with care down towards the opening. They were only out of sight briefly in the fogou, before they emerged again, gesturing to have stretchers lowered.

Lucy's heart sank. How badly were Anna and Mike hurt? Surely if they could walk Mike at least would have insisted on coming out by himself.

Tom Peters caught her eye. 'Standard practice,' he said quietly. 'They'll have taken a knock or two, the medics won't risk letting them walk.'

Lucy nodded. Of course. He was right. He had to be right.

The watchers had fallen silent. But somewhere a bird was singing, the sound incongruous as Lucy recognised it. The nightingale, out of sight and probably far away, but its notes rang piercingly sweet and clear.

When the first stretcher was lifted out of the pit a soft sigh rippled through the crowd. Lucy moved forward, desperate to see what was happening, and people parted, letting her move along as far as possible.

It was Anna on the stretcher. Lucy recognised her long black curls instantly, although they were greyed and dull with dust. They lay smooth and flat on either side of her pale face, which was marred here and there with blood. Her eyes were closed so that she appeared to be sleeping, but her body was strapped tightly under blankets into an unnatural rigidity. Lucy could not see any movement in that still form and her own breath caught in her throat.

'The air will have been bad down there,' Tom murmured. 'That's probably why she's unconscious.'

His words burned through the mist that was filling Lucy's mind. Of course. That must have been what Hugh was worried about. She glanced around, wondering where he was now. Surely, Lucy thought, he'd come out of the pit now that the paramedics were bringing Anna and Mike up. But if he had there was no chance of spotting him in the crowd, for people were all falling back, creating a path for the next stretcher.

Lucy hesitated as it was borne past her. Bryony was next to her, and for an instant Lucy caught sight of her face. The blank expression had been replaced with one Lucy could not understand. It was almost as if Bryony was seeing something she had suddenly remembered, something she was afraid of.

There was no time to wonder about it. Anna had been carried carefully off towards the house, and the second stretcher had reached the surface. Mike too lay pale and motionless, his tousled red hair also drained of colour by the grime that covered it and by what looked to Lucy's anxious eyes like the dark matting of blood.

She was torn, keen to go with her friends, but growing concerned about Hugh. Where on earth was he? She was looking around the milling figures, all beginning now to move away. All except for herself and Bryony, who still stood beside her, staring at the pit.

The rescuers were gathering their belongings, and Lucy suddenly moved, keen to thank them. Perhaps too that was where Hugh was. She had only just taken a step closer to Tom Peters who had been rejoined by Rob, when she bumped into Cal.

'Sorry,' he said, steadying her with a quick hand. 'I thought you'd want to know. About your friends. They've been quite badly knocked about, especially the bloke. There's nothing obviously life-threatening wrong with them though. But the air was bad down there, and there's no knowing how long they've been unconscious.' Cal frowned. 'I don't know why that other bloke's gone back down. We can't be sure it's safe.'

'Who?' Lucy demanded, grasping Ben's collar as the dog

shifted beside her. 'Who's gone down there?'

'The bloke who was helping us. Used to do potholing, he told us. He was the first one in. They were his friends, he insisted on it, and he knew what he was doing too.' Cal saw Lucy's face. 'You must know him as well.'

She nodded, feeling her head move stiffly on her neck. 'My husband.'

Cal's face changed as she spoke. 'Lord, I'm sorry ...' he began.

Before he could say more, Ben slipped away from under Lucy's hand to greet Hugh, who was suddenly there in front of them, almost unrecognisable under a layer of soil and dust.

'Elliot,' Hugh's voice was curt as he called out to the inspector. 'This business isn't finished yet. There are bodies in there.'

All those who heard him turned to stare at Hugh. The silence was profound until Cal laughed in relief. 'Of course there are, mate. We always thought it was an ancient tomb, even if the experts said different. Although,' his voice grew quieter, 'I don't remember ...'

Hugh interrupted impatiently. 'I don't know whether the place was originally a tomb or not, but these bodies are recent. Fairly recent,' he amended quickly. 'Virtually mummified by the dryness of the atmosphere in there, but wearing modern clothes.'

The inspector had frozen half in, half out of his jacket, whose immaculateness contrasted strangely with his dirty shirt and trousers. He finished pulling the jacket on, shivering in the cold night air as he asked, 'Bodies. How many?'

'It's hard to be sure,' Hugh replied. 'I haven't moved anything. But at least a couple.'

They all turned away from him, inspector, sergeant, Lucy, Hugh, Bryony and Cal, to stare at the fogou. Lucy heard faint monotonous muttering and glanced at the woman beside her. Bryony's lips were shaping words, almost soundlessly, and one of her hands had moved, gripping Cal's sleeve tightly.

The little group moved forward slowly towards the local constable who had been left on guard near the pit. She stared at them curiously, but stepped aside as they reached the narrow slope that led down between plank-buttressed walls to the opening, larger now, through the wooden screen that had barred the entrance.

Pausing, a hand held out to stop the others, Rob Elliot looked at Hugh. 'There isn't likely to be much evidence left around the bodies after all this time and tonight's disturbance, but I must have a look down there,' he said soberly. 'How safe is it?'

Hugh shrugged, eyeing the slope, still lit by the few remaining arc lights. 'Safe enough, I think. There's been a lot of toing and froing, but no sign of any further land movement. Still, the fewer people down there at any one time the better.'

The inspector nodded. 'Of course.' He walked across to one of the arc lights, which Aaron was helping a fireman to dismantle.

They looked up, startled, and listened intently as Elliot spoke to them. The fireman nodded, bending down and handing over a powerful torch.

The inspector came back, torch in hand, Aaron at his heels. 'They'll leave the remaining lights until we've finished here. Now,' he glanced around the group, 'I'll go down. It doesn't need anybody else.'

Five people stepped forward, Sergeant Peters, Lucy, Aaron and Cal Tregonan, and Bryony. Hugh watched, a smile twitching his lips. 'It seems you've got volunteers, Rob.'

The inspector stood staring at them, a frown on his forehead. 'It's too many.' He pointed. 'You, Tom, yes. The rest of you, no.'

'I'm coming,' Cal said bluntly. 'You'll need somebody to assess any potential shifting.'

'He's got the right of it,' Aaron said. 'He'll be of more use to you than me.'

Elliot nodded. 'Okay. But that's it. Nobody else.'

Bryony spoke for the first time in Lucy's hearing, her flat monotonous voice coming from the depths of her hood. 'I'm coming too. You can't discriminate against us just because we're women.'

The inspector sighed. 'I'm not,' he said bluntly. 'But both the men coming with me have uses that are to the purpose. You don't, unless you're a bone specialist.'

Bryony shook her head and the hood fell off, revealing the white streak running right through the long dark hair that fell dead straight on either side of her narrow face. There was expression now on her previously blank face, a sullen smouldering resentment. Aaron spoke sharply, 'Don't be foolish, girl. You don't have a place down there.'

Hugh laid a hand on Lucy's arm. 'There's no need to go, nothing to achieve,' he said. 'You'll only see a sad bundle of bones and withered skin in clothes that crumble to dust at the slightest touch.' He jerked his head slightly towards the collie. 'And Ben will try to go with you. He's already anxious enough.'

Lucy glanced down at the dog, who had pressed in between her and Hugh. Ben had heard his name and was looking up enquiringly, so that she could see how dark his normally golden eyes were.

'Okay.' She reluctantly accepted the truth of what Hugh said, and stood still next to him, only half conscious that his arm had gone round her, pulling her to his side. Her eyes followed the three men who were walking cautiously in single file down the slope. The police constable had come closer, quietly standing between the onlookers and the approach, but leaving their line of vision clear down to the entrance.

Again, time seemed to drag. It felt like an hour before Tom Peters led the men out of the fogou, but she knew it could not have been much more than ten minutes. Their faces, lit by the lights into theatrical prominence, were solemn.

As they reached the top of the slope Bryony made a small, quickly controlled, movement.

Lucy glanced at her and saw with surprise that her gaze was fixed on her cousin, Cal. Cal looked stunned.

Aaron had noticed too and took a swift step forward, placing his hand on his nephew's arm. 'What is it, boy?' he demanded.

Cal shook his head dazedly, but said nothing.

It was Rob Elliot who spoke as the little group joined the watchers and the constable moved off to a discreet distance. 'There are two bodies down there,' he said bleakly. 'A male, judging purely from the trousers, and a female in a dress. There's no superficial way of telling their ages. Have you any idea who they could be?'

Aaron stared at him in disbelief. 'No, how could I? For that matter, how could they be down there? I thought it was a mistake, what you said about it just now. It had to be a bundle of rags, rubbish dumped down there before the entrance was blocked.'

'When was that?' the inspector demanded quickly.

The older man frowned. 'Years back. The early 1960s, I reckon. The old lady, Mariot Lanyon gave orders for it to be done. She was concerned that children had been playing in it.' The frown deepened. 'There was some kind of accident with her grandson.' He shook his head. 'But nobody died, and bodies wouldn't have been left down there if they had.'

'Did you get any idea from the clothes,' Lucy asked, 'how long the bodies have been there? Style, I mean, any indication of fashion.'

'Not really,' Hugh said. 'But the woman's dress could be from the Sixties.' He refrained from saying what a shock it had been, when he had seen the bodies, to see the bright blue rags of the dress still vivid in the light of his torch, and the brittle blonde hair that hung over the top of the body, half concealing the withered face. He did not add a surmise he had made, and was sure Elliot at least had also made, that the couple had been alive when they had been shut into the fogou.

Cal spoke suddenly, his voice strained, almost unrecognisable. 'The man had a break in his leg. His left leg. You could see, the way it stuck out.'

Bryony made no movement, but Lucy was aware of her frozen stillness. Turning to look directly at her Lucy saw that her eyes were dark pools in her face. The blankness had gone, replaced with an expression of intense disbelief, of horror.

'You know who it is, don't you?' Lucy asked.

The others all turned their attention to the woman. Cal stood close to her, not quite touching her as Bryony searched his face.

'Well, girl, speak up,' Aaron said. 'No point denying it, it's written all over you.'

Bryony stepped forward, right to the edge of the slope and stared down at the entrance to the fogou. Cal moved quietly to stand at her shoulder. The others waited.

It was some moments before Bryony spoke. Her voice had lost its flatness, there was a husky note in it. 'We used to meet here. It was our den when we were kids, our club,' she smiled faintly, 'that's what we called it when we were older.' She glanced at Cal. 'We came here, our group, for a fag, and a drink, and the occasional snog.'

Elliot was about to ask something, but caught Hugh's slight shake of the head and let the words die on his lips.

'There were about a dozen of us,' Bryony went on, 'all from the village, and we came over the cliff and down through the woods. Nobody knew we were here, the place was so overgrown even then that an army could have hidden in it. And then one day he came when we were there.'

She stopped, her shoulders hunching as she remembered. 'We were friends, all of us, until he came. The other girls,' again she glanced at Cal, 'were older, prettier, than me, cleverer too. They've all moved off now, married, got careers. There's only me left here. Somehow I couldn't get away. But,' she repeated without any emphasis, 'we were all friends until he came. He divided us, split us up, favoured first one, then another, until we were all set against each other. I didn't like him. He didn't like me either, he knew that I could see him for what he was. Bored, amusing himself with the yokels.'

Aaron stirred, his expression uneasy, but he said nothing.

'Then one day we were here until late in the evening. The others had gone when he came. Cal and I were just coming out of

the fogou, had just got to the top, when he was there at the side
of the pit, that smile of his mocking us. He laughed. Just laughed,
but there was something about the sound I couldn't bear. And I
thought again about doing it. I'd wanted to for a long time.'

The waiting silence hung heavily in the early morning air. All
eyes were on Bryony, but she seemed to see none of them. It was
only Cal that she seemed aware of, turning fractionally beside him
as if they were resuming their positions from that long past time
she was remembering.

Aaron made an abrupt movement towards his daughter, but
Hugh put a hand out, gesturing him back.

'I had found a way of making my mark in the group,' Bryony
said unexpectedly. 'I became a witch, a white one of course, but I
could use the dark arts if I needed to. They all came to me for
potions.' She smiled faintly, 'It was mainly love potions, of course;
I made mint water dressed up with a variety of herbs. Forecasting
the future was big too, finding out if they'd get together with the
person they fancied. Childish things, but they satisfied us.'

Her eyes were on the edge of the slope beyond her and Cal.
'And then he came. He mocked me that evening, asking if Cal was
under my spell, what I could make him do. Cal would have hit
him, but I had a better way. I cursed him,' that husky voice said
conversationally, 'I cursed him to die a horrible death.'

Not a flicker of wind, not a sound filled the open glade. Not
a person moved in the small group around the excavated pit. Only
moths flitted in the beams of the lights, dancing madly to their
deaths.

'He laughed. We stood there, Cal and I, watching him. He
laughed so much that he staggered and the side above the slope
gave way under him, sliding him down into the fogou.'

Bryony stared at the slope as if she could still see it happening.
It was a few seconds later that she said slowly, 'We could see him
just inside the entrance, the last of the sunlight shone on his face.
We knew he'd be mad with fury, but we waited for him to come
out. We waited forever. Then Cal went down to see what was

keeping him. Cal had to scramble over the rubble although it hadn't blocked the entrance that time. I was afraid that there would be another fall and he'd be trapped down there. I didn't want Cal to be hurt.'

She drew a breath and carried on. 'He had broken his leg and couldn't get out. When Cal tried to help him, he screamed and screamed, so Cal had to leave him.' She glanced at her cousin. 'Cal sent me away, he didn't want me to get into trouble. Then he went to tell the old lady, Lady Lanyon.'

Bryony put her hand on Cal's arm. 'She never said a word to me about it, she never knew I did it. I was afraid the old lady would tell Dad on you though, we were all terrified of her.' She smiled faintly again. 'We thought she was a real witch.' Bryony's expression darkened. 'And for a long time after that I thought I was a real witch too. I never dared to do anything about witch-craft again, just played with things to amuse tourists.'

She turned, looking round at the group, her gaze suddenly clearing as her thoughts returned to the present. 'But it can't be him. Old Lady Lanyon would have had him out in double quick time, her precious boy. The entrance was blocked that same night, Cal told me. We never came here again, any of us. Not until tonight, when it all seemed to be happening again.'

Bryony stepped away from the edge of the pit. 'But it can't be him,' she said calmly. 'He left with his mother the next day. She took him to a hospital in London, then they went off to Canada and never came back.'

Inspector Elliot asked what they all wanted to know. 'Who was he?'

Bryony stared at him in surprise. 'Geraint. Lady Lanyon's grandson. I suppose,' she added thoughtfully, 'he must have been the real owner of Elowen, although we all saw Lady Lanyon as that. She must have administered it for him, he was still under age, seventeen like the others. He was usually away. At school of course, although even during the holidays he usually didn't come back to Elowen. But that year he was at home for the summer.'

'Which year?' Elliot asked quietly.

'1962, 4 August 1962, my birthday. That's why we were here then.'

'It was just as she said,' Cal spoke suddenly, his voice back to its usual firmness. 'It can't be Geraint down there. I went straight to old Lady Lanyon and told her that there'd been a landslip, that Geraint had fallen into the fogou. I didn't say how it had happened or that he was nearly wetting himself in fright at being down in the dark. I didn't say that he was blethering with the pain of his leg. If she knew I'd seen that, she'd make sure I paid for it. And I didn't really fear,' he said grimly, 'that Geraint would tell her what had actually happened. He wouldn't want to be made foolish by a village girl. But I knew he'd get back at us, he was like that.'

Cal shrugged. 'Instead, he didn't come back from London. He went away forever, and good riddance.'

'I was here that day,' Aaron said. 'I was over to the sawmill that evening, collecting timber for new fencing. I remember it as if it were yesterday. The old lady sent down from the house that all hands were to come at once to block up the fogou, there'd been an accident with young Geraint and she wasn't going to risk another. There weren't,' Aaron said dryly, 'that many hands to do the work, so I went along to help.'

'Did you go inside?' Elliot asked quickly.

Aaron shook his head. 'There were three of us to do the work, none of us went in. We'd not the time, and the old lady was worried that it wouldn't be safe. None of us wanted to risk being clouted on the head in a landslip and being off work, or worse. Besides, she was there all through the work, though it was getting quite dark. I can see her now,' he pointed, 'standing just there, leaning on that carved stick of hers, watching all we did, making sure it was a proper job, even though we had to work by flashlight. Then when the planks were fixed we had to tip in the cartloads of rubble she'd sent for and put up a barrier all round the pit. She stood there until it was done, although she must have been over seventy then.'

'Would you have seen Geraint if he was just inside the entrance?' Elliot asked.

'Couldn't have missed him,' Aaron said simply. 'We'd likely have trodden on the lad if he was still there.'

'Did you see Geraint afterwards?' Hugh asked.

'No,' Aaron spoke slowly. 'But that wasn't so strange. He wasn't interested in the estate. And,' he added suddenly, 'I remember now, about Canada. There'd been talk about it around the village. His mother, Amethyst that would be, had been heard arguing with the old lady about it. She and the boy were all set to go, and word was that they planned to stay for good on one of the Lanyon properties out there.' It was clear from Aaron's expression of quickening memory that more was coming back to his mind.

'Amethyst wasn't ever happy here,' he said. 'Not even when she came as a bride from London. She knew singers, artists and suchlike there, and she found it dull shut up in the country. She wanted to be away all the time, up in town, off to friends, going to parties, and there wasn't the money to do it. The old lady controlled what there was until the boy was twenty-one, and there wasn't much. She was just trying to keep the estate together for him, thinking he'd restore it to its glory.' Aaron sighed gently. 'I don't think she ever realised he took after his mam. We all knew he'd be shot of it as soon as he could. But then he died over in Canada, and it belongs, ruins and all, to some distant cousin out there who's never been near the place.'

'Ah well,' Hugh said, stretching his back, suddenly aware of how much his muscles ached, 'those rings should help with identification, Elliot.'

The inspector glanced at him, his eyebrows a little raised. Then he put a hand in his pocket and pulled out three rings. Even through a coating of dust they glowed with colour as he held them out towards Hugh. 'Genuine, do you think?'

'I'm sure they are,' Hugh replied. 'Diamonds, sapphires,

rubies, and fine stones too.'

Aaron's breath burst out of him in an explosive gasp. His hand was trembling as he stretched it out towards the stones. It hovered over them before falling back to his side. 'But they're hers,' he said. 'How can they be hers?'

FIVE

The sun had risen by the time Lucy and Hugh finally left Elowen. Exhausted as they were, neither of them had felt like sleeping when they got back to Rossington Manor. After showering and changing they had, without even discussing it, migrated automatically, with Ben trotting at their heels, to the kitchen in one wing of the Elizabethan house in which Lucy had grown up. It was so familiar to Lucy, this big stone-flagged kitchen in her childhood home, that she was insensibly soothed as she sat at the large pine table, her hands around the mug of coffee that Hugh had just passed to her, and Ben lying across her feet.

The room was silent except for the ticking of the clock that hung on one of the walls, its pendulum swinging endlessly backwards and forwards. Early morning sunshine came through the window that opened onto the back courtyard, lighting the kitchen's white walls and sparking off the copper pans and moulds that lined them.

Her brother Will had altered nothing here since Lucy had left. The herbs hanging from the airer were dusty now, she noted automatically, and should be replaced with this year's crop. That was a job her grandmother Isobel had once done, and Lucy doubted anyone else was going to do it, this year at least. Maybe she'd mention it to Gina, who had started as their housekeeper and cook a few years ago, shortly after Lucy's father had died and

Lucy had come home to care for the house and estate until Will was old enough to manage them. Gina now came up to the manor every day, keeping an eye on the place while Will was away in India, and running the afternoon teas that Lucy had started then.

Lucy's thoughts ranged comfortably over these familiar things, keeping her tired mind away from the things she could not bear to think about. The person she knew she had become was sliding away, returning her to the person she had been, before she and Hugh had moved to their new home at Withern. He sat opposite her now, just as he had so frequently done when they had first met, when they had had so much to talk about, so many plans to make.

She started as Hugh leaned forward, lightly touching her hair. 'I like it, this new style,' he said quietly. 'It suits you.' His face was drawn with tiredness, his brown eyes strained, but he smiled at her. 'It'll be alright, Lucy. You know Anna and Mike, they'll never give in.'

'They didn't look at all good, though, when they were brought out of the fogou,' she said, reluctantly bringing her thoughts back to the present. 'I don't know whether I should be ringing Anna's father. And I haven't the faintest idea who to ring about Mike. I suppose it would be his mother, but I don't even know where she lives. Do you?'

'Yes, I do, but we should wait and see what the news is later on, before we start contacting people, and alarming them,' Hugh said, glancing at his watch. 'It's nearly seven thirty. Let's have something to eat and then ring the hospital. About nine should be a good time.'

'They won't tell us anything,' Lucy said gloomily, putting her mug down and lifting her hands to her face, forgetting that her hair was now too short to be brushed back. 'After all, we're not related to either of them, and hospital staff are always hot on confidentiality.'

'We'll get hold of Dr Chaudhry. She knows us,' Hugh said, 'and I'm sure she'll be able to tell us what's happening. Otherwise

Rob will keep us in the picture. In the meantime, let's get some breakfast, otherwise we'll be no use for anything.'

Lucy stood up quickly, the bench grating as she pushed it back. 'Ben,' she said, as the collie leaped to his feet, 'I haven't fed him since yesterday morning. He must be starving.'

Hugh got up too, coming to her side as she hurried to a cupboard. He put his hand on her arm. 'Get yourself some toast at least, Lucy. I'll feed Ben.'

'Alright,' she said reluctantly. 'But I couldn't possibly eat anything else. It's just as well I let Gina know I was going to be here this weekend. She said she'd get in the basics so that I wouldn't starve.'

Ben had followed Hugh eagerly to the cupboard, watching as food was tipped into his bowl. Lucy went to the bread bin, and took out a crusty loaf, hearing Ben crunching through his food behind her as she put the loaf on a board. As she cut slices of bread she was surprised to find it was full of raisins and smelt deliciously of cinnamon. 'This is too nice to toast, Hugh. Let's just have it with butter. I wonder if Gina got it from the village shop,' Lucy said, carrying the board to the table and sitting down again. 'Anna was saying last night that it's been completely transformed. And apparently there's a shop up at Bridge Farm too. Mike told her about them.'

'Mike told her,' Hugh repeated as he brought over plates and knives, balancing butter and marmalade awkwardly on top of them. He sidestepped to avoid Ben, as the collie licked his empty bowl so vigorously that it slid along the floor. 'I had no idea that he and Anna had become so friendly.'

'Nor had I,' Lucy admitted, looking up from the slice of bread she was nibbling. 'I was stunned when I got her text about the picnic.' She put the bread down and stared at Hugh who was putting the kettle on the Aga. 'Do you think they're actually a couple?' she asked.

'Well,' Hugh drawled, 'they showed all the signs of that when I bumped into them at the priory yesterday. Anna was certainly planning to stay over with Mike last night, although that doesn't necessarily mean what I think it does.'

'I didn't know you were over here,' Lucy said, distracted for a moment. Ben left his bowl and came across to the table, sniffing hopefully at the floor beneath it before settling down by Lucy's feet.

'There was a problem with one of the tenants,' Hugh said briefly, pouring boiling water into a cafetière. He came to the table with it and a couple of mugs. 'Look,' he said as he put them down and leaned across to pick up a grape, 'this fruit bowl is stuffed. Gina must have remembered how much you like cherries. It does look as if local food provision has improved dramatically.'

Lucy reached for a cherry as Hugh sauntered to the fridge. 'Philly said there'd been problems at the priory, and I told her I'd talk through them with her today. That's why I planned to stay here last night.' Lucy frowned. 'Her email said there'd been late cancellations because of rumours and malicious letters. Then she seemed to be getting last-minute bookings, so some of the apartments aren't empty after all. It wasn't something I could deal with by email and I really didn't have time to go into it with her over the phone, but it all sounds very peculiar.'

'Yes, I think so too,' Hugh said, his voice muffled as he peered into the fridge. 'Ah, brie and a nice piece of Cornish blue. If we see Gina today we must be sure to thank her.'

'I'm sure she'll be here,' Lucy said, nibbling her bread again. 'Rossington teas are bound to be popular today as everyone will want to hear the latest about Anna and Mike. And I'm sure she'll come up anyway when she hears about the accident.' She swallowed the last of her slice as Hugh returned to the table with the cheese on a plate. 'Only we don't know it was an accident, do we?'

'We can't be certain of anything yet,' Hugh said, cutting himself a generous portion of cheese and taking a couple of slices of bread. 'I'm sure Rob will be here before long, he'll want to hear our stories again in more detail.'

'If he's on this case,' Lucy said suddenly. 'I think he said last night that he was already on another case, a murder I suppose, which will be more his line than this. Unless, of course, Anna or Mike dies,' she finished bleakly.

'A murder?' Hugh looked up quickly. 'Did he say who was dead?'

Lucy shook her head, surprised at the concern on Hugh's face. 'I don't think so. To tell you the truth,' she admitted, 'I was so pleased to see him that I didn't really listen much to what he said. He,' she slanted a gamine smile at Hugh, 'made me eat too.'

'You're too thin,' he said soberly, looking at her slender frame with sudden attention. 'You don't eat enough at the best of times.'

She shrugged. 'Oh well, you know how it is.' Her hazel eyes sharpened as she helped herself to more cherries. 'I do believe Rob said the murder was over in this direction. Only I can't remember if it is actually a murder, or just might be.' Her expression darkened again. 'Just like Anna and Mike.'

'Well, at least Rob's going to be around, whichever case he's working on, so we'll soon find out what's going on,' Hugh said abstractedly. He shook off his concern, cutting another large helping of Cornish blue for himself, and putting a thin slice of brie on Lucy's plate with a handful of grapes. 'Try that, it smells pretty ripe.'

Lucy ignored this. 'And what,' she demanded, 'about those bodies in the fogou? That must surely have been murder. Whoever they were, they wouldn't just have laid down in the fogou and let somebody block them in.'

'No,' Hugh agreed. His mind pictured the scene in the underground chamber again. The torchlight flickering on the bare earth walls and floor, settling on the pitiful heap of huddled bones and withered skin in the incongruously bright remnants of clothes. From the way they had lain he had formed the distinct impression that they had been clawing at the wall of the fogou, close to the wooden barrier at the entrance, trying to get out. Fortunately they were on the opposite side to where Anna and Mike had been found, also a pair of bodies huddled together, but thankfully still alive.

Hugh wondered suddenly if Mike or Anna had stumbled over the bones too. Not Mike, he realised quickly. He had only had a quick glimpse of Mike's head injury, but he really did not think the archaeologist would have been in a state to go exploring. Anna, though, Hugh frowned at the thought, seemed to have been mobile before the staleness of the air had overcome her. She would have tried to get out, like the previous internees, exploring the chamber to see if there was another exit, even if it was only a hole that she could enlarge. So she would very likely have found the other occupants of the place. His lips pressed down tightly at the thought.

'What is it, Hugh?' Lucy asked, noticing his expression as she reached for another slice of brie.

'I was wondering how we could identify those bodies,' he lied. He certainly wasn't going to tell Lucy what he thought Anna had experienced down in the fogou. But if somebody really was responsible for her presence there, I'll make sure they pay a high price for it, Hugh resolved grimly.

'But surely one of them was the old lady, Mariot Lanyon,' Lucy said. 'Aaron recognised her rings. And they are distinctive enough to be memorable.'

'You're forgetting,' Hugh said quietly, his training as a barrister taking over, 'that Mariot supervised the closing up of the fogou to prevent more accidents. And,' he forestalled a retort his wife was about to make, 'she was seen alive for some years after the work was done.'

'Not much, though,' Lucy argued. 'It might not have been her.'

'It's possible, of course, but it would have had to have been a good imposter to fool Aaron. And other local people would have known her well too,' Hugh commented dryly. 'No doubt Rob will have somebody working on the identification. I suppose the bodies will have to be DNA tested. That should give the police some leads.'

'I wonder if local interest in the bodies will supersede interest in Anna and Mike,' Lucy said thoughtfully.

'Mike will be grateful if it does,' Hugh said dryly. 'Anna will revel in the attention, but Mike will blow a gasket if this story hits the national headlines.'

'It's bound to,' Lucy said, realising this for the first time. 'I'll have to get in touch with their families before they read about it.'

'Leave it for now,' Hugh said, leaning forward to touch her hand. 'Rob may already have done it. After all, he at least knows where to find Richard Evesleigh to tell him about Anna.'

'Yes, I suppose so, but I still must speak to them as soon as we've heard from Rob,' Lucy insisted. 'And Anna's father isn't at home; he's gone back abroad with Fran, some kind of additional honeymoon trip, Anna said.' She pushed back her chair and stood up. 'And I must go down to the priory and tell Philly. She'll probably have to take over the arrangements for the play from Anna.'

'Philly's quite capable of doing that, and I'm sure Anna's got everything well in hand,' Hugh said, getting to his feet, and glancing at his watch. 'It's still too early to ring the hospital. Look, I've got to go down to the priory and check on this tenant. If I see Philly I'll tell her what's happening and you can fill her in later on when we know a bit more.'

Lucy shook her head. 'No. Thanks, Hugh, but I don't want to have time on my hands.'

'Take Ben for a walk instead,' he urged. 'One of us should, and I really must see this tenant so there's no point us both going down to the priory now. You can see Philly later.'

'Perhaps you're right,' Lucy conceded, glancing at the collie, who was watching her with eager eyes. He had clearly heard the relevant word, walk, and hoped it implied what he wanted it to. 'What is the problem with this tenant? Maybe I should sort it out.'

Hugh shook his head. 'No, leave it to me. It's somebody sent down by an old colleague in London, who asked me to keep an eye on her.'

Lucy looked at him in surprise. Before she could ask more the sound of car tyres sweeping into the courtyard distracted her attention. Ben ran to the back door, barking, as she moved swiftly to the window and looked out. The car was familiar. 'It's Rob,' she said, hope warring with fear in her mind. 'He's here early. I wonder what news he's got.'

She turned as she spoke, hurrying out into the corridor and throwing open the back door. Inspector Elliot was climbing stiffly out of the passenger seat of the car as Sergeant Peters closed the driver's door. Lucy stood waiting in the house doorway, her heart pounding, but Ben ran forward, glad to see both men.

Rob Elliot bent to briefly greet the dog, and moved on towards Lucy. She was shocked to see how tired he looked. He clearly had not been home to change since she last saw him a few hours ago. He seemed younger, more vulnerable, with his usually immaculate clothes creased, and his smooth hair ruffled and untidy.

'What is it?' she asked urgently, stretching out both her hands to him.

'I've had no news from the hospital,' he said quickly, taking her hands and pressing them reassuringly before releasing them. 'Have you?'

'No.' She felt a sense of relief that at least he was not bringing the news she dreaded. 'Hugh thinks we should wait until nine to ring them.'

Elliot nodded. 'That's reasonable,' he agreed wearily. 'We'll be in touch about then too. Can I come in?'

She was startled. 'Of course. Sorry, I wasn't thinking.' She led the way back into the kitchen.

'No news then,' Hugh said, standing by the kitchen table as he nodded to them in greeting. 'But we were expecting you, Rob. I don't suppose there's any further information about the bodies in the fogou or the fleeing man?'

'Give them a break, Hugh. Let them at least sit down,' Lucy said, moving towards the kettle. She said over her shoulder to the two policemen, 'Would you like some coffee? And something to eat?'

'We can't, Lucy,' Rob said heavily, sitting down at the table, ignoring Ben as he skittered excitedly around them. 'God knows we could both do with it, but we're here on business. And not about Elowen, I'm afraid,' Elliot said. 'It's not my case now, it's been passed to another detective in the regional squad.'

Sergeant Peters had moved a chair out slightly from the table and sat down on it, planting his sturdy legs firmly and taking out a chunky notebook to rest it on his knees.

Hugh glanced at this and frowned, taking his own seat again as Lucy came back to the table and sat down too. 'I see,' he said levelly. 'I suppose the actual deaths there must have been some time ago, and there's no proof yet that they were murders. Lucy mentioned that you might be involved in a murder case already. In this area too. Is that right?'

'It's certainly my case,' Elliot said, 'although at the moment we're treating it as an unexplained death.'

'I see,' Hugh said again. 'Can you tell us who the victim was?' His voice was unusually strained.

Lucy looked up at him sharply as she bent over the collie, who was pressing against her legs. She was aware that the inspector had also shot him a swift glance.

'A man called Damian Mallinson, according to his driving licence,' Elliot said, watching Hugh closely. 'Did you know him?'

'No,' Hugh said at once, his relief quite evident. He glanced at Lucy. 'It's always good when it isn't somebody we know. But it's a shame too; somebody somewhere will care about him.'

'I gather you were involved in an angry exchange with him three times yesterday,' Elliot said abruptly.

Hugh looked astonished. His eyebrows drew together. 'Would you care to elaborate?' His expression changed, suddenly wary. 'Good Lord, Elliot, you can't mean the bloke from the priory. The tenant in Dorter.'

'We think he was. He's been identified as such by another of the holidaymakers staying at the priory, a Mr Edward Armitage. But Mr Armitage didn't know his name or anything about him. Nor did his wife when we spoke to her.'

'Neither do I,' Hugh said. 'But Philly Leygar will have all that information.'

'We've already sent somebody down to the farm to ask her,' the inspector said. 'I wasn't sure if she'd be working on Saturdays.'

'Yes, she's due to meet me at the office,' Lucy said quietly. 'And I think she's working later on Anna's Rossington Play for this summer.'

'I expect Armitage overheard me in the priory's entrance court-yard yesterday afternoon,' Hugh said. 'He popped up shortly after the incident, twittering on about bird-watching.' Hugh frowned as he recollected the incident. 'There was no row as such. The bloke from Dorter, Mallinson, if that's his name, was pestering another guest, and I warned him off. It was no more than that.'

'Who was this other guest?' Elliot asked evenly.

'The woman staying in Frater,' Hugh said. His eyes were firmly on the inspector, but he was aware of Lucy's silent presence opposite him.

'Her name?'

'Celia Vaughan. I knew she'd come down for some peace and quiet, and this bloke seemed to be constantly popping up and following her around.'

'Wasn't she capable of dealing with him herself?' the inspector asked.

Hugh gave a short unamused laugh. 'More than capable, I'd say. But he tried it on when I was there and I wasn't going to let him get away with it.'

'He must have been a determined man to try his luck again,' Elliot commented. 'I gather you were extremely forceful in your expressions when he came upon you and Celia Vaughan in the shrubbery in the morning.'

Hugh raised an eyebrow sardonically. 'That sounds like a line from a bad thriller,' he commented dryly. 'Of course I was forceful.

He wasn't the sort of bloke who understood simple language.'

'I see.' Elliot's voice was level. 'And how did you feel when he tried it on again the next time you had words with him?'

Hugh looked puzzled. 'When was that?' he enquired.

The inspector's grey eyes were very cool as he surveyed the man in front of him. 'When you and the lady went out walking in the early evening yesterday.'

Hugh stared at him. 'Good Lord,' he exclaimed, sounding amused. 'Don't tell me Armitage was around then too. Well, Mallinson emerged from cover yet again on that outing. He didn't know I was there too, but as soon as he spotted me he came up with some story about thinking it was the bird-watching tour. He must have heard me earlier telling Armitage and his wife that Philly could arrange one. I wasn't buying that, so I told him where he got off. And,' Hugh added grimly, 'I said if he continued to pester other guests he'd have to leave. He didn't like that, and got rather heated. That's probably what Armitage overheard. I don't think,' he added consideringly, 'that I raised my voice at all.'

'Where did you go walking with the lady?' Elliot asked.

'I didn't,' Hugh replied calmly, 'go walking far. She wanted to go up to watch the peregrines. I'd shown her where they're nesting earlier in the day, the first time Mallinson tried to follow us, but the birds weren't there. In the evening I just went to the cliffs with her to put her on the right track. I was due at Elowen, as you know, and I believe,' he said ironically, 'she meant to spend the rest of the evening washing her hair. No doubt Armitage saw me return, and probably her too if he's that observant. He's an enthusiastic novice bird-watcher,' Hugh added pleasantly, 'and was certainly carrying a fine pair of binoculars when I saw him.'

'It wasn't Mr Armitage who overheard you on the other occasions,' Elliot said shortly.

Hugh studied him thoughtfully. 'Well, whoever your witness was in the evening, they probably saw me return.'

'No,' Elliot said. 'Celia Vaughan was seen cutting through the shrubbery with you just after six o'clock. Not,' his voice was level, 'on the direct path to the cliffs, I believe, which is where I presume your peregrines nest.'

'Elliot, you'll make a bird-watcher yourself one of these days,' Hugh said blandly. 'You're quite right. But I wanted to take the scenic route round the manor to the footpath onto the cliffs.'

'Why?'

Hugh considered him for a moment. 'Well, I expect Celia will tell you this herself, if she hasn't already. She's a well-known photographer, mainly wildlife and social history, somewhat along the lines of the work James Ravilious did in North Devon. You know, images of traditional working life. Incidentally, she's also a very fine painter. Either way, she's hoping to do some work down here. We went the long way round to the cliffs because I wanted to show her some of Will's collection of old farming equipment in the stables. He's already got a lot of gear for the heavy horses he and Philly's father are using for farming.'

'Where did you go after the stables?'

'We skirted the South Lawn, slipping round the corner of the ha-ha that edges it, and went straight down beside the hedge to the stile that gives access to the footpath. Once on the cliff I told her where to find the peregrines.' Hugh paused, seeing Elliot's enquiring look. 'Round the corner of Hope Point,' he said reluctantly. 'But don't spread the news too far and wide. There are four youngsters in that nest and they should be making their first flights soon. I don't want the site disturbed.'

'Of course not,' Elliot agreed. 'There's no reason why it should be. But this may turn out to be a murder enquiry. So you'll appreciate that I need to get as many details about everyone's movements as soon as possible.'

'Of course,' Hugh agreed, leaning forward to put his elbows on the table and steeple his fingers together. His fleeting glance sideways saw Sergeant Peters diligently making notes. 'When we got to the path I turned east along the cliffs to take the shorter route back, by the footpath from the harbour to the priory where I'd left my car.' He glanced at Lucy's frozen white face. 'I knew I was already running late for Anna and Mike's picnic. Celia went towards Hope Point. She had some idea of going on to the old lime kiln in the cove, but I was pretty sure she'd stay on the cliff watching the peregrines once she'd spotted them.'

He frowned slightly, considering the inspector. 'Where was Mallinson found? Can you tell us that?'

'I'm sure it's all round the village,' Elliot said dryly. 'You'd have heard by now if …' he hesitated fractionally, 'if you'd been here last night. His body was found by a pair of walkers returning to the pub on Roscombe quay. He'd gone over the landward edge of the footpath up to Hope Point. Quite high up, almost at the summit of the cliff, there was a fresh slide mark down the slope through the rocks. The walkers who saw it were curious enough to investigate. They found him lying in a small pool of water, completely obscured from view by the reeds and grass around it.'

Hugh stared blankly at him, before obviously gathering his wits. 'He must have been following us,' he said slowly. 'When I branched off towards the harbour I suppose he took his chance to follow Celia again and missed his footing on the path.' Hugh frowned slightly, trying to remember. 'I don't think he was dressed or shod for cliff walking, and that's a treacherous path. It looks so easy, but it's slippery underfoot in places, whatever the weather.'

'Yes, that seems a feasible theory,' Elliot agreed.

'Then why are you treating it as a possible murder enquiry?' Hugh asked bluntly. 'You're doing more than going through the motions, Elliot.'

'There are features about the incident that make us uncomfortable,' Elliot said carefully.

'Such as?'

'The knock he'd had on the head, for one.'

'The whole area is littered with rocky outcrops,' Hugh said, disbelief in his voice. 'He could easily have hit his head on one of those.'

The inspector nodded. 'But even with a dunk on the head he's likely to have come round when he plunged into a cold pool of water.'

'Hmmm, yes, perhaps,' Hugh said reluctantly. 'Do you have a provisional time of death?'

'Somewhere between 6.30 pm and 8.30 pm at the moment, according to the police doctor. But the autopsy is being done later this morning, so we should know more soon.'

'I see,' Hugh said. 'Well, that could put me in your frame. Celia and I were both out there then. But you can check my story with Celia. She'll be able to confirm what I've said to you.'

'I'm sure she will,' Elliot agreed amiably. 'When we find her.' His words dropped into silence.

Hugh stared at him, his face setting in hard lines. 'Isn't she at Frater?'

'No,' Elliot replied. 'She doesn't appear to have slept there either. Do you have any idea of where she could be?'

'No.' The negative fell heavily from Hugh's lips. He sat very still, staring at his steepled fingers for a few seconds. When he looked up suddenly he found the inspector's eyes on him. 'I assume you're out looking for her, Elliot?'

The inspector's eyebrows rose fractionally. 'Not yet,' he said. 'I'm not aware there's any need. But there's a general alert out for her. Mr Armitage gave us a good description. As you say, he seems to be observant.'

Hugh's face was shuttered. 'I see.'

'What can you tell us about her?'

'Not much,' Hugh said bleakly. 'Celia was looking for somewhere quiet, to chill out for a bit. I gathered she's been doing some grim reality photos in London gangland, and wanted to escape to the country and do something different. I know her work, of course, but I didn't know her until she came down here.'

'Ah.' The inspector went on gently, 'Yet Mr Armitage got the impression that you were good friends.'

Hugh shrugged. 'We get on pretty well. I can't aspire to her skills in photography, but we have got the activity in common. And she's an interesting woman altogether.'

'When did she arrive?' Elliot changed tack unexpectedly.

'Monday.'

'She doesn't seem to have a car here,' the inspector went on. 'Could she have come back and driven away in it?'

'She didn't have one with her,' Hugh said.

'Did she arrive by train?' Elliot asked.

An indefinable tone in his voice made Hugh cast him a quick look. 'No,' he replied evenly, 'I brought her down from London. I knew she was coming and offered her a lift as I was coming back myself after a book award ceremony.'

Lucy's eyes were on the hand she had rested on the collie's head. Ben turned slightly to look up at her, his golden eyes shadowed.

'That was thoughtful of you,' Elliot pursued his line of questioning with deliberation. 'To know that a woman you didn't know was coming down and to offer to bring her with you.'

'There's no mystery about it,' Hugh said. 'I bumped into a friend of hers in London and we got chatting. He ended up telling me that Celia was coming to stay down here.'

'What made her choose the priory as her bolt-hole?' the inspector persisted.

'I believe somebody she knew in London,' Hugh said, 'told her about the place.'

'Do you know the somebody too?'

'I really don't think I can help you there,' Hugh said carefully.

Elliot studied him thoughtfully. 'Are you sure there's nothing else you should be telling me, Hugh?' he asked gently.

Hugh's brown eyes met the inspector's. 'No,' he said again. 'There's nothing else that I can tell you.' He let his hands drop from the table to rest on his legs. 'I'll be in touch, Rob, if there is anything that comes to mind.'

Lucy was looking at her watch. 'It's after nine,' she said tightly, getting up stiffly from the bench. 'I'm going to ring the hospital.'

The inspector had pushed back his chair and was getting to his feet. 'Do you mind if I wait to hear the news?' he asked.

'Not at all.' Hugh had risen too. 'Lucy'll have to use the hall phone, you know how difficult mobile reception is here.' He glanced at his wife. 'I'll go down to the priory office to see if Philly's there yet, and fill her in on what's happened. But I'll be straight back, Lucy.'

Lucy had reached the door into the corridor that ran the width of the house, Ben at her heels, and she did not pause or look back as he spoke. The collie hesitated, glancing at Hugh, then followed his mistress.

Hugh turned without another word and went out into the corridor beyond the kitchen. The back door banged shut behind him.

Inspector Elliot moved quickly to the window to watch him. 'Tom,' he said quietly over his shoulder, 'go after him and see where he goes and what he does. If he sees you, you're on your way down to the priory to see if Philly Leygar has talked to our constable.' Elliot frowned. 'I don't like this. I'm pretty sure he's hiding something. And I mean to know what it is.'

Detective Sergeant Peters moved away silently, leaving the inspector to his thoughts. From his expression it was clear that they were not pleasant.

The sound of footsteps roused him and he was standing close to the table, his face composed when Lucy returned to the kitchen. The dry herbs on the airer rustled as she pushed the door open, a faint musty smell of rosemary and sage drifting downwards. Ben's claws clicked on the floor as he preceded her into the room. She came up to the table without saying a word and stood opposite him, her hands gripping the back of a chair.

'They're going to be alright,' she said faintly, giving a deep sigh of relief. She seemed to waver in front of Elliot, and he moved swiftly, placing his arm around her shoulders and holding her up.

'Careful, Lucy,' he said with concern. 'Look, sit down and lower your head. You must be very tired.'

She did as he said without any resistance, sinking gratefully onto the chair and resting her head on her arms as she folded them on the table. Ben pressed against her legs, his nose nudging her knees, but she did not have the energy to reassure him. She heard the sink tap running and soon felt a cold cloth laid gently on the back of her neck and heard a glass go down onto the table.

'Leave it for a moment,' Rob said, 'then have a sip of water and sit up when you feel like it.'

There was the scrape of a bench and Lucy knew he had sat down next to her. But she felt no need to move, to assert herself, just a great relief to let her worries go for a short time.

Ben began to whine anxiously after a while, and Lucy sat cautiously up, lifting one hand gingerly to remove the damp cloth and lowering the other one to the worried collie. 'It's alright, Ben, I'm alright.' She leaned back wearily, and glanced at the inspector. 'Sorry, Rob. I guess it's all been a bit too much for me.'

'I'm not surprised,' he said emphatically.

Lucy looked at him in surprise. It was unlike him to sound so concerned. Then she realised. Of course, he must be deeply worried about Anna. She wasn't quite sure how their relationship stood. She had thought it was becoming more than friendship, but now she suspected that wasn't the case, at least for Anna. Anna had not really got over the fact that Rob had put his work before their friendship earlier in the year during the trouble they had endured at Withern in the spring.

'I'm so sorry, Rob,' Lucy said contritely, 'you must be worried about Anna. She's coming round, the ward sister said, but she'll be groggy for most of the day. It seems the bad air down in the fogou affected her more than Mike.' She smiled, a flicker of her gamine charm showing on her pointed face. 'He, of course, is awake and, reading between the lines, agitating for news. Although he had quite a nasty head wound that needed stitches, they think he'll be able to leave later today or tomorrow at the latest.'

'They'll be glad to get rid of him,' Elliot predicted dryly. 'Mike confined to bed, but awake and aware, would be enough to daunt the best of nurses.'

'Yes,' Lucy agreed, her eyes beginning to sparkle with amusement. 'And he wants one of us, Hugh or me, to go in and tell him what's happening. The sister thought it would be a good idea if we did, it might stop him fretting, she said.'

Elliot gave a short laugh. 'Perhaps. But let Hugh do it,' he said forcefully. 'You should rest, Lucy, you're exhausted. You're pushing yourself too hard.'

She was taken aback again at his concern. Did she, she wondered, really look so bad?

'I'd like to see them,' she said firmly. 'I'll come straight back and go to bed, I promise. In fact,' she added wryly, 'I think I'll have to. But,' she forestalled the protest he was about to make, 'I'll never rest if I don't see with my own eyes that they're alright.'

'I suppose so,' he conceded reluctantly. 'Well, wait for Hugh to take you then. He should be back soon.'

She glanced towards the window onto the courtyard. 'I don't know how long he'll be away. I never do these days. I'd rather just go myself.'

Rob hesitated. 'I've got to visit the hospital to see if either Mike or Anna has any useful account of what happened last night. I can take you over there with me when Tom gets back. And he can bring you home, as long as nothing else crops up. If it does, you'll need to call Hugh, no matter how busy he is.'

His final words were biting, and she was so startled she stared at him. He met her eyes, surprised and slightly wary, and held them with his own for a second. He leaned forward, saying quietly, 'I shouldn't do this, Lucy, but if you have any influence over Hugh, get him to tell me everything he knows. I'm sure he's holding something back.'

She nodded slowly, although he could not be sure what she was agreeing to, his request or his statement. 'I'm not sure what influence I do have any more,' she said slowly. She added awkwardly, 'I expect you've realised things aren't too good between us these days.'

He nodded, stretching out a hand to touch hers briefly. 'All marriages go through bad patches, Lucy. He's a good bloke, hang on in there and see if you can weather this one.' He pushed his chair back and stood up. 'Tom shouldn't be much longer. Let me help you out to the car.'

Lucy took his arm, glad of the support, but at the door she stopped. 'I'd better leave a message for Hugh. He'll want to know what's happened.'

Rob Elliot bit his lip to stop himself commenting. 'I'll help you into the car,' he said. 'You can text him from there if you can get reception, while I go and see what's keeping Tom. He's checking that Philly Leygar has been interviewed by the constable we sent down to the farm.'

It was only as Lucy sat in the back seat of the car, wriggling slightly to pull her mobile out of her trouser pocket, encouraging Ben to settle down beside her, that she fully registered what the inspector had said. She stared at his back as he walked out of her sight round the east wing of the manor, where the estate office was situated. The estate manager wasn't there, she realised, looking for his car. He didn't always come in on Saturdays. So there was nobody who could tell her what Sergeant Peters or Inspector Elliot were up to on the way to the main priory track, if they met there.

But Lucy suspected, she very deeply suspected, that Sergeant Peters had been sent down to the priory to check up on what Hugh was doing. They must have gone down past the far side of the estate office to the disused front drive that carried on down to the priory from the main approach to the manor house. So that must mean that Rob Elliot thought Hugh could in some way be involved in this business? Surely not with the murder of this man Mallinson, she would never believe that. But with this woman, this Celia, well, Lucy thought coldly, I wonder.

She sat unmoving for some seconds, clutching her mobile tightly. Ben stirred beside her, looking out of the window.

She looked to see what had caught his attention. Swifts swirled past in low swooping curves, feasting on the insects above the South Lawn, where the tables and chairs stood ready for afternoon visitors coming for tea and cake. The line of the cliffs in the distance was hazy in the morning sunshine. And over there, out of sight, was the stile that led onto the cliff footpath near Roscombe village. Surely, she thought suddenly, in this fine weather there would have been plenty of people out walking, so somebody will have seen Hugh come back that way last night.

Then she saw what Ben had noticed. The inspector and sergeant were standing at the inner corner of the estate wing, just short of the courtyard. They were deep in conversation, but she stood no chance of overhearing any of it from inside the car. And if she got out she knew they would come to meet her, talking, if at all, about something other than what she was becoming increasingly concerned about, what her husband had been doing.

Inspector Elliot had met his sergeant half way along the narrow path threading between the estate office and the laurels that screened the track linking the front and back drives. The sergeant was returning with his usual steady tread, but his face showed faint traces of concern to one who knew him well.

'Well?' Elliot demanded as he turned to fall into step with the other man. 'What is it?

'I'm not sure, sir,' Sergeant Peters said slowly. 'Hugh Carey certainly has gone to the priory office. It's in the old gatekeeper's room, where we had that trouble a couple of years back. I didn't go in, I saw Philly Leygar through the window, with young Constable Cranley beside her, so there was no need.'

They had rounded the corner of the wing as he spoke and were approaching the back courtyard of the manor house. As their car came into sight, Elliot put out a hand, pulling the sergeant to a halt. 'I've got Lucy Rossington in the car. We've got to go to the hospital in Corrington, Anna and Mike have both come round to some degree, so we're giving Lucy a lift in as well. Unless something urgent crops up, you can bring her back later on. She's too tired to be driving herself around, and I'm not sure what else she's going to have to cope with.'

Tom Peters nodded. 'Right, sir. It doesn't look too good, I'm afraid. When he left here Hugh Carey went off onto the South Lawn behind the house, before he took the path to the priory. He was walking about there on the grass for a bit, trying to get reception on his mobile. I couldn't get close enough to hear what he was saying when he did get a call through, but I could hear his voice. It wasn't a happy conversation he was having, more of an argument really, and I'd say it wasn't going the way he wanted it to. He looked pretty grim when he came back past me.'

'Did he see you?' the inspector asked quickly.

Peters shook his head. 'Not me,' he said. 'Those bushes beside the path are made for surveillance, they haven't been tidied up as much as the ones by the priory entrance. Still,' he grinned suddenly, 'I haven't any idea what I'd have said if he'd parted the branches and found me there.'

'And then what?' Elliot was impatient of this flight of fancy.

'He went directly to the priory,' Tom reported. 'Didn't look to right or left, he went straight through the cloisters and the entrance courtyard, right up to the gatehouse and in at the door.'

'So,' Elliot mused, 'does that mean it was Celia Vaughan he was arguing with on the phone, so he knew she hadn't come back to her rented apartment? Or did he see young Cranley through the window, just as you did, and think he was there keeping surveillance on the place? Which, of course, he is, now that Philly has let him into the office.'

'It could be either,' the sergeant said. 'He's not the kind to miss much. And,' he ruminated before adding, 'he's not the kind to kill a man, at least not like this.'

'No,' said Elliot forcefully. 'And I wouldn't have thought he was the kind to obstruct a police investigation either. And yet I'm damned sure he is.'

'He must have a good reason to,' Peters said. 'Other than having done it, I mean. He thinks a lot of his own judgement, Hugh Carey does.'

'Yes,' Elliot agreed. 'And so do I. I'd rather not have to follow this line, but however good his judgement he can't keep back facts in a potential murder enquiry.' He sighed. 'Well, come on, Tom. I don't want Lucy to get out of the car and join us. She's rather fragile at the moment and I have a nasty feeling things aren't going to get any better for her.'

Sergeant Peters fell into step beside him as they began to move again. 'It's a sad thing. She's such a nice young lady, and they were so happy that it was a sight to see them not so long ago. But the story going round the village here is that they've pretty much separated.'

'I don't know the truth of that,' Elliot said quietly, as they neared the car. 'I think, from the little Anna's let drop, that it's not a formal separation, just a temporary parting of the ways, and I know she hopes that they'll get over it.'

'Fat chance of it if he's involved with this woman, this Celia,' Tom said quietly. 'Still, we don't know the rights and wrongs of it yet.'

'Not yet,' Elliot agreed. 'But we will. Soon.'

SIX

The nurse at the ward desk looked harassed as she spoke crisply into the telephone receiver. She put it down at last, one hand reaching towards her cup of cold coffee. The telephone began to ring again, and her hand moved to hover over it automatically as she glanced enquiringly at Lucy. Her glance took in the two men flanking the slight, tired woman, and recognised the police.

She nodded in greeting, saying wearily, 'If it's Professor Shannon you've come to see, he isn't in his ward. He seems to have moved permanently to the women's ward.'

Lucy stared at her in surprise, thinking she had misheard. But Rob Elliot was faster on the uptake. 'He's with Anna Evesleigh,' he stated.

The nurse nodded. 'Got it in one, Inspector. I can see why you've advanced in your career. I'll pray for you to become Chief Superintendent if you can quieten him down. We're anxious for Miss Evesleigh to get some rest. Professor Shannon,' she added with careful restraint, 'seems to believe she needs him by her side to recover.'

Lucy smiled slightly. 'That sounds very like him,' she said. 'So they're both in the women's ward.'

The nurse pointed to her left. 'Down there, second door on the right. But I expect you'll hear him before you get there.'

As they set off down the corridor, three sets of footsteps

ringing out over the floor, they heard her answer the telephone at last, her voice a practised neutral. Lucy felt she was on familiar territory. She had spent a lot of time in this hospital last year, in this very same ward.

The nurse had maligned Mike. His voice was barely audible as they entered the ward, although they saw him at once, his back to them, sitting beside a bed next to the window.

Curious eyes followed them as they walked past the other beds. Only two of the remaining three beds were occupied, each by an elderly woman who turned their attention eagerly from the couple in the corner to the new arrivals. Lucy felt a brief curiosity about the empty bed opposite Anna's. Had the nurse moved somebody out for some peace elsewhere? Or was she beating off competition for it, the prime viewing site in the ward?

Mike heard their footsteps and turned carefully towards them, obviously favouring tightly bound ribs. Lucy only just suppressed a gasp of shock. His square face was multi-coloured with bruises, their colour emphasised by the white bandage he wore around his head. She felt tears spurt to her eyes as she realised that his red hair had been shaved around his wound, leaving an odd tuft sticking out on the left part of his forehead.

Anna was much less damaged, there were only a few extra scratches added to the ones she had acquired on Mike's first expedition to discover Elowen. But she lay very still under the thin sheet and bedspread, her hair neatly brushed but flat and lifeless around her pale face. Her blue eyes were darkened, set back deeply in bruised-looking sockets, and had none of their usual sparkle as they moved to look at the visitors.

Mike had seen Lucy's quickly concealed shock. He said gruffly, 'It's not as bad as it seems. The nurse went to town with bandages. I'd say that was a woman all over, but it was a bloke. And Anna's just dozy. All she needs is some fresh air and a spot of gentle exercise.'

'What does the doctor say?' Elliot enquired mildly as Lucy went to sit on the other side of Anna's bed.

Tom Peters drew up two more chairs, putting them squarely at the foot of the bed. The inspector sat down on one, smiling as he greeted Anna gently, then leaning back as he waited for Mike's reply. The sergeant pulled his chair a little further away and sat down too, planting his feet firmly on the floor.

'She wants to keep us in for observation.' Mike snorted. 'All you hear about in the papers is bed shortages, and here we are, being told to stay in the ones we've got. Well,' he said belligerently, 'I've got things to do, so I'm off home this morning.' He looked at Lucy. 'I've been expecting you. Where's Hugh?' He glanced expectantly over her shoulder, but did not wait for a reply. 'I need a lift back to Roscombe.' His attention turned to the inspector. 'Where's my car, Elliot? Please don't tell me it's been left out in the country to be stripped of its wheels.'

'It's quite safe,' the inspector replied calmly. 'Aaron Tregonan got his nephew to drive it to his farm for you to collect. When you can drive safely,' he finished pointedly. 'Aaron said he'd met you and Anna at the local pub, and you'd know him.'

'That's right.' Mike was frowning. 'What was he doing there?'

Elliot gave a short laugh. 'The entire village was there, for which you should be grateful. Most of them were involved in digging you out. There were men digging the rubble out, lines of men and women shifting it away, and Aaron there bringing in supplies of wood from the estate's old timber yard to shore up the walls of the entrance slope.'

Mike groaned. 'God, I can see this is going to be expensive. Drinks all round in the pub at least.'

'You and Anna may well owe your lives to them all, but especially Aaron,' the inspector said quietly. 'If you'd been down there much longer, what air was left would probably have run out.'

Mike lifted a hand to clutch his hair, his fingers gripping the bandage instead, causing an expression first of surprise, then of irritation to cross his face. 'And I know Aaron likes the best whisky. I suppose his will have to be a double.'

'You'll be lucky to get off with that,' Elliot said dryly. 'I should think you'll be getting away cheaply with a bottle.'

Mike grinned. Then he frowned. 'How do you know?' he demanded. 'What was happening, I mean. We're not dead, so you can't be on the case.'

'They came to help too, when they heard about it on the police radio,' Lucy said quietly, looking briefly across the bed at the men. 'Rob was digging, Tom was shifting rubble.'

Mike stared at the two policemen. 'Thanks,' he said gruffly, a tinge of red added to the blue and black shades on his face. 'I'll see you at The Lobster Pot in Roscombe sometime.'

Elliot nodded. 'Can you remember anything about what happened?' he asked.

'Of course I can,' Mike said crossly. 'I've only had a slight tap on the head. My brain still works, and so does my memory.' He scowled at Lucy, who had glanced at him with a quick smile.

'But,' he turned his attention to the inspector again, 'there's nothing useful to tell you. I was checking out the extent that the fogou ran back under the trees that cover it when I heard a lot of crashing and Anna scream.' He grimaced suddenly. 'I shot out of the trees and saw her sliding down the slope as the walls fell in on her. There wasn't time to do anything except jump in after her and shove her into the chamber. I'd seen the wooden screen on the fogou entrance was broken when I found it a couple of days ago. It was the only hope. But I didn't know if we'd get through, or,' his lips tightened, 'if the remainder of the screen would hold up against the fall of rubble.'

His eyes slid to look at Anna, who lay listening without any of her usual interest. She did smile slightly, a wan imitation of her usual brilliance, and stretched out one of the hands that had been lying still on the bedspread. 'My hero,' she said faintly, touching his hand before letting her own fall limply back onto the bed. 'At last,' she added with a faint touch of her usual humour.

Mike scowled. 'I was the only one there, and all your kung fu skills wouldn't have helped you against falling rocks.'

'Would you have expected the sides of the slope to collapse like that?' the inspector asked.

Mike shrugged. 'Who knows? Something like that could easily be unstable. The edge crumbled when I found it on Thursday, and there was a bit of a fall when I slipped over it. It wouldn't have taken much to cause another shift on the loose rubble, a deer, even a fox crossing the slope. Not necessarily Anna landing on it. But I wouldn't have expected the fall to be so severe.' His lips tightened. 'Both sides seemed to be coming down, as far as I could tell.' He glanced at the inspector. 'You'll have a better idea than I do of how much caved in.'

Elliot nodded, but did not respond to the oblique question. 'Did you see anybody else around before Anna fell?' he enquired.

Mike began to shake his head, stopping abruptly with a grimace of pain. 'No. There was only Lucy, and she wasn't in sight. And I don't suppose she suddenly felt the urge to dispose of Anna. Although, there again …' he grinned suddenly at Anna, 'I've felt it myself from time to time.'

'There was a man, Rob,' Anna said unexpectedly. 'I've just remembered. I think I was calling Mike, it was time to eat and he'd gone wandering off. As usual.' She slanted a look at Mike. 'And all of a sudden this man came bursting out of the bushes towards me.'

'Did he attack you?' Elliot asked quickly.

'No,' Anna said slowly, hesitantly. 'I thought he was going to, the way he came rushing at me, so I stepped back, then I was falling, and Mike was there pushing me further down.' Her voice trailed away.

Elliot looked at her in concern, obviously wondering whether to continue. He glanced interrogatively at Lucy.

Anna saw this and smiled faintly. 'I'm alright, Rob, just very tired. I don't know anything else anyway.' She closed her eyes and seemed to fall asleep.

'She keeps doing that,' Mike muttered, staring at Anna.

'At least she's conscious and in her right mind,' the inspector said softly.

Anna's eyes opened again quite suddenly, moving slowly round the seated men, resting finally on Inspector Elliot. 'Rob,' she said urgently, 'are you here about the bodies?'

Mike was still staring at her, his expression now tinged with anxiety. 'Trust you to tempt fate, Elliot,' he growled. He leaned forward, making an attempt to sound rational and soothing, 'There weren't bodies, Anna. We both got out safely.'

'No,' Anna stirred, becoming agitated. 'There were bodies. Rob, ...'

'It's alright, Anna,' Elliot leaned forward, catching her eyes, 'I've seen the bodies.'

Mike turned his stare on the inspector, quite flabbergasted now. His eyes flickered to Sergeant Peters, then to Lucy, obviously hoping to find one of them to support him. Then they returned to Elliot and narrowed. 'What bodies?' he demanded.

'We don't know,' the inspector said, 'but there were two bodies in the fogou. They had been there a long time, decades at least.'

'What!' Mike exploded. The nurse came hurrying in from the desk, the elderly women in the nearby beds were agog with anticipation.

'Really, Professor,' the nurse expostulated, as she reached the group around Anna's bed, 'if you can't be quieter you must leave this ward.'

'It was my fault,' Elliot intervened quickly, 'he's just had some startling news.'

'I don't care if he's won the lottery,' the nurse snapped. 'He can't disturb the other patients.'

'I don't think,' Sergeant Peters said mildly, glancing to the other beds, 'that they're complaining.'

The nurse sniffed. 'Any more disturbance and you must all leave,' she said stiffly. 'Miss Evesleigh needs peace and quiet.'

She turned and stalked stiffly up the ward and out of the door. Mike glared after her, then caught the fascinated eyes of the woman in the next bed and turned hurriedly back to the inspector.

'Alright, Elliot, whose bodies are we talking about?' he asked, attempting to mute his voice.

'As I said,' the inspector replied patiently, 'we don't know. But there were two semi-mummified corpses in there.'

Anna made a slight sound. 'Two? She wasn't alone either?'

'She?' Elliot asked quickly.

'I felt her,' Anna said, her eyes open wide now, reliving the horror of that moment, 'her bones, her skin, her skirt.'

Mike reached out, gripping her hand so tightly that she winced. 'How?' he demanded. 'How did you find her?'

'I was trying to find a way out,' she said, her voice gaining in strength. 'You were unconscious, I didn't know how badly you were hurt, there was nothing else I could do. There was no light, so I could only feel around the walls, up to the roof, down to the floor. That's how I found her.'

Mike glanced quickly at Elliot. 'Was one of them a woman?'

'Yes,' he conceded, 'and wearing rings that Aaron recognised as belonging to old Lady Mariot Lanyon, the last person to live in Elowen.'

'Well,' Mike was puzzled, 'that's one corpse identified then.'

'No,' Elliot replied, 'because Lady Lanyon was buried in Genarran churchyard, some years after these corpses were immured in the fogou.'

'Were they dead when they were put there?' Anna asked quietly.

The inspector's hesitation was barely noticeable. 'Probably,' he said, pleased to see her eyes slowly close in relief. 'But we'll soon know for sure.'

Mike had seen the hesitation and was about to pursue the matter when he caught Lucy's minatory glare. She flickered a quick pointed glance at Anna and shook her head fractionally.

Mike shut his mouth and fell silent. He realised that he was still holding Anna's hand and dropped it hastily.

Anna had missed this exchange, only opening her eyes again

now to ask, 'Who was the other one?'

'We really don't know,' Elliot repeated patiently, 'but we think it was a man.'

'There you are, Anna,' Mike said encouragingly, 'let's go home and we can give Elliot a hand in solving the mystery. Then you can write it into one of your plays. Although you could just make it up as usual, you don't need to wait for Elliot to get the facts.'

Anna's lips twitched, but she did not reply.

'Well,' Mike said impatiently, turning to the policemen, 'if that's it I'll just get on and discharge myself. And you'd better make up your mind, Anna,' he turned back abruptly to her, 'whether you're going to stay here or not.'

'I would like to come home,' she said mildly.

'Your father and Fran are still away, aren't they?' Lucy asked. 'You can come back to the manor with me, and have the room you always stayed in when we were girls. I may,' she added, thinking suddenly of the other body that Hugh might or might not know about, 'be there a little longer than I was planning, as something has cropped up.'

Elliot carefully kept his gaze away from Lucy, but his imperturbability was visibly jolted when Mike spoke.

'Anna's coming home with me,' he announced. 'You'll have your own work to deal with, Lucy, and as I've got to take it easy too I might as well have Anna around to nag me and make life interesting. And if,' he added hopefully, glancing at Anna, 'you've got first aid skills to match your self-defence ones you can do a better job of this, so that I don't go through the village worrying all the old ladies, and exciting Tilly Barlow's sympathy.' He touched his bandage gingerly, attempting to look pathetic, and failing so abysmally that Lucy had to bite her lip not to laugh out loud.

Rob Elliot helped Anna climb gingerly out of the front of his car after a gentle drive from Corrington hospital back to Roscombe. Mike had pushed Ben off his lap and got out of the back seat with alacrity as soon as the car had stopped. It had been crowded, with Mike sandwiched between Lucy and Rob Elliot, as Sergeant Peters drove them slowly through the town and the winding lanes. Mike was obviously in a hurry to get into his home, but he slowed his pace on the short path as he approached the front door of his cottage, fumbling in his trouser pockets for the key.

Lucy held open the gate that had bounced shut behind Mike. Ben had gone springing after him, but he hesitated now, looking back at Lucy as she waited by the gate for Rob to pass through it with his arm around Anna. Anna was concentrating on putting one step in front of the other, unaware of the flurry of excitement in the nearby cottages as their arrival was noted. Faces were pressed against the small windowpanes. Some were openly staring, pale distorted ovals pressed against the glass, others were just shadows peering around twitched curtains. Here and there a front door swung open as the bolder observers hurried out in the hope of speech, in one case stumbling down steps and tripping over an awkwardly placed flowerpot.

Rob was also aware of the eager onlookers, and led Anna as quickly as he could up the path, keen not to use his police persona to deter them. Lucy closed the gate firmly behind the two of them and lingered, pressing her back against it, watching them make their slow way to the door. Mike had disappeared inside, leaving it wide open, and Lucy wondered for a moment why he was in such a hurry to get home. Ben had come back to join her, pressing against her legs, keen that she should hurry in with the others. She felt him stiffen and turn towards the street.

Her heart sank as a light breathless voice called her name. 'Lucy!' The voice came again, totally familiar and nearer to hand, so Lucy turned reluctantly to face Tilly Barlow.

Tilly was hurrying towards Lucy, who blinked at the sight of her. Her long black skirt was embroidered in vivid pink and orange swirls, and clung to her legs as she moved, impeding the speed she was trying to achieve. A lime-green tunic reached to her knees over the skirt, and was slashed very low in the bodice, revealing an expanse of sun-reddened skin. Several strings of beads swung backwards and forwards, bouncing up and down in what Lucy felt could only be a painful way.

'This is lucky, isn't it? Catching up with you like this, I mean,' Tilly said, panting a little as she reached Lucy. 'I'd heard they were badly hurt. Anna and Mike, you know. I hadn't expected him to be home so soon. And Anna too, I see. Is she staying here with him?' Tilly was forced to pause as her breath ran out.

'We've only just got back,' Lucy said firmly, leaning against the gate, determined not to open it for Tilly, 'so I don't quite know what arrangements are going to be made.'

'The police too,' Tilly said, staring avidly at the cottage door, which Rob had closed firmly behind him. 'Of course they'll be around anyway with this murder on the cliffs, but then Inspector Elliot is so friendly with Anna, isn't he? No doubt he's told her, and you too, I expect, all about it. But then again,' she said archly, 'maybe not.'

The man who had come up to stand behind Tilly spoke unexpectedly, his voice nasal and congested. 'Come on, Tilly, you know you were warned not to talk about it.'

Lucy had been vaguely aware of his presence but now she focused on him for the first time. Before she could comment, Tilly hurried on, 'Oh, of course, yes, I hadn't forgotten.' She saw Lucy looking at the man, whose loose t-shirt hanging over his jeans failed to conceal a paunchy stomach. He was not at all familiar to Lucy, and she wondered if he had recently moved into the village.

'Silly me, I forget you don't live here now, Lucy,' Tilly said with a titter. 'You always knew everything when you did, a real lady of the manor. But you won't know Clive, he's my lodger, at least until he finds somewhere of his own to live. And he's a very fine plumber, you ask Jack Leygar up at Home Farm.' Tilly waved a thin hand wildly. 'He's putting in Mary's bathrooms, although really, of course, I tell him he's being a traitor. Mary's going into the bed-and-breakfast line too, you know, so it's more competition for little me. And it's difficult now, with people not having so much money to spend on holidays. But then,' she said complacently, 'I've got Clive, and my regulars nearly all come back again. It'll take Mary a while to build up the kind of business I've got.'

'Come on, Tilly,' Clive said impatiently, without looking once at Lucy. 'I've got to get back to work at the farm. Otherwise I won't be earning the money to pay the rent.'

'Oh yes, of course.' She caught his arm, ostentatiously tucking hers through it. Her voice drifted over her shoulder as he dragged her away. 'And, of course, Philly's had all those cancellations at the priory. Strange, but that's how it goes. Such a shame, though, it'll only be adding to your troubles.'

Lucy stared after her, a slight frown on her face. She started as Rob Elliot spoke at her shoulder. 'Sorry, Rob,' she said apologetically, while Ben sprang to greet him as if he had not seen him for days, 'I didn't hear you coming.'

'I'm not surprised,' he commented, one hand absentmindedly stroking the dog. He was not looking at her, but after the figures of Tilly and Clive as they dwindled away, vanishing altogether as they turned through the gates onto the back drive to the manor. 'That woman can talk for fifty. I suppose she'd come to muscle in and offer help.'

Lucy smiled. 'The first, yes, she wanted to know what was happening, although she talked so much I didn't have to stonewall. The second, no. She's scared of Mike, so she wouldn't dare to interfere, even under the guise of helping. He doesn't suffer fools gladly, and as far as he's concerned she fits very firmly into that category.'

'I know.' Elliot sighed. 'Unfortunately I sometimes have to suffer them where Mike can just shut them up. Did she say anything worth listening to?'

'I'm not sure,' Lucy said slowly. 'She seemed to know something about the death of this man on the cliffs. Something she's obviously bursting to tell me, yet she didn't. Although,' Lucy admitted, 'that may be because the man with her stopped her.'

Lucy was watching the inspector's expression closely, but learned nothing from its impassivity.

'Where was she going?' he asked. 'I thought she worked in Coombhaven in the mornings.'

'You know more than I do, then,' Lucy said as the collie came back to sit by her feet. 'She said I was out of touch with local affairs, and she seems to be right. Still, maybe she doesn't work weekends.'

Elliot looked startled. 'Of course,' he said, 'I'd forgotten what day it is. It's Saturday, isn't it?'

'Yes, but it's not surprising you didn't know,' she reassured him, 'I barely know which day of the week I'm on at the best of times, let alone with all that's happened in the last eighteen hours. And you've had more to deal with than I have, with this new death.'

'Perhaps,' he agreed. 'But I think you were already tired out before yesterday's traumas, Lucy. You're pushing yourself too much. Take care. And look after Anna, if you can.' He smiled suddenly. 'I've left her stretched in artistic languor over Mike's sofa. He's already ferreting round in the dining room, although I don't know why he calls it a dining room. It's a cartoonist's idea of how a professor would work, surrounded by piles of books. And in this case bits of rock and, for all I know, bits of bones. God knows what he's looking for that's so important right now.' He drew a deep breath. 'Can you stay with her for a bit? I can't imagine Mike's going to remember why she's there.'

'Of course I can,' she said readily, standing aside to let him open the gate. 'I was planning to. We might just as well rest together. You're right,' she said slowly, as Sergeant Peters went past her to the car, 'I am tired, and Mike's unlikely to notice I'm here as well if he's got some bee in his bonnet. But,' she remembered abruptly, 'I need to speak to Philly about some trouble with the priory holiday bookings. I'd almost forgotten, but something Tilly said reminded me. If she knows about it I'm afraid it must be more serious than I'd expected. And if she knows the whole village will too. Still, I'm sure Philly will come down here when she has a chance, once she knows we're here.'

Elliot paused with his hand on the gate, looking back at her. 'What kind of trouble is there at the priory?' he asked curiously.

'Not police trouble,' she said quickly. 'At least, I hope not. I'm not really sure, to be honest. I know several recent bookings were cancelled at the last moment, and Philly mentioned one or two people saying they'd received anonymous letters warning them not to come. I think somebody was told there was a rat infestation, and somebody else that there was dry rot and fungus growing on the walls behind the furniture. It sounds mad, doesn't it?'

The inspector was staring intently at her. 'Was it recent, this spate of anonymous letters?' he demanded.

'Mmm,' she said, surprised at his interest. 'The whole of last week's bookings were wiped out, so we were lucky to have so much late interest. Some of the apartments are occupied in spite of the cancellations.'

'Very lucky,' he said smoothly. 'So all these people staying at the priory now have come as last minute bookings.'

'Yes, that's right,' Lucy said slowly.

'Including Damian Mallinson?'

'I suppose so. I don't really know much about the priory bookings; it's my brother's concern really,' Lucy admitted. 'Philly only got in touch with me about this because she thought I ought to know as Will's away in India.'

'That's very interesting,' Elliot said, shutting the gate. 'I'll have a word with Philly Leygar about it. She'll be at the priory now, won't she?'

Lucy glanced at her watch, taken aback to see it was only eleven thirty. 'I should think so. She doesn't do fixed hours, especially on Saturdays, she just does the time it takes to get the work done.'

'I'll chance it, and see if I can catch her there,' the inspector said, moving towards the car. 'After all, if she isn't at the priory she's likely to have gone back to the farm for lunch. Why don't I ask her to come down and see you here, if you must talk to her?'

'That's a good idea,' she said gratefully.

He raised a hand in farewell as he opened his car door and slid into the passenger seat. Sergeant Peters started the car and lifted a hand in farewell as he drove down to the quay, where Lucy knew he would turn round to go back up Roscombe's main street.

Calling Ben to her side she moved slowly to the front door, where she stood screened by the prolific curtain of jasmine that overhung it, breathing in the honeyed scent that seemed to cling to her. Sure enough, the car came sweeping past only a minute later.

Lucy went quickly back down the short path and leaned over the gate, watching the car turn in through the gate piers of the manor's back drive. So Rob was definitely going up to the priory. But was he planning just to talk to Philly? Lucy had an uneasy feeling that he was also keen to catch up with Tilly Barlow. And Tilly Barlow knew something about the death on the cliffs, something she had really wanted to tell Lucy, something she felt sorry for Lucy about, or pretended to at least.

Lucy returned to the front door, thinking hard. She pulled her mobile out of her pocket and scrolled through it. There were three messages, but not one from Hugh. She frowned. Where was he? And just what was he doing? She tapped out another short message to him, telling him where she was. At least he shouldn't complain, she thought grimly, that she didn't let him know what was happening.

Lucy put down her mug of tea and glanced at Anna, who lay dozing lightly under the patchwork quilt that covered her. Mike had brought it down from one of the bedrooms when she had asked for a cover. In spite of the increasing warmth of the day it was cool inside the cottage and Lucy was keen that Anna should not get too cold.

As she looked at her friend now, Lucy was convinced that a faint tint of pinkness was returning to her pale face. Anna's eyelids flickered occasionally, her breathing was light and steady. But from time to time her hands scrabbled over the bedspread, the fingers first spread out, searching, then digging deeply into the quilt.

Lucy reached out to hold one hand, murmuring softly, and Anna quietened again. Ben lay in front of the hearth, his head lifted to watch them. He turned away, sniffing in a desultory fashion at the pottery pieces in the nearby basket, before lowering his head with a sigh and shutting his own eyes. The open door to the right of the fireplace led into the dining room, where Lucy knew Mike worked when he was at home. He was in there now, and had been since they got back. She had been aware of him moving piles of papers, lifting books, muttering to himself most of the time. He had quietened down now as well, so she wondered what he was doing, and whether he too had fallen asleep. She considered going to look, and decided against it. If Mike had dozed off in his chair, she was pretty sure he would have slept in more uncomfortable places on one of his digs.

Lucy gently removed her hand from Anna's and let her eyes rest on the quilt. She had been surprised when Mike had produced it, it was a finely worked piece, with cotton squares and lozenges carefully fitted together to produce a harmonious whole in creams, pinks and roses. She must remember to ask Mike about it, for she was sure her grandmother Isobel, with her interest in historic fabrics and designs, would be keen to see it. The thought of Isobel made Lucy wish she was at her mews house in Coombhaven rather than at her flat in Italy. She should be back soon though, and Lucy was surprised how much she was looking forward to seeing and talking to her.

Lucy was startled from her thoughts as Ben stirred, looking up hopefully. She was suddenly aware that Mike had come in noiselessly from the dining room and was amazed, he had moved so quietly that she had not noticed him.

He was standing behind the sofa staring down at Anna. 'She's looking better,' he said hoarsely. 'Isn't she?'

'I think so,' Lucy agreed softly. 'I'm sure all she needs is rest. It's a shame she wouldn't go up to bed, she'd be more comfortable.'

'She needs her friends around her, she doesn't like being on her own normally, let alone now,' he said firmly. 'And she probably needs food. It must be time for lunch.'

His voice had risen to its usual pitch, Ben sat up, and Anna stirred. Her fingers began to roam feverishly over the quilt again, while her head started to roll from side to side.

Mike leaned across the back of the sofa and put a blunt-fingered hand over one of hers. 'It's alright, Anna. It's lunch time.'

Her eyelids flickered and rolled open, her dark blue eyes dazed and confused as they looked up. They cleared as she focused on Mike. 'Mike.' She smiled a little. 'Always thinking about food.' She struggled to sit up.

Lucy bent forward to help her, but Mike came round the end of the sofa and nudged her away. 'I'll do it, you get us something to eat. There should be soup and bread in the kitchen. And maybe eggs. She should,' he said authoritatively, 'eat something light.' He glanced, suddenly uncertain, over his shoulder at Lucy. 'Shouldn't she?'

'Both of you should,' Lucy replied, entertained by his assumption of knowledge and strangely touched by his concern for Anna. A twinge of regret stabbed her. Hugh had been like this once. Hugh. At the thought of him her mind fell into the well-worn treadmill that she was trying to avoid. Where was Hugh? What was he doing?

Beside her Anna was sitting up, still looking fragile and interesting, propped against the arm of the sofa. She was resisting Mike's attempts to stuff more cushions behind her back. 'Lucy,' she appealed, 'tell him I don't need them.'

Distracted, Lucy opened her mouth but before she could speak they were galvanised by knocking on the front door.

Lucy froze but Mike leaped forward. 'At last,' he ejaculated. 'I wondered what was keeping Hugh.' He wrenched the door open

and stood still, taken aback at the sight of the person in front of
him.

'Is Lucy here?' Philly Leygar demanded, her round face
troubled under her short black curls as she fended off the excited
collie. 'The inspector said she was, and Anna too, and that Lucy
wanted to talk to me.'

'Come in,' Mike said, 'quickly, before the rest of the village
materialises as well.' He took her arm, virtually yanking her
through the door and down the shallow step, sending Ben agilely
skittering aside as he peered suspiciously over her shoulder at the
village street.

He was just in time. On the opposite side of the street a door
opened and a woman appeared, waving energetically.

Mike ignored her, slamming the door shut. 'What's the news?'
he demanded.

'I don't think there's anything new,' Philly said. 'The inspector
came into the office with Tom Peters to ask me a couple more
things, and now he wants me to go into Coombhaven to make a
statement.'

Mike frowned. 'About what?'

Ben wandered over to Anna, pressing up against the sofa
beside her. Philly hurried over too, ignoring Mike's question, and
briefly pressing Anna's hands. 'I'm so glad you're alright, Anna,'
she said. 'There were awful stories going round the village. About
you both.' She glanced over her shoulder at Mike.

Mike grunted derisively. 'There were bound to be. It's been
very quiet around here lately. I suppose,' he went on with forced
humour, 'we were terribly injured, or dying slowly in our own
blood.'

Philly grinned. 'Something like that. And buried alive with the
living dead.' Her grin faded at the expression on Mike's face.
'Sorry,' she said.

'Don't be silly,' Anna said faintly. 'You couldn't know. And
we weren't buried for long and the bodies weren't still living.'

Philly stared at her, horrified. 'Were you really then?'

'Buried? Oh yes, with Mike, who saved my life with great gallantry.' Anna's voice grew stronger, her eyes had a sparkle and her hands fluttered expressively as she continued, 'And we were dug out by a band of heroic volunteers, led by the local octogenarian with important knowledge that saved us in the nick of time.'

Philly was still staring, unsure whether to be amused or not.

'I told you she was feeling better,' Mike growled to Lucy, his face reddening between the motley bruising. 'I'm sure of it once she begins to turn facts into a fantastic story.'

'It's pretty accurate, though,' Lucy demurred, enjoying his embarrassment. 'After all, I was there and at least saw you both being dug out of the fogou by the massed ranks of villagers.'

'It's past history,' he grunted. 'We need to be concerned about what's happening now. What's Elliot's concern here? Surely not another murder?'

Lucy sighed. 'I tried to tell you when we got back,' she pointed out, 'but your mind was elsewhere.'

'I was still dazed,' he said reproachfully. 'I had a knock on the head, you know.'

'And the effects have cleared up miraculously after you spent a couple of hours ferreting among your books and papers rather than resting,' she retorted tartly.

Mike ignored this. 'Well, what about this murder?'

'I'm not sure they know it's a murder,' Lucy demurred. She caught sight of Philly's face and demanded sharply, 'Do they?'

'Umm,' Philly mumbled uncomfortably. 'They seem to. I don't know what's changed, but Tom Peters took a call just after he and the inspector turned up in the office. They went off together for a bit, then the inspector came back and told me it was a murder enquiry. That's when he asked me to go to the station to sign a formal statement. That's why I've come really, to let you know I can't stay and talk to you right now.'

Lucy's mind reeled as she stared at her, only pulling her wits together with an effort at the sound of Mike's demanding voice.

'Well, who's been killed?'

'A man staying in one of the priory apartments, I forget his name.' Lucy glanced in query at Philly.

'Damian Mallinson,' Philly supplied. 'He was found dead on the cliffs, and Celia Vaughan has disappeared from one of the other apartments too.' She looked wide-eyed at Lucy, oblivious to Mike's startled expression. 'I really don't know what to make of it all. The local policeman, Darren Cranley, has been in the office all morning. He's watching Celia's apartment in case she comes back. And Mr Armitage has gone in to speak to the inspector again, he's been going around looking awkward for a bit. I think,' she said slowly, 'he hadn't told them something earlier.'

Mike was staring at her. 'I'm having difficulty following this,' he complained. 'Who's this Armitage bloke?'

'He's another guest at the priory,' Philly said. She looked at Lucy. 'Inspector Elliot seemed very interested in the cancelled bookings.'

'What cancelled bookings?' Mike interrupted forcefully.

'A lot of bookings were cancelled recently, for this week particularly,' Philly explained quickly. 'And a couple of the people cancelling mentioned anonymous letters telling them bad things about the priory. Things,' she added indignantly, 'that aren't true. And this is just what we don't need when we're trying to build up custom.'

'But you've got all these people staying there, haven't you?' Mike was puzzled and growing irritable. 'Even if they are disappearing, or getting themselves murdered.'

Philly nodded. 'They're all late, chance bookings.' Her eyes returned to Lucy. 'He thinks it's suspicious,' she said. 'Inspector Elliot, that is. All these cancellations and late bookings. He wanted to know why I didn't report the anonymous letters.'

'Why didn't you?' Mike asked.

Philly's eyes flickered away from Lucy to him, then fell to her feet. 'I told Hugh about them when he rang at the weekend to see if we had a free apartment. He said it wasn't worth bothering the police about them just yet.'

'Did you tell them that?' Lucy asked quickly.

'I didn't mean to,' Philly said miserably. 'Inspector Elliot sort of boxed me in and I had to. And…' Her voice tailed away.

'Did you tell them about the row Hugh had with that visitor?' Mike demanded. 'Dear God, don't tell me it's him that's dead?'

'Damian Mallinson. Yes,' she said. 'I just said he and Hugh had been talking with Celia, but I couldn't hear what they were saying.' She shivered. 'He really pressed me about it, what their body posture was like, whether the window was open, could I hear their voices. I didn't say anything I didn't have to.'

Mike was looking relieved. 'Thank God for that,' he said. 'I've rarely seen Hugh so angry, it wouldn't do to pass that on to Elliot.'

'He already knows,' Philly said dismally.

'What! How?'

'Mr Armitage heard them too, so I suppose he told the inspector all about it.'

Mike's face was dark, grim, now. 'What does Hugh say about it?' he asked, swinging round to Lucy.

Her lips were tightly pressed together. It was with an effort that she prised them open. 'Not much. I've barely seen him since this morning.'

'Where is he?' he demanded. 'I thought he'd come to the hospital with you.'

'He went off first thing, as soon as Rob Elliot had finished talking to him. That's why Rob brought me into Corrington.'

'Hugh's been in the priory office all morning too,' Philly said unexpectedly.

Philly flushed as Mike and Lucy turned to look at her in surprise. 'He said he wanted to talk about the priory apartments, and what to do about this business, but,' she sounded awkward, 'he spent a lot of time just looking out of the window. I could see Darren, the policeman, you know, was surprised and wanted him to go, but didn't know how to make him. After all, Hugh has worked with the inspector before, and that must make it awkward for Darren.'

In more ways than one, Lucy thought bleakly. And for Rob Elliot too.

'What was Hugh doing?' Mike demanded. 'Surely he had better things to do than just hang around there.'

'It looked like the same as Darren,' Philly said reluctantly. 'I thought he was watching Celia Vaughan's cottage as well, in case she comes back.'

'Or in case somebody else goes in,' Lucy added. Unwillingly she wondered about a third option. Was it Hugh who was waiting for a chance to get in there unobserved?

'Anyway, Hugh left just before the inspector came into the office. He'd got your text message, Lucy, so he said he'd come down here after he'd made some calls,' Philly said. 'I thought he'd arrive before me. In fact, the inspector wants to talk to Hugh so I said he'd be here.' She saw the concern on Lucy's face and said quickly, 'I think he's probably talking to everyone again. He was outside the gatehouse when I left the office, Tom Peters was there too and seemed to have brought Tilly back from the farm with him, and Clive, her lodger. Well,' she added reluctantly, 'I'd better get over to Coombhaven to make this statement. Shall I come back here again afterwards, Lucy, if you still want to discuss this bookings problem?'

Lucy collected her thoughts with an effort. 'Yes, perhaps that would be best,' she said, glancing at Anna. 'If anything changes I'll ring you on your mobile.'

'Okay.' Philly hesitated at the front door, looking back at the three people in Mike's sitting room. 'Take care.'

Mike closed the door firmly behind her, his hand hovering for a moment over the bolt at the top of it. 'Better not,' he muttered to himself.

'Well,' Lucy said, suddenly feeling exhausted, 'I'll see about lunch. You stay with Anna, Mike.'

She had only just turned towards the kitchen beyond the

sitting room, when they heard brisk footsteps approaching on the front path, and Ben sprang towards the front door.

'Bloody hell,' Mike snarled, 'we're supposed to be resting in peace and quiet. It'll be one of those damned women from the village, with a pie or a cake, bursting to interrogate us.' He took two hasty steps and jerked the door open, almost knocking the collie over.

His scowling face lightened as he saw who stood there. 'About time,' he growled. 'Get in quickly before the whole village comes visiting.'

Hugh entered without haste, bending over the excited dog as he said appreciatively, 'I see you're feeling better, Mike.'

'It was only a bump on the head,' Mike growled. 'So much fuss about nothing.'

Hugh ignored this, flicking a quick smile at Lucy as he crossed with Ben at his heels to Anna's side. He looked down at her, and nodded. 'You're looking better. How do you feel?' He bent to kiss her cheek.

'I'm fine,' she said valiantly. 'Mike and Lucy are taking great care of me. And you're just in time for lunch.'

'Lucy,' Hugh turned to his wife, holding out his hands, 'I'm sorry to have left you in the lurch. There are a couple of issues I have to sort out.'

She ignored his hands. 'Philly says Rob Elliot wants to talk to you again.'

He let his hands fall to his sides and stood quite still for a second, before saying levelly, 'He'll want to check the details we've all been giving him, to create as accurate a timetable of movements as possible.' Hugh frowned. 'He does seem to be taking this to the next stage of investigation.' He looked penetratingly at Lucy. 'Have there been any developments?'

'Celia Vaughan hasn't turned up, if that's what's bothering you,' Lucy said as Ben lay down beside the sofa, looking anxiously between his master and mistress. 'But Rob is now dealing with a murder enquiry.'

'I see,' Hugh said, on a long sigh. 'I wondered when I saw uniformed police knocking on doors on both sides of the street as I came here.'

'Hugh,' Mike said quickly, 'do you know it's that bloke that you had a row with yesterday?'

'It was hardly a row,' Hugh demurred. 'But yes, I know who the dead man was.' He glanced round, one brow quirking upwards. 'I didn't kill him, you know,' he said gently, watching their faces.

'But you know something, Hugh, don't you?' Lucy asked. 'Is it about this woman, Celia Vaughan? Who is she?'

'So many questions,' he said gently. 'Don't you trust me, Lucy?'

'I can turn that round, Hugh,' she said quickly. 'Don't you trust me, all of us, enough to tell us what you know?'

'It isn't that simple, I'm afraid,' he replied.

'It seems simple enough to me,' she said.

'Hugh,' Mike began urgently, 'you know …' He broke off as a brisk tattoo was hammered on the front door, which he was still standing next to. Taking a quick step sideways he peered out of the window, trying to see round the jasmine that screened the path. He could not see the visitor, but beyond the gate was parked a car he knew.

'It's Elliot,' he said quietly. 'Hugh, …'

'You'd better let him in then,' Hugh said firmly. 'He's a busy man.'

Without another word Mike opened the front door and stood back, letting Inspector Elliot and Sergeant Peters come down the shallow step into the sitting room before he shut the door firmly behind them. Ben looked up, wagging his tail slowly, but did not come to greet them.

The inspector looked quickly across the room to the sofa where Anna lay. A faint smile touched his mouth as he saw her sitting up, more colour in her cheeks. It faded as he saw the anxiety in her eyes, and disappeared altogether as his gaze fell briefly on Lucy. He moved his attention on to Hugh with an effort, speaking in an unusually formal tone. 'We are, you may know, running a murder investigation now. In the light of that, do you have anything you want to add to, or change in, your original version of your activities?'

Sergeant Peters stood at Elliot's shoulder, his bulk seeming to support the stiff figure of the inspector. Both of them were looking intently at Hugh. So were his wife and friends.

Hugh answered immediately, aware of the waiting tension in the room. 'There's nothing more I can tell you,' he said quietly.

Elliot's lips tightened. 'Then, in the light of the evidence that I have, I must ask you to come to the station in Coombhaven for further questioning,' he said grimly. 'You know that you are entitled to have a solicitor present if you wish.'

'I shan't need a solicitor, thanks all the same,' Hugh said quietly. 'If it comes to it, which it won't, I'll represent myself.'

'As you like.' The inspector indicated the door. Mike moved away, letting the inspector open it to lead the way out, Hugh close behind him, with Sergeant Peters bringing up the rear. The sergeant cast Lucy a brief commiserating look as he shut the door, closing off the sitting room from the outside world that was swallowing Hugh.

SEVEN

Lucy glanced again at her watch. It was nearly four o'clock. Hugh had been gone for almost three hours, and there had not been a word from him or the police station. She wondered again how she would know if he was charged. Surely, she thought, Rob Elliot would tell her.

Anna had seen the action. 'He'll be back,' she said reassuringly. 'You know he can't have killed that man.'

'He's hiding something though,' Lucy said bitterly. 'He knows what happened, and I think he's covering up for that woman.'

Anna bit her lip, remembering the scene she had witnessed in the priory yesterday. She was quite certain Celia Vaughan would be capable of killing a man. But surely Hugh couldn't be so besotted with her that he'd cover up something like that.

Lucy looked at her friend with concern. 'You don't need this, Anna,' she said. 'Try not to think about it.'

'Huh!' Mike said loudly from the dining-room doorway. 'This sort of thing is meat and drink to her. The excitement will do her good.' He gestured towards Anna. 'Look, she's virtually back to normal. Bursting to sort it all out.'

Anna's brilliant smile was almost as bright as usual. 'Then let's think about what Hugh's up to,' she said. 'I'm sure we can work it out.'

'Why not?' Mike said, his voice vibrating with triumph. 'After all, I've just solved the first murder mystery for Elliot.' He waved a small book, its Italian marbled paper cover mottled with damp spots.

Lucy and Anna looked at him in surprise, both distracted by his words. Before he could speak again there was a gentle tap at the door and Ben exploded into a frenzy of barking.

All three people in the room turned as one to stare at the door. Mike put the book he held carefully down on the mantelpiece and went to see who the visitor was. He already knew it would not be Hugh, or Rob Elliot, who would knock more firmly.

It was Philly who stood there again, clutching a large cake tin. Nobody spoke as she stepped down into the room, brushing past Mike. The only other movement was the wagging of Ben's tail from where he stood at his post beside Lucy. Mike shut the door behind Philly and leaned his back against it. They were all remembering that she had been at Coombhaven police station that afternoon, and thinking that she might have seen Hugh.

'I went back to the farm to let Mum and Dad know what was happening,' Philly said, pushing the tin towards Lucy. 'Mum sent you this. A light sponge, she thought it would be just right for Anna and Mike.'

'Thank you,' Lucy said automatically, taking the tin and clutching it rather uncertainly.

Anna reached across and took it from her, putting it carefully on the table. 'Thank her very much, Philly,' she said. 'I do fancy something like that. We'll make some tea in a minute and we can all have a piece of it.' She smiled at Philly, patting the sofa next to her. 'Come and sit down and tell us how you got on at the police station.'

Philly sat as bidden, Ben wriggling beside her with excitement as she briefly stroked him, before folding her hands tightly together on her lap. 'Is Hugh back?' she asked. 'I saw him at the police station.'

Lucy shook her head. She found she could not speak.

'Who else was there?' Anna asked. 'Didn't I hear Tilly Barlow had to go in too?'

Mike snorted, coming further into the room and flinging himself down on an armchair, wincing as he jolted his head. 'That sounds too good to be true. Tilly as the murderer.'

Anna shot him a reproving glance, but could not stop herself from smiling.

'Yes, she was there,' Philly agreed, 'and Clive too. They were leaving just as I arrived.'

Lucy saw Mike's frown and explained, 'You know, Mike, Clive is the man who's lodging with Tilly. I met him with her earlier on. Not a very chatty sort.'

'Well, Clive was back at the farm when I got home,' Philly said, 'telling Mum and Dad all about it.' She stopped suddenly, looking distressed.

'About what?' Lucy asked quietly. She saw Philly was reluctant to speak, and said gently, 'I know it's about Hugh, Philly. I'd rather hear what's being said before it's spread all round the village. If Tilly's involved everyone in the place has probably already heard about it.'

Philly nodded, the embarrassed colour running into her cheeks. 'It was about yesterday evening. Tilly comes up most evenings to meet Clive when he finishes work, you see. I think they go walking on the cliff, or something,' she said vaguely.

Mike made a muffled sound. When she glanced at him, he waved a hand, encouraging her to go on.

'Anyway,' she said, 'she was walking up the priory's back drive and had gone into the bushes to look at some flowers …'

This time the sound Mike made was definitely another snort.

'I know,' Philly said, 'but that's what she says. Anyway, while she was there, for about twenty minutes between six twenty and six forty, she saw Hugh and Celia coming out of the priory gatehouse and going through the shrubbery towards the lake. Shortly afterwards Damian Mallinson came out and went the same way.'

She looked round at them. 'You know Tilly. She says it was

such a nice evening she decided to wait there under the trees, enjoying nature,' Philly looked nauseated as she repeated the phrase, 'until Clive came.'

'Then she must have seen Mallinson come back,' Lucy said quickly. 'Hugh said they'd had words and he sent him off with a flea in his ear.'

Philly shook her head slowly. 'She's quite definite that he didn't come back while she was there,' she said. 'The only one they saw later, both of them, Tilly and Clive, was Hugh, coming through the old cemetery below the priory church. They said he was looking very hot and bothered.'

'Well, that's a point in his favour,' Mike commented sarcastically. 'If he'd just killed a man he'd be making a big effort to look calm and collected when meeting Tilly Barlow.'

'They didn't think he saw them, he was in such a hurry,' Philly reported miserably. 'And it seems there's an issue about the time when they saw him. Tilly says the inspector kept coming back to it, but Clive's adamant it was about seven fifteen. He knew he was later than he'd expected to be, so he'd just checked his watch before catching sight of Tilly on the track.

She'd wandered on to meet him, and then turned back towards the gatehouse with him. It was shortly after they'd passed it when they saw Hugh, presumably going back to his car, which they had noticed was still in the car park.'

Brows drawing together, Mike gritted his teeth. The timings were bad. Hugh had said he arrived at Elowen at about nine o'clock. Mike knew perfectly well, as did the women, that the drive to Elowen only took about nearly an hour. What the hell was Hugh playing at, he thought irritably.

'They certainly noticed a lot,' Anna commented dryly. 'It's just as if they were spying on Hugh.'

Mike looked sharply at her, a startled look on his face. Ben began to bark, springing towards the front door, eager to get outside. Mike moved quickly, reaching the window before anybody had time to speak. 'It's Elliot's car,' he said, 'but I can't see who's in it.'

'I'll go,' Philly said, hurrying to the front door, 'and come back later. Give me a ring if you need anything, Lucy.'

Mike opened the door for her and went through it behind her. His attempt to shut it was thwarted. Lucy was there, Ben sliding past her onto the path, and Anna was close beside her.

'What's this?' Mike demanded, glaring at them. 'A welcoming committee?'

Philly had slipped through the gate, carefully leaving Ben on the inside. She waved a hand in farewell and walked quickly up the street out of sight. Ben reared up on his hind legs, planting his front feet on the upper bar of the gate, wagging his tail furiously.

Lucy tried to peer through the darkened windows of the car, but could not make out any passengers in the back. She needed only one look at Inspector Elliot's grim face as he got out of the front passenger seat to know that the situation was as bad as ever. Her lips tightened, and she greeted him with constraint when he edged past the excited collie, pausing only to give him a perfunctory pat.

Sergeant Peters got out of the driver's seat and waited by the car, beckoning to the two uniformed constables who had been left to make enquiries in the village. The two young men had worked separately down the street, revisiting each house and cottage that had been empty on their earlier trawl. They had just met up on the quay, near the pub, and looked up at the car when it arrived, recognising it at once. As soon as the sergeant summoned them, they hurried the short distance to the front of Mike's cottage. On all sides of the street there was furtive movement at windows, but the police presence quelled those who might have been brave enough to venture outside to see what was happening.

The inspector had come to a halt on the cottage path, where Lucy and Mike confronted him, with Anna standing by the front door. They all stared at him for a second.

It was Mike who spoke first. He tried to mute his voice, without much success, as he demanded, 'Well?'

Elliot looked past him to Lucy. 'I'm sorry,' he said flatly. 'We're detaining Hugh for further enquiries.' He stepped forward hastily, his hands outstretched to catch her as she swayed.

'No,' she said with an effort, waving him away. 'I'm alright, really. It was just a shock.'

'For God's sake, man,' Mike said furiously, his fists clenched, 'couldn't you have been a bit more careful?'

Ben whined softly, pressing anxiously against his mistress. Her hand went down automatically to rest on his head, as Anna came to stand beside her.

'If you can find a better way of telling the truth, you'll have to let me know,' Elliot said brusquely. 'It doesn't please me to have to say it any more than it does you to have to hear it. Nothing's going to change what has to be said, however much I pussyfoot around it.' He shook his head. 'Hugh won't say anything more, he just repeats that there's nothing else he can tell us.'

'Well, then …' Mike began belligerently.

'And that won't do,' Elliot cut him off forcefully. 'We have a witness who saw Celia strike Mallinson on the cliff path, knocking him down the slope. He also saw first Celia, then Hugh go down to look at Mallinson after the first blow was struck. There are further witnesses who saw Hugh later, looking worried and overheated. And the timings Hugh has given me don't agree with the timings of the witnesses. Faced with all that, he just repeats that there's nothing more he can tell us.'

They were flabbergasted. In the silence Lucy could hear her heart beating, thump, thump, getting louder and louder.

Elliot put one hand on her arm. 'Look, let's go indoors. There's no point standing out here in the street giving the neighbours a show.' He turned her gently and began to steer her up the path to the front door, adding, 'Hugh has at least agreed to ring his solicitor, an old friend of his apparently from his London days. You may know him too, Dominic Etheridge.'

Anna stared after them as they went into the cottage. 'I don't believe this,' she said softly, turning her eyes to Mike's face.

Mike was looking particularly grim. 'But if somebody saw him there Hugh's got some explaining to do.'

'Whoever it was must be lying,' Anna said firmly.

'Why should they?' he asked flatly.

'I don't know,' she said impatiently, 'but I don't believe Hugh would kill anybody.'

'He didn't,' Mike said. 'It sounds as though Celia Vaughan did, and Hugh's covering up for her. Why the hell would he do that?'

Anna looked unhappy. 'Well, he must care about her in some way,' she said slowly. 'Hugh of all people wouldn't do something like this lightly.' She straightened her drooping shoulders. 'We just have to find out what's behind it.'

She glanced at the gate, where Sergeant Peters was obviously relaying new instructions to the constables. 'Tom must know all about it. I'll see what he'll tell me.'

Mike groaned. 'He's a policeman, Anna, he'll know what you're up to. He can't tell you anything.' Nonetheless he followed her to the gate.

She leaned over it, watching the constables turn away, back down towards the quay. 'We're just giving Lucy some time with Rob,' she said quietly to Sergeant Peters as he approached her. 'This seems so unbelievable we're all in shock.'

Tom Peters nodded. 'It's a bad business,' he said in his deep voice with the soft local accent that she normally loved to hear.

'Have they found out anything useful?' Anna enquired, gesturing towards the constables who were skirting around a woman who was striding confidently up the street.

Anna's eyes widened. She leaned forward, staring at the woman who was moving with loping pantherish grace towards them. The sun fell on her uncovered face framed in short light brown hair. The camisole top and very short shorts seemed to be the ones she had worn yesterday.

'That's her,' Anna said loudly, making Mike jump. 'That's Celia Vaughan.'

Mike brushed against her, leaning over the gate too. 'Bloody hell, so it is,' he blurted out. 'Here, Anna, out of the way. I want a few words with her.'

'Stay there, Professor,' the sergeant said sharply. 'I'll speak to the lady.' He was moving off as he spoke, adding over his shoulder, 'Let the inspector know she's here.'

Anna turned, but Mike was gone, racing up the path and flinging his front door open. She heard the urgency in his voice as he conveyed the news, but not the words he used. That they were effective there was no doubt, for Inspector Elliot came purposefully towards her, with Mike close behind him. Lucy appeared in the doorway, looking dazed and white, one hand on Ben's collar.

Celia Vaughan seemed unaware of the group of people staring down the street at her. Her long strides had brought her almost to the gate of Wheelwright's Cottage while her eyes ranged over the village taking in the curve of the street, the pots of plants on the cottage windowsills, the splashes of colour that the geraniums made against the whitewashed cottages, the feathery tamarisk that softened the outlines of the buildings. One hand loosely clasped the straps of the camera cases that hung over her shoulder. The hand slipped down to loosen the fastening of one case and her pace slowed. She was clearly taken aback when Sergeant Peters stepped in front of her, discreetly showing his warrant card.

She gave an incredulous laugh. 'What's this? I've only been gone twenty-four hours, and Hugh's called in the heavy brigade.'

Her expression of scornful disbelief raised Mike's hackles at once. Anna was leaning against him and felt him stiffen. She put her hand on his arm. 'Don't, Mike,' she said softly. 'Let Rob deal with her.'

'Where have you been, Miss Vaughan?' the inspector asked her, after showing his own identification.

'I don't have to explain myself to you,' she said. 'Or Hugh, for that matter. Neither of you are my keepers.'

'It's not a role any sane bloke would want,' Mike muttered.

Anna suppressed a smile, but kept her attention on the scene in front of her.

'You're mistaken, Miss Vaughan,' Elliot said calmly. 'We have been trying to contact you. And I need to know a great deal more than where you've been since yesterday evening. But we'll start with that.'

She stared at him, her brows knitted. 'It's Ms,' she said, almost automatically, 'not Miss. Look, what's this about?'

'I'm asking the questions,' the inspector said, ignoring Mike's derisive grunt. 'Where have you been?'

She shrugged, pushing her hands into the pockets of her shorts, her stance combative as she considered him. 'For what it's worth, I've been on an island just off the coast.'

'What were you doing there?'

Her lips tightened. 'Taking photographs,' she said shortly.

Elliot sighed. 'Alright, Ms Vaughan, let's do it the hard way, down at the station.'

'The police station?' she demanded. 'You must be joking.'

'Not at all.' He gestured to the car, where Tom had opened a back door. 'I am investigating a murder, and have every reason to believe you can tell me something about it.'

She stared at him, and it was hard for the watchers to tell if she was shocked or not. Her face had stiffened, her expression was, Anna thought, suddenly wary. 'I don't know what you're talking about,' she said, her tone more amenable, 'but if I can help, of course I will.' Concern touched her face. 'It's not Hugh, is it?'

'Why should you think it would be?' Elliot queried, not sure if she was referring to victim or perpetrator.

'Well, he's the only person I know down here,' she pointed out.

'Crimes don't always involve people we know,' Elliot said, 'but that doesn't mean we aren't connected with them.'

'Okay,' she smiled suddenly, 'I'll take that. Just tell me the corpse isn't Hugh, because I'd really feel responsible for that, even if I didn't wield the actual dagger.' She saw the alertness of his expression and laughed sardonically. 'I'm speaking metaphorically, of course. Look,' she glanced at Mike and Anna who were leaning over the gate, 'I don't know who's involved in this, but I don't particularly want to go to the police station. Can't we deal with it here? I've met Mike and Anna, I'm sure they'd be more than happy to offer us their house.'

Anna felt a jolt of surprise at being linked to Mike so publicly. She wondered what Rob Elliot was thinking of Celia's assumption that they were a couple. Not, she admitted to herself, an unfounded assumption, given the roles she and Mike had played yesterday. Then her mind sharpened. Hugh had not introduced Celia to them yesterday, so he must have told her who Anna and Mike were.

The inspector's face was unemotional as he looked enquiringly at Mike. 'What do you think?' he asked. 'I'd prefer to get Ms Vaughan's information as quickly as possible.'

Mike looked undecided. He glanced over his shoulder to where Lucy stood, then back at Elliot. The archaeologist leaned over the gate, saying as quietly as he could, 'I'm not sure, Elliot. Lucy's already had a bad shock. I don't want her to go through any more traumas.'

'Lucy? Hugh's wife?' Celia Vaughan queried, glancing up the path to where the white-faced young woman leaned against the doorframe, the collie once again beside her. 'I can't see why anything I've got to say should add to her problems.'

Anna's fingernails dug so deeply into Mike's arm that he winced, scowling down at her until she relaxed her grip.

He swung back to face the trio outside his gate, the two policemen flanking the woman, all waiting for his decision. 'Alright,' he said abruptly, pulling the gate open. 'But,' he glanced at Anna, 'not for too long. Anna's supposed to be recuperating as well, not getting over excited.'

Celia had set off up the path and glanced speculatively back at Anna. 'It sounds as though I've been missing all the excitement,' she said.

'You could have had my part any time,' Anna said with excessive sweetness.

Celia had reached the door, where she nodded shortly to Lucy as she passed her, stepping down into Mike's front room. The others followed her in and Anna gritted her teeth. Celia had assumed the lead and they had all fallen in tamely behind her.

Celia swung round one of the upright cane chairs Mike had against the far wall and straddled it, her chin resting on the hands she had folded across its back. Anna left the sofa to Lucy, who still looked worryingly pale, and strangely vulnerable with her new short hairstyle. Ben was staying close to her and pushed his nose up into her hand as she sank onto the soft cushions, encouraging her to stroke his head. Anna sat down herself in the armchair beside the front window, careless of the light that fell on her strained face.

Both Elliot and Mike stood facing Celia, who was quite undaunted by their stance. She glanced briefly at Sergeant Peters as he moved a chair out for the inspector, and put another a little out of range of the others and sat down on it, pulling out his notebook. As he took his own seat the inspector took the opportunity to jerk his head at Mike, encouraging him to move away too. It was with reluctance that Mike did so, going to stand beside Anna's chair, one fist firmly clenched on its back.

'Well, get on with it,' Celia said, her eyes on Inspector Elliot. 'But before I answer any questions I want to know who's been killed.'

'A man called Damian Mallinson,' Elliot replied.

Celia looked blank. 'Well, that's easy,' she said breezily. 'I've never heard of him.'

'He was a fellow guest of yours at Rossington Priory,' the inspector said, watching the expression on her face, aware already that she had formidable control over it.

'Dark glasses, straw hat, pushy, thought a lot of himself, fancied he had a way with women,' Celia reeled off. 'If that fits, I've met him.'

'I don't know about his manner,' Elliot said. 'By the time I met him he was lying dead on the cliffs.' He fancied the woman facing him stiffened imperceptibly.

Not a word was spoken. The room was very still. Suddenly Celia spoke, startling them all. 'He was alive when I left him.'

They all looked at her, but she was unconcerned at being the focus of so many eyes. Her own attention was centred on the inspector.

'He was a pest, but not a serious one. I've dealt with many worse than him. Hugh saw him off a couple of times, but there was no need. I'm quite capable of dealing with my own problems. He must have followed Hugh and me onto the cliffs and kept a low profile until he saw Hugh leave. Then he tried it on again. When his charm,' she emphasised the word brutally, 'failed, he got more direct. I gave him a shove, quite hard, he was grabbing at my camera cases and I won't have them damaged. He staggered back, slipped on the rocky surface and fell down the landward slope.' Her eyes were fixed on the inspector, every word she spoke was said clearly and evenly. 'I looked over and saw that he was getting to his feet, winded, maybe even a bit stunned. I didn't wait around for more trouble.'

'We have a witness who saw you go down to him,' Elliot said.

She stared at him scornfully. 'They're lying. I didn't go down.' Her expression of scorn deepened. 'And,' she added, 'I certainly didn't see anybody else about.'

'Did Mallinson make a noise when he fell?'

Celia frowned. 'Between a shout and a yell, I suppose. It started off as a profanity and just became noise.'

'Would Hugh have been close enough to hear it?'

Her frown deepened. 'I don't know. I don't think so. Why?'

Elliot ignored the question. 'What did you do after Mallinson fell?'

Celia looked puzzled. 'I've just told you.'

'After you'd looked down and seen him moving around?'

'I went on up the cliff, of course.' She sounded surprised. 'I'd come to see the peregrines that Hugh had told me about, so that's where I went.'

'How long were you there?'

She shrugged. 'I wasn't watching the time.' She thought for a couple of seconds. 'I was taking photos, they'll be timed, so that could give us an idea.'

'And then?'

Celia looked blank. 'Then what?'

'I presume you didn't stay watching birds for twenty-four hours,' Elliot said, holding onto his patience. 'Where does this island come in?'

'Actually, that's just what I did, watch birds for most of the time,' she said.

'The peregrines?' he asked.

She laughed. 'No, of course not.'

'Ms Vaughan,' he allowed his temper to slip slightly, so that his voice was icy, startling Anna who had never heard the tone before, 'I am investigating a murder. A man has been killed. A man who seems to have given you cause to dislike him. You were identified at the scene of his death, at the time it happened. You were involved in a physical struggle with him then. Perhaps you won't waste my time with your word games, but will spend a little of your own considering your position.'

Celia straightened, raising her chin from her hands. Her eyes blazed, then the fire faded out of them. She sighed. 'Sorry. I've never liked explaining myself. But you're right. He was a foul specimen, but no doubt he had a mother or some other misguided woman who cared about him. He probably even had redeeming features. I just didn't see them.' She ran her hands along the back of the chair, out and back to meet in the centre.

'I went on down to the cove below the headland,' she said abruptly. 'There are some interesting industrial buildings there. A limekiln, Hugh said. While I was prowling around a boat put in. The bloke in it, Jon, was from the nearby village, going out for a night's fishing. He was a birder too, and had stopped off to look at the peregrines. We fell to talking and he told me about the island just off the coast. Gull Rocks, it's called, and that's all it is really, just a pile of rocks with a few strips of land between them. But there used to be a small settlement there, and one of the ways the people kept themselves was to take eggs from the breeding gulls on the ledges, and collect guano for fertilising their tiny fields. Both practices are finished now, of course, but the birds still nest there in thousands.' She shrugged, suddenly fed up with the explanation. 'I wanted to go and see it. He agreed to drop me off there for the night, and collect me on his way home today.'

'Rather a sudden decision,' Elliot commented dryly. 'To go off with a man you'd just met. You can't have had anything with you.'

Celia looked at him sharply. 'I'm a photographer, Inspector, I had my cameras, and that's all I need,' she said, 'I take opportunities when they crop up.'

He nodded. 'I believe that.'

She gave a short bark of laughter. 'It doesn't make me a murderer,' she said. She looked thoughtful. 'Although I can see it might.' Glancing down at the cameras, she said, 'I suppose you'll have to look at all my pictures. Can you copy them onto a memory stick? I don't want any old plod messing around with them.'

'We're quite adept at photographic work these days,' Elliot said mildly.

She made an amused sound. 'No doubt. But I make my living at this, these photos are for my next exhibition and I don't want them being shown all over the place before that. I can't expect you to understand, I suppose.'

'Oh, I know the importance of your work, Ms Vaughan,' the inspector said. 'I saw your last exhibition.'

Celia was clearly startled. She laughed derisively, but it was plain she was laughing at herself. 'I should never underestimate a policeman, should I?'

'It doesn't pay to do so,' Elliot agreed. He stood up and looked down at her. 'I'd like you to come to the police station and sign a statement when Sergeant Peters has typed it up. And I'm afraid we'll have to ask you some more questions, as there are a number of discrepancies I have to resolve.'

She stood up too, swinging one leg over the seat of the chair, before stooping to gather up her camera cases. 'Where is Hugh?' she asked suddenly.

'He's at the station,' Elliot replied. 'Helping us with our enquiries,' he added mendaciously, thinking of Hugh's unexpected refusal to co-operate.

Mike scowled, but Anna's hand on his arm kept him from speaking. He yanked the door open to allow the policemen to escort Celia through.

She paused on the threshold, obviously struck by a sudden thought. 'How did this bloke, whatshisname, Mallinson, die?' she demanded. The hand clasping the camera straps tightened, the knuckles whitening. 'Did he hit his head?'

'No, it wasn't the fall that killed him,' Elliot replied. He paused, noting that the tension in her hand relaxed. 'He drowned, and it looks as though he was held under water until he died,' he finished, and saw at once that he had startled her.

One hand on her elbow, he urged her onwards. Silently she moved down the path towards the car.

Anna took her place in the doorway, Mike peering over her shoulder. 'You'll let us know, Rob,' she called urgently.

'When I can,' he answered, sparing her a quick look before his gaze passed on to Lucy, just visible inside the sitting room. 'I'm sure,' it was to Lucy that he spoke now, 'that we'll have things sorted out soon.'

It was the banging of crockery that woke Lucy. She stared around the room, unsure for a moment where she was. Pins and needles prickled in her right arm, which was awkwardly folded under her body. She sat up, wincing at other aches and pains, recognising Mike's sitting room, realising she must have fallen asleep on his sofa.

The collie who had been lying beside the sofa had lifted his head hopefully when she first stirred. Now he sat up too, his eyes eager as he watched her.

Lucy looked round the room, memories of the last couple of days flooding back relentlessly into her mind. Anna was in an armchair, turned to face the window, but sound asleep, quite undisturbed by the noise in the kitchen. As there was nobody else in the sitting room Lucy guessed that it was Mike who was clattering around. She glanced at her watch, taken aback to see that it was after six o'clock, although sunlight was still bright outside the windows of the cottage. Perhaps, she thought hopefully, getting carefully to her feet, Hugh has come back and is helping Mike.

She stood for a moment, one hand clutching the arm of the sofa, Ben pressed against her legs, as she willed a sudden dizziness to vanish. The collie whined softly, looking across the room.

Mike had appeared in the kitchen doorway, a large tray in his hands. 'For God's sake, Lucy,' he said in alarm, 'sit down again. You're as white as a sheet.'

'I'm alright,' she protested, but she was glad to follow his advice, shaken that she felt so feeble. She glanced across at Anna, who had stirred at the sound of Mike's voice, turning in her chair to look at them. Her blue eyes were bright and clear, looking so alert that Lucy felt immediately worse.

'What's this, Mike?' Anna enquired, staring at the tray. 'Surely it's not teatime already?'

'You've both been sleeping for more than an hour,' he commented, putting the tray down on the low table in the centre of the room. ' A fine pair of snorers you are, too.'

'Nonsense,' Anna said indignantly. 'You're making it up.'

Her eyes ran over the tea tray, taking in the cake. She was touched to notice that he had put it on a plate, but she felt a bubble of amusement as she saw that the sugar sat in its bag, the milk in its bottle. She bit her lip, determined not to comment, surprised that he had bothered at all.

'Is Hugh here?' Lucy asked abruptly.

Mike's face darkened. He shook his head. 'I haven't heard anything,' he said gruffly, meeting her gaze fleetingly.

'That can't be good, can it?' she asked.

'It doesn't look like it,' he agreed reluctantly, 'but I really can't believe…'

A soft knock on the door interrupted him. Both women turned to stare at it as Mike sprang forward, almost tripping over the collie as they both leaped towards the door.

Mike flung it open to reveal Philly, who stood there, taken aback to see them all staring at her. 'I'm sorry,' she said, 'I don't mean to keep disturbing you. I just wanted to see if there's anything I can do.'

Mike stood back. 'Come in,' he ordered. 'It's beginning to feel as if you live here anyway. Have you any news?'

She shook her head. 'It's hard to believe anything's happened now, the priory is pretty much back to normal. The cloisters and Dorter, where Damian Mallinson was staying, are still cordoned off, but that's out of my sight from the office. Otherwise it all seems to be going on just as usual. Tilly called in on her way up to the farm to meet Clive. She had his cousin Bruce with her, and although he'd brought over more tourist leaflets they were really just nosing around to see what was happening. Mr and Mrs Armitage were kitting themselves out for a spot of bird-watching, they don't seem to be much bothered by what's happened.' She smiled suddenly. 'I think they must be pretty new to bird-watching, everything they've got seems so immaculate, and he's always consulting his book. I'm not really sure that Mrs Armitage is enjoying it, she generally looks rather fed up. She keeps looking at leaflets for places to visit, but they never seem to go anywhere.'

Mike had flung himself into a chair and was scowling blackly as he stared at Philly. The young woman had taken a seat next to Lucy on the sofa and was gently stroking Ben who was between the two women. 'Really, it's more obvious out in the street that something's happened,' Philly continued. 'There's still a policeman at the lodge gates, keeping people out. Dad says there's one at the entrance to the farm lane too. I can't believe so many people have just come out to stare. There are cars all over the place. Dad's had a struggle to get the tractor down the street. And there are reporters too, they tried to stop me when I came out of the lodge gates, but I just ignored them.'

As Philly was speaking Anna had busied herself pouring tea and cutting cake. 'Mike, can you pass things round?' she asked.

He started, turning his stare on her. But he got up without a word, seizing a plate and mug.

'Here,' he said, putting them down on the small bookcase that stood near Lucy's end of the sofa. 'Are the police still up there?' he demanded over his shoulder, turning to pick up a mug and plate for Philly.

'No, they've been gone for a while,' Philly replied, 'ever since Celia came back.'

Mike froze abruptly, slopping the tea over the top of the mug. 'Came back,' he repeated. 'When was that?'

'Mike, we all saw her get back a couple of hours ago,' Anna remonstrated, pulling a tissue out of her bag and mopping up the spill on the table. 'We know when it was.'

'Philly wasn't here when Celia came swanning up the street,' he pointed out, his attention on the young woman. 'And Celia was driven straight off to the police station then, not back to the priory.'

'I expect Rob contacted the constable at the priory,' Anna said reasonably, dropping the wet tissue on the tray. 'There'd be no reason to keep them there once Celia had been found.'

'Mike's right, Anna, this has only just happened,' Philly said, leaning forward to prise her mug and plate from Mike's grip. 'Celia came back to the priory just before I left, the police brought her, I think, because one man came in at the same time and took away Darren Cranley. He'd been in the office for a long time, so he was glad to go.'

Lucy was clutching the plate and mug she had picked up,

without attempting to either eat or drink. 'Was Hugh with her?' she asked bluntly.

Philly shook her head, looking surprised. 'Oh no, she was on her own. She didn't look very, ummm, happy,' Philly said. 'I thought Hugh would be here.' She stopped, suddenly embarrassed.

Lucy put her plate and mug down carefully on the table and pulled her mobile out of her pocket. She scrolled across the screen, her pale lips tightening. 'No calls, no messages,' she said.

'Try him,' Mike urged. 'See what's going on.'

Lucy pressed the buttons and they all sat silently, waiting for Hugh to reply to her call. 'His phone is switched off,' she said at last. Her hazel eyes clouded. Hugh's phone had been switched off once before, when she had needed him badly. The memories of that terrible time began to form, edging into her mind. With an effort she banished them. 'It isn't good, is it?' she asked again.

Mike had been standing, his arms hanging loosely at his sides. Suddenly his fists clenched, and he turned away, bumping into the corner of the table in his haste. The collie leaped up, startled, jogging the plate that Philly held, sending the last part of her cake sliding to the floor.

'Mike!' Anna called after him in alarm, quickly swallowing a mouthful of sponge. 'What is it? Where are you going?'

He paused, his hand on the front door latch. He turned stiffly towards her, his face set in determined lines. 'Celia Vaughan knows what's going on,' he said harshly. 'I don't know whether Rob Elliot got it out of her, but I'm damned well going to.'

Anna stood up hastily. 'Wait,' she said urgently, 'I'm coming too.'

'And me,' Lucy said, getting to her feet. Ben gulped down the dropped cake and moved to the door. Mike looked down at him and then round at the women.

'I don't need the cavalry,' he growled irritably, 'I can manage on my own.'

'Of course you can,' Anna said quickly. 'But we need to know what's going on too, Mike, you must see that.'

'Oh alright,' he snapped crossly. He glared at Anna as she moved towards him. 'But no heroics, mind.'

EIGHT

The desk sergeant at Corrington police station looked round, a phone held limply to his ear, and knew who the man was at once. A pinstripe suit that had been made to measure, and a fancy bow-tie to make him look more human. The sergeant uttered mechanical replies to the person on the other end of the telephone line, while his cynical eye assessed the briefcase his visitor had propped on the desk. Worth a packet. He'd be lucky not to have that nicked if he left it lying around.

There was no doubt in the sergeant's mind that this was the high-powered London solicitor that Hugh Carey had rung up a few hours ago. The sergeant glanced at the clock, uttering a silent whistle as he saw that it was getting on for five thirty. The bloke certainly hadn't wasted any time. Either Hugh Carey had a lot of clout, or this solicitor thought his client was in real trouble.

None of these thoughts showed in his face as he finally managed to shut down old Mrs Blount, who was again giving him her views on the immorality of the sunbathers in the public park. He put the telephone receiver down firmly and turned to the visitor who was looming over the desk with ill-concealed impatience. 'I'm sorry to keep you waiting, sir,' the sergeant said blandly. 'How can I help you?'

The visitor eyed him with a weary eye. 'I'm Dominic Etheridge,' he said, enunciating the words slowly. 'Hugh Carey called me and asked me to come down.'

'His solicitor, are you, sir?' the sergeant queried, enjoying himself.

'I'm sure you recognise a solicitor when you see one, constable, ah, sorry, sergeant,' Dom Etheridge said, his eyes flickering over the stripes on the other man's uniform. He fished into his pocket and brought out a card case. Snapping it open he flicked out a card, heavily embossed in dark Gothic script, and handed it to the sergeant. 'Just to convince you.'

The sergeant took it, feeling his day was being well enlivened. He'd have the canteen in fits tomorrow when he described this encounter.

'That's all well and good, sir,' he said, reading the card carefully, 'but it's easy to forge these things.' Looking up he caught Dom's eye and decided he'd had as much fun as he could get. 'But Inspector Elliot gave me your name. I'll let him know you're here. If you'd like to take a seat I'm sure the inspector won't keep you waiting long.'

Dom Etheridge grasped his briefcase and turned away, hiding a grin. He sat down on one of the chairs, looking round appraisingly. He didn't often spend time in police station waiting rooms these days, but as they went this one wasn't too bad. Clean off-white walls held the usual posters, but the plants in pots looked alright. Dom did not know one plant from another, and certainly had no ambition to, but he could tell the difference between a healthy green plant and one that was dying, dusty and unwatered. He cast a disparaging glance at the well-worn magazines on the nearby table, and was surprised to see there were more than the few women's ones and the motoring and gardening ones that usually leavened the feminine bias.

He almost picked up a *Country Life* that he had not read, sure that would confirm the impression he had been at pains to create for the desk sergeant. It not only lightened the man's dull routine, but it never hurt to create an impression of buffoonery, thought Dom, one of London's brightest barristers. He hesitated, torn between the magazine, rereading *The Times* that was in his case, ostentatiously flicking through the brief he had been working on during the train trip, and the novel he was longing to get to the end of.

Dom was relieved to have the choice taken out of his hands when he saw Inspector Rob Elliot walking towards him. He stood up, a genuine smile on his face as he held out his hand to shake the other man's. 'It's good to see you, Elliot. I knew you'd moved out to the sticks, but didn't really expect to be dragged down to them myself. Thank God it's not raining. Now,' he fell into step with the inspector as Elliot opened a door into the private section of the station, 'tell me what old Hugh has been up to. Surely he isn't under arrest?'

The door shut firmly behind the two men and the sergeant sighed. Ah well, he thought, he couldn't really expect to hear any more.

Elliot glanced at Dom Etheridge as he led the way to an interview room. The two men knew each other from the London legal scene, just as they both knew Hugh from the same background. The inspector was well aware that Dom liked to play up his image of the upper-crust solicitor, but he also knew that the barrister's mind was razor sharp and that he was more frequently involved in unsavoury criminal cases than in high society social upsets or marital breakdowns. Hugh's reputation as a young barrister had been impressive, so his contemporaries and colleagues had been startled when he gave up his predicted meteoric career to vegetate in the country over books and photographs. But in Elliot's opinion Dom Etheridge was Hugh's equal in the profession, and he had developed a sharp cutting style in recent years that often disconcerted people who had rashly accepted his dandyish appearance as indicative of the man.

'No,' he replied to Dom's question as they seated themselves, 'Hugh's not under arrest. But he's refusing to co-operate in a murder enquiry. He hasn't put himself in a good light during our investigations, but he hasn't been cautioned. Yet,' Elliot added pointedly. 'He asked to ring you, as of course he's entitled to do.'

'Who's been murdered?' Dom demanded.

'A man called Damian Mallinson,' the inspector said, his eyes narrowed. He could not be sure, but there had perhaps been a note of unexpected anxiety in Dom's voice.

'Ah,' Dom said. 'Did Hugh know him?'

Elliot was sure now that the solicitor was relieved. Why, he wondered silently. Out loud he answered the query. 'Not really. But Mallinson was staying in one of the holiday apartments at Rossington Priory, part of Hugh's brother-in-law's home. Hugh has been over there a lot this week and recently was heard to have a couple of rows with him.'

'What about?' Dom asked sharply.

'Mallinson appeared to be bothering one of the other guests, a woman, and Hugh objected to this, rather forcefully according to some onlookers.'

'Who…' Dom broke off as there was a knock on the door

It opened and Hugh was ushered in by Sergeant Peters. The two men in the room stood up, Dom stepping forward to shake Hugh's hand. 'I came as soon as I got your message. Luckily I was at my parents' house in Wiltshire, so it didn't take too long,' he said, as they sat down round the table with the inspector. Sergeant Peters took up his usual position next to Elliot.

'This conversation is at the moment informal,' Elliot said, 'to put Dom in the picture, such as it is. But then it will become a formal recorded interview.'

Hugh nodded, his eyes fixed on his ex-colleague. 'How much has Elliot told you?' he asked.

'Who was the woman?' Dom's question shot across the room at the same moment.

Hugh looked puzzled, glancing from Dom to the inspector, then back again.

'The woman this bloke was pestering,' Dom elaborated impatiently.

Elliot sat still, waiting, aware of the mounting tension between the two men in front of him.

Hugh's eyes closed wearily for a moment, then opened and fastened on Dom again. 'Celia, of course,' he said flatly. 'You've heard about the murder?' Dom nodded, and Hugh added grimly, 'Celia's missing. I'm under suspicion of killing this bloke Mallinson. I've made a right muck of it.'

'She's missing?' Dom sounded incredulous. He turned to the inspector. 'Surely you've some idea what's happened to her?'

'We put out an alert,' Elliot replied, 'but that's been sorted now.'

Dom swung back towards Hugh, demanding, 'Did you recognise Mallinson?'

Hugh shook his head. 'No, and Celia was convinced he was a common pest, nothing more.'

'Why should he have been something more?' Elliot asked. His quiet voice startled the other two, breaking into their private exchange.

Hugh glanced at Dom Etheridge. 'He should know, especially now she's missing,' he said quietly. 'That's why I rang you from here. I've been trying to get you since I first heard. But it's up to you what you say.'

Dom's gaze shifted, staring past Hugh as he considered. He decided quickly and turned to Elliot, who sat back in his chair watching them both. 'Hugh has been doing me a favour,' Dom said, all trace of affectation gone from his manner. 'I'm sorry,' he glanced briefly at Hugh, 'that it's got him into difficulties.'

Dom leaned forward, his eyes fixed on Elliot. 'I can only tell you this if you can guarantee that it won't go any further than the four of us in this room.' He saw the inspector's reaction, recognising his resistance at once. 'Unless it's of relevance to your case, of course,' he said impatiently, 'that's understood.'

Inspector Elliot considered him for a moment. 'Very well, I'll hear what you say. And unless it's of importance to this murder there should be no need to use it.' He glanced at Sergeant Peters, then back to Dom Etheridge.

'You'll understand why I asked,' Dom said heavily. 'Celia Vaughan is a protected prosecution witness in a very important case that's coming up shortly in the High Court. It's enough if I say that she was unwittingly in a position to take some very important photographs in an extremely unpleasant bout of gang warfare. And she's willing to stand up in court and identify the men involved in a nasty murder.'

The barrister's lips tightened. 'Inevitably she's had death threats, and in fact some narrow escapes from peculiar incidents. It became quite clear that somebody in the police force was informing on her movements and the plans we had to keep her safe.'

The inspector was frowning now. 'Those plans must have been kept to a pretty small circle.'

'Yes,' Dom agreed, 'but we don't yet know who in it has been selling information, and how many people outside that immediate circle could be involved. That's where Hugh came in. I bumped into him at a book award ceremony last weekend, and we got chatting. I heard all about this place, Rossington Priory, and Hugh heard about my current problem with Celia. It seemed the obvious solution when he offered to set her up in one of the apartments there, and brought her down himself. She's got no links to the place, or to him, so there should have been nothing to lead them to her there. Nobody except the three of us knew where she was. And Hugh agreed to say nothing to anybody about her, including you, Elliot. Not,' Dom added quickly, 'that either of us doubted you, but we didn't want to put you in an awkward position.'

Elliot nodded. 'I appreciate that.' He glanced at Hugh. 'And where does Mallinson come into this?'

'I don't know,' Hugh said. 'I didn't think he did, but I was anxious about him pestering Celia. I didn't want her drawing attention to herself by creating a scene with him.' He groaned, putting his head in his hands. 'I seem to have done that quite spectacularly myself.' His voice was muffled.

'Well, she's confirmed your story,' Elliot said. 'But there's still a discrepancy between her account of her own actions and ones we've got from other witnesses. And there are still some details to iron out in your movements,' he added, frowning. 'The witness statements about seeing you don't fit with your accounts.'

'She's confirmed my story,' Hugh repeated. 'Do you mean you've found Celia?'

'In a way,' Elliot said. 'Anna spotted her walking up the street in Roscombe. She'd gone off with a fisherman to spend a night on an island and take photos of birds.' He watched their expressions, where disbelief warred with anger.

'Dear God,' Dom exploded. 'Will she never learn?'

'Where is she now?' Hugh said urgently.

'Dom just missed her. She was taken back to the priory just before he arrived,' the inspector replied. 'Why?'

'Do you still have a police presence there?' Hugh was curt.

'No, it was withdrawn when she returned,' Elliot said. 'Is there a problem?'

'I don't know.' Hugh shifted in his chair, glancing at Dom. 'I just don't like the feel of this.'

Elliot pushed his chair back and got smoothly to his feet. 'Then I'll send a couple of constables over there to keep an eye on her. And I can imagine what she'll say about that.' He turned to Sergeant Peters. 'See to it will you, Tom. As a priority.'

Hugh had got up as well. 'Am I free to go?' he asked shortly.

The inspector frowned. 'I'd like to go over these discrepancies,' he said. He studied Hugh for an instant. 'You're really worried about her, aren't you?'

'Mmmm. I've just got a bad feeling about this,' Hugh said defensively. 'I know that's usually Lucy's line, but ...' His voice trailed off.

'I'll get over there,' Dom offered, getting up too. 'She's really my problem, after all.'

'We'll all go,' Elliot said firmly. 'You're beginning to infect me with your worries.'

Gravel crunched noisily under Mike's feet as he strode along the track towards the priory, the collie running eagerly ahead of him. Anna was out of breath as she struggled to keep up with Mike, realising just how weak she was after the previous day's experience. She wondered briefly whether she should use her unexpected feebleness to keep Lucy with her, away from the interview they were all storming towards.

As they approached the priory the east end of the little church was to their left, beyond the crooked gravestones that rose through the rough turf of the old cemetery at its feet. The long south wall of the guesthouse within the enclave was just ahead of them, and the barn that hid the gatehouse, so if she was going to act Anna knew it must be immediately. She glanced sideways at the two women who kept pace with her. Philly was beside her, her rosy cheeks contrasting with Lucy's pale face on her other side.

One look at Lucy was enough for Anna. Her friend's face was set and determined. Anna knew that she could not be persuaded to stay out of the coming confrontation, not even to provide succour for her best friend. Philly would undoubtedly be detailed to the task. After all, Philly was not intimately concerned with this trouble, she could be left to look after Anna. Lucy was concerned, and she obviously meant to find out what was going on.

Anna let out her breath in a sigh and slipped unexpectedly, missing her footing on the gravel. She regained her balance at once, but Mike paused, looking frowningly back at her. To her surprise he said nothing, just waited for the women to catch up with him. The collie hesitated too, turning to look at them from the edge of the barn, before running back to Lucy's side.

It was Philly who spoke in some surprise, looking through the bushes that half hid the guest car park from sight. 'That's Bruce's car, the man who brings over the leaflets from the Tourist Information Office. I know he was here earlier, but I wasn't expecting him to still be around.' She glanced at her watch, surprised to see how late it was. 'I wonder if he wants me for anything.' She looked apologetically at the others. 'He may be out walking with Clive and Tilly, of course, but I'd better see if he's waiting in the gatehouse.'

Mike disregarded this, barely noticing her pass him as he fixed Lucy and Anna with a minatory glare. 'Let's get our strategy straight,' he said. 'We don't want to get into a row with the woman, we just want some answers from her. All it needs is clear questioning, so leave the talking to me.'

Anna bit her lip. 'Let's see how it goes,' she said evasively. 'You start things off, by all means, but you might need some back up. She's a determined woman, she won't talk to you if she doesn't want to.'

'There's no point standing around here,' Lucy said. She walked forward, brushing past Mike, Ben bounding ahead of her.

Mike glanced at her, then at Anna as she came up to his side. Before he could say anything there was the sound of running footsteps. They both looked towards the gatehouse, still out of sight, and saw Philly come running past the far corner of the barn towards them with Ben leaping beside her.

'Come quickly,' she shouted, stopping abruptly, waving her arms at them. As soon as they reached her she gestured towards the gatehouse and the entrance court that lay beyond its shaded archway. 'There's been trouble,' she gasped, '... bodies in the courtyard.'

Mike brushed past her, with Anna and Lucy close behind him as he ran through the open gates, Ben at their heels, all of them suddenly aware of the high wailing noise that rose to meet them. He stopped so abruptly that both the women bumped into him, clutching at his arms to keep their balance as they stared at the scene in front of them. Ben slipped around the frozen group and stopped too, his ears down, his tail drooping.

Anna winced at the sound of a woman's shrill keening, which filled the air, piercing their ears. To her amazement it came from Tilly Barlow, who was crouched over a man's body, which lay crumpled on the paved courtyard. Her long black skirt with its pink and orange swirls was billowed around her, her faded blonde curls hung wispily from her bent head, and for an instant Anna thought she looked like a large rapacious bird guarding its prey.

Tilly lifted her head to look at them, her face ravaged with crying, tears running down into her gaping mouth. Anna thought the man seemed strangely familiar, but she did not know him. From Tilly's reaction though, Anna guessed this must be the plumber that lodged with her. Beyond them was another man, stirring feebly, trying to lift himself off the ground. As he raised his head Anna felt a start of shock. She recognised him. The man from the pub at Elowen. Bruce Riley, she dredged up the name, Bryony Tregonan's boyfriend, the man Cal Tregonan described as a know-all. What on earth was Bruce Riley doing here?

'He's dead,' Tilly wailed, her hands scrabbling at the shirt of the man who lay beside her. 'Clive's dead. They've killed him.'

'Who?' Mike demanded sharply, striding towards them. 'Who's done this?' He bent over the man's body, lifting his wrist to feel for a pulse. Anna hurried past him to Bruce Riley. 'Help me,' she called to Lucy who still stood, her hand on Ben's collar, staring at them as if stupefied.

Lucy shook her head as if clearing it, released her hold on Ben and went quickly to Anna's side, watching as Anna ran her arms over Bruce's arms and legs. 'Can he get up?' she asked.

'I don't know,' Anna said. 'He hasn't broken any limbs, but there may be other injuries. Hush,' she added quickly, 'he's trying to speak.' She bent over the man, her long dark curls brushing against his bruised and cut face.

'In there.' His voice was hoarse. He stopped to cough, and a dribble of blood ran down his chin. 'The woman. They've taken her in there. Tried to help her.' He slumped forward, lapsing into unconsciousness.

'Mike!' Anna sat back on her heels and looked across to where the archaeologist was checking over Clive, fending off a hysterical Tilly with one arm. 'Celia Vaughan's in trouble. In the apartment.'

Mike stood up quickly. 'Right. This one's not dead. Knocked

out, but alright otherwise, as far as I can tell. Stay with them. I'll sort out the rest.' His face was grim as he turned to the closed apartment door. As he turned the handle his mouth tightened. Locked.

Lucy moved over to Clive, Ben close to her side, as Anna shifted Bruce competently into the recovery position. Behind them Mike burst the apartment door open. Bang goes any element of surprise, Anna thought. Whoever's in there will be waiting for him.

Tilly's hysterics were making it difficult for Lucy to touch Clive. Anna gave an exasperated sigh, torn between going to help Lucy or going after Mike. Mike, she decided. His need was obviously greater.

Light footsteps came running towards them. 'I've called an ambulance and the police,' Philly said breathlessly. 'Rob Elliot is already on his way, they put me through to him on his mobile. He says we're to stay well clear, that the people responsible for this are likely to be armed and very dangerous.' She looked round at the fallen men. 'Can we move them?'

'No,' Anna said shortly. She ran towards the door and disappeared into Frater, ignoring Philly's anxious cry.

Thuds and grunts came from the main room, the old monks' dining room beyond the half-panelled hallway. Furniture crunched, china smashed, Mike was grunting with effort. The front door slammed shut behind Anna and a dog began to bark, repeatedly, desperately.

She glanced over her shoulder and saw Lucy behind her. 'Take care,' she whispered, turning to move lightly past a small bench towards the open archway into the room. She paused beside it, peering round its edge, Lucy at her shoulder.

The room seemed to be full of struggling people. Mike had managed to get one arm around the neck of a man whom Anna could not quite place. But the sight of the woman wrestling with Celia Vaughan took Anna's breath away. Her faded hair and bleached skin, beige trousers and top would have easily made her disappear into a crowd, yet Anna recognised her at once, with a sense of incredulous disbelief. She was Karen Armitage, that faded woman trailing along behind her husband that nobody had really noticed. And her appearance belied the ferocity with which she fought to subdue Celia, who was strapped into a chair with a thick band of cloth. A glint of light shone for a second on something the woman held in one hand.

A knife, Anna thought with a thrill of horror, as she sprang towards the struggling women. With one deft kick she knocked it out of Mrs Armitage's hand and saw it fall to the floor, rolling out of reach. The woman turned with unexpected speed, hitting Anna hard across the face with one arm.

Anna fell back, dazed, with blood pouring from her nose, tears streaming from her eyes. Blearily she caught sight of Lucy dashing past her, bending to scrabble at the floor, trying to retrieve the weapon. Mrs Armitage lashed out, kicking quite as deftly as Anna had. Lucy screamed, rolling into a ball as she clutched her stomach.

Anna's head was ringing as she tried to reach Lucy. Suddenly she realised there was another noise, the thudding of feet, many feet, in the hallway, bursting into the room. 'Police,' a voice was shouting. 'Don't move, nobody move.'

The action ceased as if a movie had been suddenly cut. Mike had been in the act of banging the man's head against the wall. The two of them fell back from it, Mike's arm round the man's neck again. Anna was halfway across the room, almost beside Lucy as she lay groaning on the floor.

Then one person moved. Mrs Armitage grabbed the fallen weapon as she turned swiftly to Lucy. Jerking Lucy's head back the woman held it to her throat. It was only then that Anna, the closest to the pair, saw that the weapon was a syringe.

'One move and she's dead,' said Mrs Armitage. 'Let him go,' she instructed Mike, nodding her head slightly towards the man he held. Of course, Anna realised, he was Eddie Armitage, his face oddly different without its expression of amiability.

Mrs Armitage pulled Lucy up off the floor, and Anna marvelled at the strength she displayed. She dragged Lucy round, pressed close against her own body, the syringe rigidly held to her throat. She began to move backwards towards the archway, watching everybody in the room with hard cold eyes. Armitage began to move towards her, a slight smile twitching his full lips. His complacent expression changed suddenly to one of horror and his mouth opened. But he was too late to utter a warning.

With a ferocious snarl the collie sprang, launching himself full onto the back of the woman who threatened his mistress. Karen Armitage reeled forward, dropping the syringe, releasing her hold on Lucy.

Anna moved without thought, one foot kicking the syringe towards the group clustered on the other side of the room. At the same time she grabbed Lucy and pulled her roughly away from the woman. Mrs Armitage fell heavily to the floor, the dog leaped clear and spun round, his lips rolled back to expose a terrifying display of white teeth, a low ominous growl rumbling from his throat.

Mike seized the stunned Armitage again, grabbing both arms and twisting them behind his back. Sergeant Peters hurried over, pulling out handcuffs and preparing to snap them onto Armitage's wrists. Inspector Elliot had taken hold of Mrs Armitage, while keeping a wary eye on Ben as Hugh took the dog's collar and pulled him back. Dom Etheridge hurried over to the chair where Celia Vaughan was straining at the twisted cloth that bound her arms.

Hugh ignored the sudden burst of activity in the room, looking anxiously to where Lucy lay in a heap, her chest heaving. 'Is she alright?' he demanded, striding over, pulling Ben with him.

'She took a terrific kick in the stomach,' Anna said, her expression worried as she bent over her friend. She glanced at Hugh and saw his face pale as he took in the implications. Lucy had been badly injured before. They both hoped that no further harm had been done. 'I think she'd better go to hospital to be checked over,' Anna declared, letting the dog wriggle past her to lie beside his mistress, frantically licking at the small portion of her face that was visible.

'Hugh, I'm sorry,' Celia Vaughan said, laying a hand on his arm. 'This is all my fault. It would never have happened if you hadn't taken pity on me.'

Anna stared at her with cold dislike. 'It's too late to be sorry now,' she said stiffly. Her eyes moved to Hugh, including him in the judgment.

Lucy stirred, one hand reaching out to the dog who nudged it vigorously, encouraging her to get up.

Above the sound of Sergeant Peters reciting the standard formula of arrest and warning came the shrill wail of sirens. Lots of sirens, it seemed to Anna, wincing at the pitch and volume. Urgent voices, loud footsteps and the room that already seemed full was suddenly packed with more people, police and paramedics.

It seemed no time at all until the hubbub swirling around Anna had subsided, sweeping away the Armitages with Sergeant Peters and Inspector Elliot, Lucy, Bruce and Clive with the paramedics, Celia Vaughan with an unknown man in a bow-tie who Anna knew was a friend of Hugh's. What on earth was he doing here, she wondered vaguely, as the sirens faded when the police turned theirs off and the ambulances drove away.

The priory courtyard was still, the four people left behind stood motionless, looking dazed after all the action had ceased. It was Philly who spoke first, almost apologetically, her voice sounding unusually loud in the silence. 'I'd better get back to the farm,' she said. 'Mum and Dad will be wondering what's happened up here, with all the sirens going.'

She took a few steps and hesitated, looking back over her shoulder. 'Do you know what happened to Tilly? She was in a fair state, she shouldn't be on her own. I expect Mum'll go down to her cottage if Tilly's gone back there.'

'The men were taken off in one ambulance and she went in the other one,' Anna said. 'With Lucy, thank God. At that time I thought Celia Vaughan would be taken to hospital too, and even Tilly's company will be better than hers.'

Hugh stirred. 'It's not what you're thinking,' he said mildly.

'I'm thinking,' Anna snapped with unusual sharpness, 'that Lucy's in hospital again thanks to you and Celia Vaughan.'

He nodded, his eyes shuttered, his face closed. 'I can't deny that. I'd better get over there. Will you look after Ben until we get back?'

'Of course.' Anna put her hand on the dog's collar, fastening on his lead, murmuring soothingly to him as Hugh walked across the courtyard and out of sight under the arch of the gatehouse.

Ben whined, pulling to follow him, but Mike came over to join Anna and fussed over the dog. 'It's not entirely Hugh's fault Lucy got hurt,' he ventured, glancing at Anna's rigid countenance. 'She didn't have to burst in on the fight. Nor did you.'

'Did you really think we'd stay outside wringing our hands listening to it, wondering if you were being beaten to pulp or worse?' Anna demanded angrily, glaring at him, her hands on her hips.

Mike stood up, turning to face her. 'If I ever did, I've learned better,' he commented wryly. 'Don't condemn Hugh unheard, Anna, we don't know what's been going on. And I'd trust him with my life.'

She shook her head, her curls swirling around her shoulders. 'I know. But that's not really the point. Do you think Lucy's going to feel happier with Hugh as a result of this experience? He's hardly been very communicative or considerate of her feelings, has he?'

'Urrr,' Mike mumbled. He glowered. 'I see what you mean. But she should give him chance to explain.'

'I'm sure she will,' Anna said. 'But that doesn't alter how she's likely to feel. Oh damn,' she said vehemently, 'I'd so hoped things were getting better between them.' She scrubbed impatiently at her eyes as tears filled them.

Mike reached out, grabbing her shoulders and pulling her close to him. Beyond them Ben yanked on his lead, straining to get to the gates.

Anna sat in the armchair by the window of Wheelwright's Cottage, staring out at the street. Ben lay beside her, his whole body taut with expectation. Mike had lost patience with their vigil, stamping out of the sitting room into the dining room that was littered with his work. From time to time a muffled oath drifted out, accompanied by the shuffling of papers and occasionally by the thud of a heavier object being moved.

But when Anna called out Mike was instantly in the sitting room, flinging the door open. Hugh was walking wearily up the path, his face drained of colour. Ben ran eagerly down to meet him and Hugh paused, bending to fuss the dog.

'Don't hang around outside,' Mike called. 'You'll encourage the whole village to come out and talk to you.'

Hugh looked up with a faint smile. He stepped down into the room, Ben springing along beside him, and allowed Mike to bang the front door shut.

'Drink?' Mike demanded, shooting a quick look at Hugh's face.

'I'd give a lot for a brandy,' Hugh admitted, sinking into another chair, 'but I ought to wait until I get back home.'

'How's Lucy?' Anna asked anxiously, her hand going out to the dog's head as he returned to sit beside her again.

Hugh looked across at her. 'They don't think that any major harm's been done, thank God. Just bruising. But they're keeping her in overnight. I can pick her up tomorrow morning, after the doctor's been round.'

Mike passed him a glass of brandy and flung himself down heavily onto the sofa, making it creak in protest. He had poured himself a beer and now he took an invigorating gulp. 'So,' he said, 'are you going to tell us what's been going on?'

'I owe you that much,' Hugh said, 'and now I'm free to speak.'

'Why couldn't you before?' Anna demanded.

Mike held up a hand. 'Let the man speak,' he said firmly. 'We'll be here all night if you keep interrupting.'

Anna's delicately arched eyebrows drew together, but she said nothing, turning her attention to Hugh.

'You may remember Dominic Etheridge,' he began, confounding her.

She shook her head, puzzled. 'I've never heard of him.'

'Maybe I didn't introduce you,' Hugh conceded. 'I bumped into him at the book launch you came to with me in London last weekend. He's a barrister too, still practising. We trained together, and were friendly enough. In fact,' Hugh frowned, sipping at his drink, 'you must have seen him a couple of hours ago at the priory. The smart dresser with the signature bow tie.'

Anna nodded, frowning.

'What the hell does he have to do with anything?' Mike demanded.

'I thought we weren't interrupting,' Anna said indignantly.

Mike grinned over his beer tankard.

Hugh carried on, 'He was seriously worried about a case which he's prosecuting. His most crucial witness was under threat, and the police protection she'd been given had been compromised a couple of times. He was afraid there was a leak in the force and wanted to tuck her away in some unknown place.'

'Celia Vaughan,' Anna exclaimed, ignoring Mike's admonitory gesture.

'Yes.' Hugh shrugged. 'When he told me about it, I rashly offered one of the priory apartments. Philly had emailed me to say there had been a whole spate of cancellations, so I knew there'd be a vacancy. In fact, I expected the whole place to be empty. Anyway, I picked her up on my way home on Monday and brought her down here.'

He leaned back in his chair, holding his glass lightly in both hands. 'I knew at once she'd be difficult to keep under wraps. She was much too keen on having things her own way.'

'You do surprise me,' Mike muttered sarcastically.

'But I also knew she was a photographer as well as an artist,' Hugh went on, 'and in fact I admired her work. I thought I could use that as a common interest, to try to keep close to her, keep tabs on her activities.'

'And Mallinson,' Mike said, 'the man who was killed. What about him?'

Anna bit her lip, deciding not to reproach him for interrupting. After all, she had been about to ask the same question.

'He seems to have had nothing to do with this,' Hugh admitted. He took a deep draught of brandy. 'The man was a genuine last-minute booking who tried his luck with Celia. I over-reacted when I found out about it, but I was pretty anxious about all these sudden new visitors.' Hugh sighed. 'He was a pest, who paid a high price for being in the wrong place at the wrong time.'

'Who killed him?' Anna asked quietly.

'Armitage has spilled the beans,' Hugh said grimly. 'He's blaming his wife for the whole thing, she planned it all, put it into operation. He just got carried away with an opportunity to finish their commission. Somehow word of Dom's contact with me must have reached his employers and Armitage came down here with his wife. They traced Celia quite simply.'

Hugh ran a hand over his eyes. 'She simply couldn't be made to keep a low profile. She wanted paints, so she went to the Art Shop in Coombhaven without a thought for her safety. As luck would have it, the Art Shop is where Tilly Barlow works, and Tilly turned out to be a great fan of Celia's work. And the Art Shop was the place where another keen fan enquired about her where-abouts. Tilly said that Eddie Armitage came in saying he'd thought he'd seen Celia Vaughan. It was just a try-on, but he struck gold. Not only had Tilly seen and recognised Celia, she was able to tell him where she was staying. I believe she even had some thought that he was a boyfriend of Celia's.' He sighed. 'Pure bad luck.'

'What,' Anna demanded through gritted teeth, just beating

Mike to speech, 'was the whole thing Armitage got carried away with?'

'A plot to discredit Celia Vaughan, or to blackmail her into refusing to give evidence,' Hugh explained evenly. 'Armitage kept a close eye on her.' His fingers clenched. 'I should have seen through that bird-watching façade.' He relaxed. 'Ah well, I'll look at novice bird-watchers a damn sight more closely in future.'

'Hugh,' Anna's voice was low, but dangerous.

'Sorry,' he said, brushing a hand across his forehead. 'I'm tired, I can't believe I'm digressing like this. Anyway, Armitage knew about the peregrines and was lurking on the cliffs, waiting for Celia and me to go up there. He watched us approach, saw me branch off to the village, and spotted Damian Mallinson trailing her. I don't know quite what Armitage had in mind when he followed Celia and Mallinson. We can't know if her murder was part of his brief. And she wouldn't have been the first person to be pushed off the headland. Still, when he saw Mallinson get the brush off and fall down the slope he saw a chance to fulfil his commission in a different way.'

Hugh took another slow sip of brandy before continuing. 'Mallinson was scratched, bruised, dazed, but not seriously hurt. Armitage went down himself, coming up behind Mallinson as he tried to get up. A knock on the head with a handy rock and Mallinson was unconscious. Armitage swears he didn't realise he'd fallen into a pool of water and would drown. He just wanted to blacken Celia's reputation, and was ready to swear, as he did, that he saw her go down to the man she'd pushed over. I was added into the scene in an attempt to discredit me. I think the idea was to be that Celia repelled Mallinson again, killing him, and I was covering it up for her.'

'Do you believe this bloke?' Mike demanded.

Hugh put the empty brandy glass on the table, leaned back wearily, resting his arms on the chair and steepling his fingers together. 'It's a good story,' he said slowly, 'it fits in with all the pieces we know. In fact, there are other strands of evidence that support the story too. Tilly Barlow saw Armitage going up to the cliffs just before we did. There are minute traces of mud from the pool on his trouser legs. But all of that could be excused away, and I haven't heard what Karen Armitage has to say. Elliot was just going to interview her when I spoke to him.'

Hugh studied his fingers for a moment, then glanced round at the watching faces. 'My gut instinct is that Armitage was the moving force in the pair. He took his opportunity unhesitatingly when he saw Celia push Damian Mallinson. I rather think,' a faint smile touched his mouth, lighting his sombre eyes, 'that Karen Armitage provided the muscle and not the brains.'

Mike snorted with laughter. 'Maybe it's as well I left her to you,' he said, looking at Anna.

'Where is Celia now?' she asked Hugh.

'I don't know, and don't particularly want to,' he said. 'Dom's responsible for her, and he's got another week to go before the trial starts and she gives her evidence. I think he's going to take her to his place. I certainly don't envy him the task.'

'Right,' Mike said briskly, banging down his drained tankard on the table. 'Now I've got something much more interesting to tell you. Just let me get the book.' He bounded up and strode into the dining room.

Hugh looked at Anna, raising an eyebrow in surprise. She shook her head, quite as much in the dark as he was.

Mike was back almost at once, clutching a small book that Anna recognised. He stood facing them, just as if, she thought with a spurt of laughter, he was going to lecture them. She bit her lip as she realised he probably was.

A staccato rapping brought Ben to his feet, barking furiously as he rushed to the front door. Mike swore, his brow darkening. 'If that's an offer of more cake,' he muttered, striding towards it. He seized the handle and flung the door open, his countenance anything but welcoming.

It was Inspector Elliot who stood there, his own face as tired as Hugh's and so drained of colour that it matched the grey suit he wore.

Mike's expression lightened, although it could hardly be described as welcoming, Anna thought. He seized the inspector by the arm, urging him into the room. 'Just the man, Elliot. You're in time to hear how I've solved one of your mysteries.'

'Oh?' Elliot sounded no more than politely interested as he stepped into the sitting room. He glanced with a slight smile at Anna.

'Come and sit down, Rob,' she said. 'You look worn out.'

'I've felt better,' he agreed, sinking down into a chair near her and thankfully stretching his long legs out in front of him. He looked across at Hugh. 'You'll be glad to hear that it's all sorted. We've charged Eddie Armitage with murder, and Karen Armitage with attempted murder. Celia Vaughan has been taken into safe-keeping by Dominic Etheridge.'

'Right, about time,' Mike said, flinging himself back down onto the sofa. 'Now …'

'And,' Elliot went on smoothly, 'I've solved the riddles of the cancelling guests and the mystery man in the garden.'

Hugh's eyebrow rose again. The inspector felt a faint satisfaction. It was never easy to surprise Hugh Carey.

'The two men in the priory courtyard with Tilly Barlow proved to be rather interesting,' Elliot said.

'Oh yes,' Anna interrupted, remembering, 'I've met one of them. So have you, Mike,' she added, glancing across at him. 'Bruce Riley. He was in the pub we went to after exploring the garden at Elowen.'

Mike was staring at her blankly. 'You know,' she said impatiently, 'his girlfriend runs the Witches' Shop in Coombhaven, and I think he works there too.'

'He does,' Elliot confirmed. 'In the Tourist Information Office.' He let the nugget of information fall into the room like a stone.

Hugh was watching him closely. 'And?'

'And he was very helpful, bringing out leaflets to Philly for the priory information room. He chatted to her, hearing all about what was going on. And he chatted to Tilly Barlow, whenever he bumped into her. After all, he knew her as his cousin Clive was her lodger.'

Anna drew in a sharp breath. Even Mike was listening, fascinated, his own attempt at story telling forgotten. Temporarily at least.

'The two cousins had different agendas, but they were used to co-operating. They grew up together, and have stayed close, both wanting to move down here where they spent childhood holidays.'

'They do look a bit alike,' Anna said. 'I felt I'd seen Clive before, but of course I hadn't, it must just have been his resemblance to his cousin Bruce.'

A low growl warned her that Mike's impatience was being strained and she fell silent, waiting for Rob Elliot to continue.

'Clive felt very strongly that Tilly Barlow was losing business because of the priory holiday apartments. Apparently things have got so bad that she's taken this part-time job in Coombhaven. He seems,' Elliot could not quite control the amusement in his voice, 'to be very fond of her, and he wanted to help. He decided the best way was to put people off the priory apartments and started a series of rumours that his cousin Bruce subtly promoted from the Tourist Information Office. And Bruce helped the scheme go a stage further, when he managed to glimpse the booking information in Philly's office. Clive began to send out little warning letters to booked clients. He had one of them on him when he was taken to the hospital, that's how the whole thing has come to light so quickly.'

'Was Tilly involved in this?' Hugh asked.

'I don't think so,' Elliot replied. 'Clive says very definitely that she knows nothing about it.'

'I'll bet she's got a damned good idea,' Mike growled.

'Perhaps not,' Anna said slowly. 'She's nosy and pushy, but not malicious, you know.'

'Mmmm,' Hugh murmured thoughtfully. 'I'm inclined to

agree with you. Perhaps we should suggest that Will looks into some way that she could be linked into the priory lettings. Maybe promoting her Bed and Breakfast for people who don't want to self cater.'

Mike ignored this. 'What about Elowen?' he demanded, his eyes fixed on Elliot. 'That's what you meant, isn't it? The man in the garden there on the night of the landslip?'

'Yes,' the inspector agreed. 'Bruce benefited from the cousins' interchange with information from Tilly, who is really extremely good at picking it up. She knew,' he glanced at Anna, 'about your plans for a midsummer picnic, and she passed them on to Clive, who let Bruce know.'

'But why on earth was he interested?' Anna felt as though she would explode with frustrated curiosity. 'Do get on with it, Rob.'

He grinned suddenly. 'Bruce is a frustrated garden historian. He was sure that this was his chance to make his name, discovering the hidden gardens at Elowen once he learned of its existence. He thought it would be as big a find as Heligan. And he was terrified that you'd find something exciting there before he did.'

The inspector sighed. 'He didn't intend to harm anyone, he was alarmed when Anna nearly spotted him and even more alarmed when he heard the sound of the landslip behind him as he raced past Lucy.'

'How did you find out?' Hugh asked.

'He told us,' Elliot said simply. 'It's been preying on his mind.'

'So much for the great criminal investigation,' Mike said. He stood up, and held out the shabby book he was still clutching. 'Now this is the result of research. It gives us, me, at least,' he amended smugly, 'the answer to the Bones in the Fogou mystery.'

Rob Elliot was amused. 'Alright, Mike,' he settled more comfortably in his chair, 'the floor's all yours.'

Mike seemed to swell with satisfaction. 'I had a slight advantage,' he admitted fairly, 'because I've already done quite a lot of research into the garden at Elowen. I had a faint recollection of skimming through the old lady's diaries and seeing something odd. It didn't seem relevant then, after all I was only interested in garden details and I just picked it up because she mentioned filling in the fogou. It was the first confirmation I had that it had still been accessible in recent times.'

'What old lady?' Hugh asked when Mike paused for breath.

'Mariot Lanyon,' Mike said, rather surprised. 'Of course, you didn't get to hear about the family, did you?'

He did not wait for a reply but grasped the book more firmly. 'This is one of her diaries. She was the last of the family to live in the house, or part of it, as it fell into disrepair after the Second World War. She was riddled with family pride, she'd married a cousin who died in the First World War and brought up a son who died in the Second. His son, her grandson, was her hope for the future. Everything she did was to maintain the house and grounds for him. So she tolerated his mother Amethyst, a London singer, with whom she had zilch in common.'

Mike paused again, but nobody interrupted him this time. He held his audience rapt with interest. He smiled, pleased.

'Amethyst hated the place, but couldn't leave as she had no money, no means of supporting herself and her son.'

'She could have if she really wanted to,' Anna pointed out. 'Other women had to work and bring up children after the war.'

'True,' Mike conceded. 'Perhaps she liked the lifestyle, just not being buried in the country. But her chance of escape came at last, when her son was left a small property in Montreal. A town, and she seemed to crave town life, and a huge distance between herself and her mother-in-law.'

'What did Mariot think of it?' Hugh asked.

'Not much,' Mike said, flicking through the pages of the book. 'She didn't intend to let the boy go. She even tried to bribe Amethyst, offering her the jewels, the rings and necklaces that belonged to the Lanyons that she had never surrendered to her son's bride. Amethyst took them, but she still threw a spanner into the works.'

Anna leaned forward, her eyes bright with interest.

Mike glanced at her. 'With your imagination you can probably guess. She told the old lady that the boy wasn't her grandchild, the son of her son, but the child of an itinerant actor who wouldn't marry her when she became pregnant. Denzil, Mariot's son, was more obliging and certainly more gullible.'

Nobody moved as he smoothed out the page he had been searching for. 'Here it is,' he said. 'Mariot wrote it all down, describing how she had gone out into the garden to her husband's memorial, horrified at what she had heard. She, with her pride of family and place, to leave the Lanyon estates to a bastard who bore her name. She couldn't do it. But how could she avoid it without revealing how her son had been deceived?'

Mike drew a breath, so deeply involved in the story that he barely noticed the others. 'And at that moment,' he said sombrely, 'her chance came. At any other time she may not have taken it. But at this time she did.'

'What was her chance?' Anna asked quietly.

'Can't you guess?' he enquired.

She nodded, her face full of horror. But she did not speak.

'It came at the moment,' Mike continued, 'that Cal Tregonan came running up to her to say her grandson had fallen into the fogou, breaking his leg, and needed help.'

Mike pulled a face. 'Did Mariot decide then and there, or a little later? I don't know, and she doesn't say. She sent Cal off to the sawmill for men to help, and she went back herself to the house to collect Amethyst, the boy's mother. At the fogou they called and called the boy, but he couldn't get out on his own.

So Amethyst did what any mother would, she slithered down the slope and through the gap into the fogou. And Mariot followed and did the deed that would save the estate.'

Mike shook his head. 'In her eyes, at least,' he said heavily. 'She biffed Amethyst across the head with the walking stick she always used and left her there with her son Geraint, the boy who was not a Lanyon, not Mariot's grandson. The old lady wrote it down without equivocation. I imagine she must have seen to Geraint too, although she doesn't mention it.'

Mike's expression was grim as he finished the story. 'Mariot was back up top, leaning heavily on her walking stick, when Aaron arrived with the men from the sawmill. She told them that Amethyst had taken the boy back to the house and the entrance was to be sealed at once. And it was done. Amethyst and her son were walled in to die.'

'But people must have missed them,' Anna exclaimed. 'The servants, the villagers.'

'By then there was only one old maid in the house who did the cooking,' Mike said. 'When she died Mariot stayed there alone until her own death. And the villagers were told that Amethyst and the boy had gone to a London hospital and then on to Canada. They weren't to know otherwise. No doubt there'd been gossip about Amethyst's Canadian project.'

'Was it true?' Hugh asked. 'About the boy's parentage? Or did Amethyst just use it to get away?'

'Who knows?' Mike said. He closed the book. 'If I can get funding, I'll have DNA tests done on the remains. That should tell us.'

'Why did she write it all down?' Anna asked.

'She had nobody to tell,' Rob Elliot answered, 'probably nobody even to talk to by then. It sounds as though she lived pretty isolated from the locals.' He ended on a questioning note, glancing at Mike.

Mike nodded. 'Yes, that seems to have been the case. Perhaps she didn't want them to see how the house and gardens were going to rack and ruin. They knew, of course, but that didn't bother her.'

'Did Mariot kill them when she hit them or did they suffocate down there, Amethyst and the boy?' Anna's voice held a note of horror.

'I don't think her blows would have killed them,' Hugh said slowly, remembering the position of the bodies he had seen.

'They would have run out of air,' Mike said practically. 'Just gone to sleep really.' He looked appraisingly at Anna. 'Don't dwell on it. The garden is still lovely, it's not responsible for the bad things done in it.'

'No,' she agreed reluctantly. 'But still …'

Rob intervened. 'Make a play out of it,' he advised. 'It'll be a way to exorcise the ghosts.'

Anna brightened, shooting him an appreciative glance. 'Maybe, but it would be a tragedy, I've never written one before. Still, I could try.' She subsided, obviously already adjusting her thoughts.

Rob met Mike's eyes for a moment and a tremor of amusement passed between the two men. 'How is Lucy?' Rob asked, turning to Hugh.

'She's going to be alright,' he said. 'I collect her tomorrow morning after the doctor's seen her again.' His voice was completely even as he added, 'She insists she's well enough to go back to work in Hampshire next week. Until then she wants to be here at the manor.'

'Oh well,' Anna broke the awkward silence that fell, 'I expect she wants to sort out the apartment lettings with Philly. I'll be here a lot, so I'll keep an eye on her. But perhaps,' she amended hopefully, 'you're staying too, Hugh?'

'No.' He was aware he sounded curt, and tried to soften the negative. 'I'll get back to Withern. One of us needs to be at home or we might as well not keep the place. And I've work to do. In fact,' he pushed himself up, 'I'll get home now and make a start on it.'

'Stay to dinner,' Anna urged. 'Mike's cooking.' She ignored Mike's startled look. 'And you, Rob, you can stay, can't you?'

He shook his head. 'I'd love to, Anna. I've never sampled Mike's cooking. But there's still a lot to sort out. I shouldn't really be here at all, but I wanted to let you know what's happening, and get the latest news on Lucy.'

'Another time then,' Mike said heartily, pulling the front door open. 'Take it easy, Hugh,' he added more quietly, putting a hand briefly on Hugh's shoulder as his friend went past.

Hugh nodded, and without another word walked slowly down the path. Ben hesitated for a second, glancing around at Anna and Mike, then raced after Hugh.

Rob Elliot stood on the doorstep, staring after them. 'You'll keep an eye on things,' he said, with again the slight questioning inflection.

'Of course,' Mike said gruffly.

He shut the door firmly and leaned back against it, looking across at Anna.

'It's not good, is it?' he asked.

'No. They seem even further apart than ever,' she agreed reluctantly.

'Well, we'll have to see what we can do,' he said firmly, coming back into the room. 'Now about Elowen …'

With a groan she sank down onto the sofa with him. But already she knew that somehow Elowen was going to feature in her future too.

MARY TANT's Rossington series

1 *The Rossington Inheritance*

Lucy Rossington has put a promising career on hold, so that she can keep the family home going for her young brother Will – not an easy task, when home is an Elizabethan manor that the family have lived in for generations.

When the taint of avarice and deceit from the past seems to stain the present, she had to know who she can trust, not only for her own happiness, but also for the safety of her family and friends. Will she find out in time?

2007   £6.99   PAPERBACK   ISBN 978-1-903152-21-8

2 *Death at the Priory*

Lucy Rossington doesn't need any more trouble just now. She's got plenty of that already at the family manor in an idyllic West Country valley.

So it's really the last straw when odd incidents plague the priory excavations, under the leadership of the mercurial Mike Shannon. Does the death of an archaeologist mean more than a temporary disturbance? Is Lucy imagining evil where none exists? She is soon to know.

2008   £7.99   ISBN 978-1-903152-17-1

3 *Friends... and a Foe*

Life looks promising for Lucy Rossington and her family – there is no way they could guess that in just a few days their happiness might be shattered for ever..

Old friends rejoin the family circle – one of them brings in their wake a secret that somebody would kill to keep. How could the Rossingtons know that this secret will cost them dearly?

2009   £7.99   ISBN 978-1-903152-22-5